More praise for *Unfeeling*

'An outstandingly gifted writer and a dauntingly brave one
too . . . Holding's novel is written with a devastating blend of
control and anger'
*Scotsman*

'Remarkable . . . the novel's construction is a tour de force, a kind
of narrative corkscrew . . . gripping'
*Sunday Independent* (South Africa)

'His surefooted prose gives this novel a devastating punch . . . a
commanding picture of the land and nature as the ultimate power'
*Metro*

'Controversial and powerful . . . Through the eyes of his teenage
protagonist Holding charts the horror and fear of those who
suffered eviction and watched as the livelihood they had fought
for was torn out from underneath them' *The Big Issue*

'Narrated in spare, unfaltering prose, the novel is freighted with a
profound sense of foreboding . . .'
*Courier Mail* (South Africa)

'Riveting'
*Time Out*

Ian Holding is 28 years old and lives in Harare. This is his first novel.

# Unfeeling

## IAN HOLDING

POCKET
BOOKS

LONDON • SYDNEY • NEW YORK • TORONTO

First published in Great Britain by Simon & Schuster UK Ltd, 2005
First published by Pocket Books, 2006
An imprint of Simon & Schuster UK Ltd
A CBS COMPANY

1 3 5 7 9 10 8 6 4 2

Simon & Schuster UK Ltd
Africa House
64 -78 Kingsway
London WC2B 6AH

www.simonsays.co.uk

Simon & Schuster Australia
Sydney

A CIP catalogue record for this book is available
from the British Library

ISBN-13: 9781416522485
ISBN-10: 1-4165-2248-4

Typeset in Granjon by M Rules
Printed and bound in Great Britain by
Cox & Wyman Ltd, Reading, Berks

*For the victims*

# Acknowledgements

For their help, advice and friendship, I am grateful to Seranne Nield, Ling Cooper, Jennifer Barclay, Charles Buchan.

For their professional expertise and guidance: Bruce Hunter and my other agents at David Higham Associates, London. My wonderful editor Ben Ball: a genius, perfectionist and advocate. And Rochelle Venables, Hannah Corbett and the great team at Scribner/Simon & Schuster UK.

A special thanks to my parents.

And finally to my good mate, Mathew – remember, my friend, read books, play sport. Thanks for the good times. Thanks for the inspiration.

On a morning like this I could kiss everybody,
I'm so full of love and goodwill.

'A Wonderful Day Like Today'

LESLIE BRICUSSE AND ANTHONY NEWLEY

1

The boy with emerald eyes everyone calls Davey sits on the veranda of Aunt Marsha's farmhouse, hugging his knees in the searing morning sun. He is shaking, his mind restless, thinking of Edenfields – the Cape Dutch house clutching the hill, just above the cathedral-like tobacco barns and the cluttered chemical-smelling sheds, then down to the brown Broadlands Dam lying beneath the hill, and the fields rutted and rugged, spreading beyond. From the hill's summit at Eden's View he could stand squinting and know that everything he could see belonged to Edenfields Farm.

Aunt Marsha's veranda is a smooth stretch of glazed red granite. The rich stench of floor polish makes the boy queasy as he stares at his reflection, still on the stone floor. Looking up to steady the spinning in his head he is lost in a blurred haze of khaki: branches, twigs, leaves, moss. The landscape won't settle, something in the air seems to reject him, the sudden wild squall of a bird perched high in a dry tree.

Up, out and beyond, he can feel the heavy silence, the flustered settling of the wild.

But in his head strange noises trouble him, grating and scratching about like the snorting of a pig. His hands, stiff and skeletal, shake continually. Sporadically, he claws at his skin with filthy nails, scraping grooves through days of dirt and grime. His body is battered and bruised. His guts shift and stir – he leans forward, grips his stomach, throws up on the steps below.

From the deep shadows of the veranda, Aunt Marsha rises from her wicker chair and moves forward to put a cool hand to his shoulder.

'There, there,' she whispers.

Nothing brings him relief. He cannot focus on a thought, hold an image still long enough to recognize what it is or means. Sudden snatches of memory swim across his vision, cancelling out the blotted garden. Sitting back against the cream pillar, his teeth chattering, his hands shaking, he is aware that Aunt Marsha stands, mutters something, withdraws. It feels like the removal of a gag. Alone, his body exhales. A convulsion follows, the breaking of a fresh sweat and a coldness creeping on him, a bone chill.

Only when he finds himself clutching a cold glass and glimpses again the haze of Aunt Marsha above him does he surface to feel the dull throb of pain at his temple, the roller coaster wobble of nausea. He lifts the rim of the glass to his soured mouth. He tastes the sweetness of the Coke, then the rush of rum and throws up again. He sits back, clutching his tender stomach, hearing the bird complain at him invisible in its tree, and then, a moment later, the sun's heat escalates.

He had taken a bottle of Captain Morgan's as he left Edenfields, the shotgun tucked under his arm. He'd planned to retrieve the gun from its hiding place, kick down the living-room door, blow away everyone who moved. Instead, he'd inched down the passage, utterly exhausted, battling to hold the heavy gun steady, the barrel constantly bearing towards the floor.

Being back in the house had done nothing to appease him. Its life-force had gone: he felt no slow pulse rise from its foundations, no current move through the sunken pipes and trusses. There was nothing to suggest what it had been. He'd thought the house would have spurred him on, that being there inside its walls, under its roof, would have filled him with family memories, steeped him in the essence of what he'd lost, if just for a moment. Instead, the place seemed sterile, or, worse, indifferent to him. She had spread her terminal gloom to it. The evening was still, the air warm and stale and hard on his lungs as he moved deeper inside – to his left a crescent-shaped table bearing the brass bulldogs he'd once given Ma for a birthday present, on his right a series of teak-framed lion photographs he remembered her hanging on the wall. Ahead: the bedroom, drawing him in like a vortex, for the next act. But in the end he took no delight in pulling the trigger.

Thinking about it now, he realizes he should have expected this anticlimax. He had long ago learnt that death is a strangely quiet thing, even for people. On that night a couple of months before, as he reeled against the cupboard in his parents' bedroom, the bed red and soaked, a pool of blood edging towards him along the beige carpet like a snake across stone, it had been pure silence pounding in his ears.

Being back in the house disturbed him in other ways he didn't anticipate. The memories that he had cherished since that night soured and after a while he withdrew as quietly as he'd come, taking only the bottle of rum from the bar counter in the lounge. Purposeless now, he wandered down the hill, through the cream-pillared gate, and didn't look back at the tight grip of the house, fort-like on the kopje, betraying him with its stubborn stillness. Even though the woman was now dead, Edenfields didn't seem cleansed or redeemed. Nothing had been restored, nothing replaced. He wanted to get far away.

He walked over the red soil, along the dusty road that cut through the scorched fields. The sky darkened; shrill insects seemed to berate him. The wind shifted every now and then, washing him in the evening's coolness. There was not another soul about, but in any case, the last couple of days had left him far beyond caring whether he was seen or not. He walked steadily through the quick fall of night, climbed to the peak of the high kopje, to the sacred place his great-grandfather had named Eden's View — a place he knew the fat woman would never have invaded — and there he leant against a rock face, exhausted, delirious, drained of will or reason.

With darkness blurring the edges of the tobacco barns, swallowing up the blue hills, there was nothing between him and the murderers. The militia had appeared from nowhere, caught them unawares, permeated the farmhouse like vapours. And now they were beginning to come again, this time through his ears, his eyes, the soles of his feet, the hardness of the rocks, from out of Edenfields itself, a shroud of killers, a shimmer of raised pangas, just when he should have defeated them.

Then the haunting sound of a boar rose again, sticking hard in his skull like a razor-edged arrow splintering the bone, slicing cleanly into his brain. In pain, he drove his body hard against the boulder, bruising his spine, cutting his shoulder blades on stone shards sharp as glass. The blood welled through his skin, dampening the grime on his shirt.

But there was no boar. Insects buzzed in his ears, nestled in the dampness of his sweaty arms. Below him the land stretched black and boundless, fold upon fold, dale upon dale, burnt and barren. When the wind blew, he pictured ash rising in a great grey gust across the vast wastelands of the farm, his Edenfields.

So in fact he hadn't taken the farm back, hadn't achieved what he wanted to. He couldn't raise the dead after all.

He broke the gold bottle-top seal with a quick turn of his hand and lifted the liquor to his lips. He left the gun by his side, waiting.

Then the night condensed into a black shadow, surrounded by sunlight, and the shadow took his head on to its shoulder. It was Aunt Marsha: a featureless angel etched in gold, her words distant, incomprehensible, but calm and caring. She moved forward, peered into him. He saw there – he can't remember – something soft, motherly in the spark of her eyes, a connection.

Then she shook, spun away. A shatter of glass as the emptied rum bottle smashed against rock, a shudder within him, a fall again into darkness.

At Summerville Farm, Marsha is troubled. She sits at her desk in the office, clutching a pencil, poised over a notepad. Someone once told her that she should plan what to say when confronting people, write down what angle to take. She's never had to try it before – she never has cause to disagree with Mike, never did with Leigh either – but she knows she will need to be prepared when Davey finally shows up. She jots down a few points, tearing the lines out of herself.

1) You know we're always here for you Davey.
2) Blaming yourself or anyone else isn't going to help matters.
3) We understand your hurt, the pain you're going through.

Then she stops. She may as well be fighting a fire with a cake of soap. Who wrote these words? she wonders. Looking down at the paper with its silly little point-form platitudes, she is overcome with a new wave of apprehension. She screws the paper up, discards it.

She's been anxious for two days, ever since the headmaster called to announce that Davey was missing. The call brought it all out into the open again, forcing her again to confront these dreadful past few months, months in which innocence was lost, lives were taken, everything snatched away in the night. Months in which they've all, each and every one of them, been afflicted, but somehow, with the boy neatly tucked away and out of sight, they've been able to cover it up, pretend it was all okay.

But, to be honest, she's been expecting it. She's had an inkling something like this was going to happen. It is their fault; it is her fault. The simple truth is that poor Davey Baker was forced back into the living, working, breathing world far too quickly after the whole awful ordeal. At the time the community gathered round him, told him that putting his best foot forward was the one way to overcome his grief. They said, 'Be strong and tough young man, be brave, they'd have wanted you to.'

And however sincere this advice had been, Marsha wonders how many of those giving it knew the truth, that it was said merely to remove the source of their own shock and pain, to bury the evidence. Seeing him off back to boarding school with their tearful faces, their gifts of fudge and koeksusters, had been an act of cowardice.

My God, she thinks, angered by this sudden bitter truth, the poor kid was shipped off at the beginning of the new term, just three weeks after his parents were hacked and bludgeoned to death, and everyone breathed a sigh of relief. She could almost hear the community exhale for the first time in weeks. But what gave them the right? And what cruelty: their thin solace was at the expense of the person meant to matter most — the victim, the orphan. Underneath that tough farm boy tan he's really always been a sensitive child. Surely she should have realized he would have been this vulnerable, this fragile? She had done everything for herself: they all had. They'd let him down.

Yes.

The guilt hits her and with it her opportunity to atone, when he makes his appearance, as he certainly will. She has felt the signs all along: her prickling fingertips, a sudden shudder in the night, and now that she thinks about it she realizes that he'd even tried to tell them what he was going to do. There can be no denying what crisis, what dark storm has been brewing.

When Davey first went back to school, Marsha moved in with old friends in town and went to see him every day. She stayed a week, arriving at the school at lunchtimes and in the early evening after he'd finished cricket practice, and he'd come to the car or they'd sit silently on a bench beside a brick-lined path that ran through the plush lawns. She tried to comfort him, cheer him up, but knew that her grief was plain to see. So she addressed herself to his stomach, plying him with chocolates, pizzas, chips. He ate slowly and silently and neither of them cried.

One afternoon she took him shopping. He'd lost everything, literally – she bought him a whole new wardrobe, new school uniforms, a new cricket bat and kit – and while she was writing out the cheque in Sportsman's Paradise, it struck Marsha that 5000 hectares of prime farming land and all the carefree promise in the world were now reduced to this chunk of willow and the torment of desolation. For a minute her hand trembled, her breath quickened, she couldn't remember whether the word 'million' had one 'l' or two. A couple of days later she decided she had done what she could.

Back at Summerville she took to calling Davey up regularly. At first these conversations were no easier than sitting on the path bench. Marsha was astonished at how difficult she found it to say anything beyond bland, pointless pleasantries. She desperately wanted to find the phrase that would lance his grief, that would release him to tell her what was going on inside, and therefore be free of it. But each time she thought she might try, she felt herself pushing him away, and stopped.

'How are you Davey?'

'Fine.'

'How's school coming along?'

'Okay.'

'Is there anything you need?'

'No thanks.'

She turned over his monosyllables like crossword clues. At first he spoke with a neutral gravity that implied he was treading lightly in his new being, behaving well, but falsely. But after a few weeks he began to assert the rights of his pain, and Marsha was relieved, though torn, when the phone would ring in the middle of the week and Davey would say, 'Aunt Marsha, I'm not well – it's a bug going round.' She was delighted he wanted to come to her, but then she'd have to fob him off: they couldn't leave the farm, or petrol was a problem. It was heartbreaking. But that's what they had decided.

'Perhaps it is sensible for him not to have to see the unfortunate situation developing out there,' his headmaster had advised. 'Instead, I've taken the liberty of telephoning one of his friend's parents who reside here in the city and they're more than happy to have him for the weekends, look after him and all. I assure you, Mrs De Wet, it's for the best.'

Mike agreed. 'It's better he learns to stick it out at school. There're far too many disturbing things around here for him now.'

Initially Marsha resented the idea. It was such a typically male thing to suggest. This tough farmer stoicism wasn't going to help the boy one bit – he needed motherly care, a sympathizer, someone to grieve with. And, of course, Leigh would never have left him in need; she'd have been there in an instant, she'd have travelled through the night if she thought her son was unwell and needed care. But in the end Marsha resigned herself to hardening her heart, because she saw their point. She'd been forced to acknowledge what she couldn't have conceived of when she first came to Summerville – that farms were no longer places for children, that the horrors he'd witnessed weren't one-off, random acts, that an organized system of violence had been instigated, and they had to find a way of living with it. Perhaps her days of being what Mike called, affectionately, an eternal idealist were not eternal after all. Although she ached for the sight of Davey, the comfort she'd bring him and the comfort he'd give her as his mother's son, she had to be realistic.

But a few weeks later, the headmaster made the first of what became regular phone calls. He'd start off, 'I don't want to alarm you Mrs De Wet', and she would know at once that David had been up to something: smoking, fighting, swearing. 'Of course,' he would say, 'we do appreciate he's going through a bad time and we all sympathize with him deeply, but I must warn you that although these incidents may be relatively trivial within themselves, we don't want him becoming something that he really isn't – a thoroughly nasty young man.'

'Yes, I see,' she'd replied curtly, wounded. The words 'thoroughly nasty' seemed brutal, cruel – as though they were directed at her. She understood what the head meant to suggest, of course she did, but a part of her was angered by this crude branding, herding Davey in with other normal, naughty schoolboys.

'Perhaps he needs special care?'

'Quite honestly, Mrs De Wet, the worst thing for him is to be treated differently.'

'But he is different. He needs some guidance and understanding surely?'

For a while they found themselves in polite deadlock, until eventually they agreed in principle on a revised strategy: he was to go for counselling with the school chaplain. As soon as she'd put the phone down, she knew he would hate it – all that well-meaning obfuscation. She knew he was far too much a farm boy to go in for that nonsense, for talking like a woman, getting in touch with his inner self; he's far too proud to show emotion, sentiment. Still, what could be done?

And then the half term break began to approach, Davey would have to come back. Marsha dreaded it more and more, longed for it more and more. She didn't know what to expect from him, how he'd cope returning to the district, how he'd assuage this wild, erratic rage of his, yet at the same time she needed him to come, she needed to bask in his survival. She made up a room for him, removed all the flowered vases, embroidered pillows, and put in a study lamp, an ethnic print duvet, newly made curtains, and a few posters of flashy sports cars and pouting girls in swimsuits on the cupboard doors.

He seemed excited to be coming, almost manic. The whole way back in the car he talked about everything, nothing. At the farm he tore around, ate ferociously, ran amok with the dogs, kicked about in the pool.

'The kid's looking much better,' said Mike. 'Let him do what he wants, whatever makes him happy. He's only a boy after all.'

Marsha wasn't so sure, but tried to ignore this nagging, useless doubt. They indulged him. Mike took him fishing. Marsha baked his favourite carrot cake and milk tart. They went to the sports club to play tennis and socialize, although the club gatherings lacked their old zest. They'd all been so depressed, so down. Now, though, it was halfterm, all the kids were back, and they tried to make it like old times even if they all knew that the old times were fast becoming incomprehensible, like an era before their birth.

Davey seemed at ease around the community, even if the community wasn't entirely at ease around him. Marsha felt the smiling discomfort, the accepting hostility. How dare they, she thought, how dare they be so damn cruel? Don't they know it must be obvious to him, must scream out at him even as they chat blandly away? Men asked him about sport, women about school – only the other kids seemed to retain a bit of honesty, not really knowing what to do, awkward in their affection. She tried to ignore what she felt beneath the surface, and in the teeth of everyone's anxiety to remain calm (to the point of paralysis) she took charge of arranging the mixed doubles and drinks orders herself. The tennis was ordinary, the drinks muzzled the panic.

But it was to no avail. By the time they came back from the club Davey's mood had changed entirely. He dropped the fake normality (Marsha was partly relieved – the front had been as much a drain on her energy as him) and retreated to a hard moodiness. Marsha soldiered on through carelessly made comments, pregnant silences, the terrible wrench at realizing how Davey might have taken something, and her own desperate, repeated prayer to avoid anything risky or sensitive.

In this state Davey generated a power of his own. Perhaps this was what he was like at school. Marsha never thought a boy would throw her composure, skittle her nerve so easily, especially sweet Davey. There were moments when she positively shook from the inside, sitting across from him in the lounge, not knowing what to say other than offering him yet another ginger biscuit. It was almost like first love – young, unknowing love. And when she made herself dig down beneath his tanned crust, when she pressed into his supple skin, or when she entered through his emerald eyes, it was him – it was Davey – and his being there meant that for a day or

14

two she could be the person she longed for and missed. She could be Aunt Marsha again.

But the next day at church matters came to a head. The three of them were sitting near the back while Pastor Fellows gave his usual pithy sermon. Over the years he'd learnt to make it short if he wanted any kind of attendance. The day's theme: forgiveness. Marsha stopped breathing when he announced it.

'We must never underestimate the blessing of forgiveness, the one true gift of the Lord to mankind.'

She sat as still as the pew, sensing the tension rising in David, feeling it steal over her. She looked across to see him clenching his hands, flexing his jaw, his cheeks flushed. Jesus, she thought, please make him stop. But no: Pastor Fellows ploughed on, driving home his point. 'Forgiveness is a powerful tool indeed in the hands of mankind.' At each intoned phrase Davey inhaled more audibly, drawing his face into a pained, angular tightness until Marsha saw a vein surface and bulge in his temple.

As she reached out to put a comforting hand on his knee, he snapped. Swearing loudly, he rose to his feet. Marsha tried to pacify him, clutching at his knee, but to no avail. The congregation gasped, spinning round on their pews. 'David,' she whispered sternly, trying to pull him down, but he struggled free. He stumbled his way through the sea of knees and then stormed out, muttering angry threats she couldn't understand.

Shock froze the congregation. A few elderly ladies had raised their hands to their mouths to contain their disbelief, and signal their disapproval. Pastor Fellows quickly announced the next hymn and the thumped opening chords of 'Praise My Soul' sounded.

'I'm sorry,' she said afterwards, outside, bursting into tears. 'I'm sorry, he's just not himself. He doesn't mean it. He's just not over it yet.'

Everyone consoled her, said how they sympathized. 'It's tough, we know it's tough.' But, of course, it remained shocking: it left the impression of violence in people's minds, stirred their own nervousness. Poor Davey, she thought, was a walking, talking, breathing nightmare for them all, an icy plunge into that deep level where trauma and dread and violence are kept locked away. He stripped back layers of their own blindness to show what the future might hold, the plight of the survivor. Floating between the tea tables outside the church, occasionally snagged by people she'd thought she knew, Marsha glimpsed a dark secret: the unspoken acknowledgement that it would have been better if Davey had perished with his mother and father, so that Edenfields and the Bakers just didn't exist any more. Total obliteration would have been tidier, less of a hassle to deal with. That was really what these churchgoers were saying to one another when they carefully talked about some subject other than Davey.

On the way home he sat silently on the back seat. She didn't know what to say to him. The pressure weighed like stone on her shoulders, almost unbearable. In the last couple of months she felt she'd become the community's flagship, the one they all checked to see was still sailing, still ignoring what the dismal future held in store, and therefore somehow holding together the pieces of a quickly disintegrating flotilla. Or maybe it was Davey they were looking to, and she was just the link: people measured their own sense of wellbeing, their own ability to cope on how he held up. If he cracked, they would crack. And she was responsible for him, wrapped around him, protecting, insulating.

And perhaps Davey just needed the opposite. Perhaps he had

done what he needed – shock them – and now that he had reminded them of his pain, he could concentrate on dealing with it properly. Outwardly they all hoped it was so. At church the next week, when Davey was back at school, she made up an announcement on his behalf. 'He wishes to apologize to everyone for his outburst. He knows it wasn't the time or, certainly, the place. But he's truly sorry and wants me to tell you all that he's now much better and more at peace. He's much more his old self.'

The community, in his absence, patted him on the back, pleased to see him doing his bit, calming their own fears and anxieties. But it was cosmetic, for all of them a lie. She knew. He wasn't calm. Wasn't at ease. He hadn't got over anything at all.

And then three nights ago Davey called them up late. He sounded agitated, excited, spoke at a rate of knots, saying the same thing over and over.

'I know what I'm going to do, I know how to deal with these people. I've got the solution. It's all okay now, it'll be all okay.'

She didn't know what he was talking about, but tried to calm him. 'Now just try to get a good night's sleep.' Eventually she got him to agree to go to bed and think things through in the morning, but she knew it was a reprieve, not a victory. She told Mike.

'Just ignore it, the kid's having a bad time that's all. He's probably homesick, been in a punch-up or something.'

Marsha knew that wasn't it. There was something horribly determined in his voice, something steadfast, resolved. She felt another layer of denial slip away, and spent the whole night restless and unsettled, thinking over and over what he'd said, how hard she'd needed to work to get him to breathe, to talk slowly, to remember that she was there on the other end of the line. And really she knew what he meant to do, and wondered how she could talk him out of it. It wasn't going to be easy, especially when, with the mounting anger in her heart, she'd like nothing better than to do the same herself. But she knew it was her duty to try to pacify him, help him accept what had happened.

And now he's run away. She tries to pull herself together. Sitting in the office, tapping a pencil against a screwed-up ball of paper isn't going to make him appear with an innocent explanation. She's been stupefied by inaction: all these mounting worries – this anger she has inside her against something she's powerless to overcome – have weakened her, made her ineffectual. She tosses the pencil aside, throws the paper into the wastepaper basket, taps her twitchy fingers on the desk calendar, stops. She closes her eyes for a moment, to marshal her thoughts, to try to see what to do now. She knows he must be coming back, somehow, travelling back towards her, towards Leigh, towards Edenfields. On the back of her eyelids, in the blackness, she sees him, a shape in the distance, a figure struggling, labouring along the hot surface of a weltering track, a shape broken up by the haze of the heat, into a head, a body, for a moment a limb. Marsha feels the heat, a blast from a furnace. Her breath quickens, her cheeks burn, and then the figure is gone, in the yellow sun.

She opens her eyes, and sits for a while. She goes through to put the kettle on for tea, allowing her mind to settle. She wanders round the kitchen, hacks a chicken from the depths of the deep-freeze and leaves it on a plate to thaw for supper. Waiting for the water to boil, she knows that he needs her – not just in a protective, motherly way, but physically needs her. She doesn't know why or how, but nevertheless he does. She flicks the kettle off. The bubbling water comes to quick rest. She walks through to the passage, picks the keys to the truck off the key rack.

A few minutes later she's on her way to Edenfields, to Eden's View, ignoring the dangers, the armed militia who have fortified the farm. She drives, pulled towards the base of the hill. No one stops her. She parks the truck slightly in the bushes to conceal it from the homestead and begins picking her way through the tall unruly vlei so that she can climb the hill (thankful she's at least wearing track shoes) to find the boy who's spent the whole night there, waiting for her. The boy who ran away three days ago to come and do what needed to be done.

The view from the summit is heartbreaking. It has been so long since she's come up here, since she's wallowed in the expanse of flaxen bush, the gold crop thick and full on the fields. Not that the crop is there now. As she made her way up the hill, she tried to find in herself the grief and longing that had brought Davey to this place. What was it that had lured him, like her, to come here for help? She wants to know what he sees.

But she can't. She can't make sense of anything when she stands here at the top, saddened and shocked to witness the desolation rolled out below her: red soil roasted black, the squashed, trodden remnants of the winter wheat charred crisp and slick.

From behind a large boulder comes a hard choking heave. For the first time she is apprehensive, but nevertheless sure of what she'll find. It's him, of course. Beautiful Davey Baker, her joy, her hope. He's utterly filthy – that's the first thing that strikes her – huddled against the grey rock in smeared, soiled rags, his hair damp with grease and dirt, his skin spattered in dried mud, dried blood. He is gazing ahead, seeing nothing. Her heart aches for the child, a genuine stab in her chest, but here, in front of her now, faltering at her feet, the child has disappeared. In an instant she flounders, her eyes filled with a watery gleam. Not tears – she's promised herself – but certainly a twinge of emotional weakness, a glint of fear, sadness for what they've all lost. She moves forward, takes his head to her shoulder.

*

The shotgun disturbs her, even though she had expected it. The boy is not only in a sorry state – dishevelled, drunk, dirty – but she can't see in his face what she'd hoped for: a family likeness in the eyes, traces of what she can't mourn for. Nevertheless she will protect him, shelter him. Whatever he has done, she'll accept it, wipe the slate clean.

Her problem is logistics. She's come alone, and how does one get a drunk, semiconscious teenage boy all the way down a perilously steep escarpment? She should've waited until Mike was ready to come with her. She should have told him what was up, her fears, forebodings, even if he'd just dismissed it as one of her whims, told her again she was just being overemotional. She shouldn't have been so impulsive.

She props herself on a rock next to him. He seems to be asleep. She takes a deep breath and the notion suddenly comes to her that she'll hold the breath in, let it fill her whole self, so that perhaps when she exhales, all her cares and concerns, the worries and anxieties she's been accommodating these last few months will simply be pushed out, gently into the mid-morning air. She'll leave them here, like Davey seems to have. She wonders, with inexplicable optimism, whether there's a chance their lives will settle down, now that Davey's clearly done whatever he was threatening to do. Perhaps with this act Davey has brought them all to a turning-point, a resolution of sorts.

She thinks of the strain on Mike – the increasing pains in his chest, the pointless inactivity, the daytime drinking (but can she honestly blame him?). He'll never give in. He won't roll over and surrender his family's legacy that easily. Although she wouldn't admit it, she hasn't got his fight, the simple refusal to give up and let go if they arrived tomorrow, crawling up the driveway in some ominous expensive car and demanding the farm. She knows they probably will one of these days, and when the time comes, then she's more than prepared to accept reality and quietly depart. But then, she wasn't born here.

She looks far out over the lands. There is the African sun blazing in a blue sky. It is a blue clearer and purer than anything she knows. She considers it untouched and untainted, a pure dome like the heavenly ceiling of a cathedral or the deepest hollows of a cave unreachable by human hands. There is a kind of sanctity in this blue dome. Its purity holds her in, keeps her here under an African sky, so that despite the brutality and the killings, the fear and trauma raging below, she wants to stay here, do her best to hold on to her life. She believes there's some hope in this view, in this seamless stretch of sky, an aspiration that makes her not want to give in and flee to a foreign, unwelcoming place. From where she sits it's clear to see that old Oupa Baker hadn't named this place Eden's View for nothing.

She sits and muses, working her long bony fingers through the boy's greasy, unkempt hair, trying to disentangle it, avoiding touching his scalp with her cold fingertips, and waits patiently for him to stir.

When at last he does she helps him to his feet. They stumble down the hill, stopping every few metres. She repeats over and over again how important it is they make their way back to Summerville. She's soon exhausted, cut on rocks and trees, and it seems an age before she finally bundles him into the truck and drives off at high speed in a swirl of dust. This isn't their land. She hates to think what would befall them if they were discovered trespassing.

He's difficult. He kicks and struggles. He mutters and groans drowsily, saying that they could all go to hell, fuck off. Then he makes a quick snatch for the gun, with a speed she didn't think he had in him. She is quicker, composed, knowing that this language and behaviour is the booze, the journey, not her Davey.

Back at Summerville, when he is sick over the edge of the veranda, she rises from her wicker chair, pats him on the shoulder, soothing him as he vomits red rum, sickly sparkling in the sun on the steps, and says, 'There, there boy, it's okay now, everything will be okay.' His reply, after a laboured moan, is a stifled 'Oh fuck', and he retches again.

The sight of him throwing up doesn't disturb her. She's seen too many stillborn piglets expelled in a gush of dark slime on to concrete floors, too many heads severed from roaming chickens, too many grotesque things on farms. What upsets her is what it suggests. That it's not finished. For now though she brushes this aside. He's clearly dehydrated. She stands, retreats into the coolness of the house where she takes a cold Coke from the kitchen fridge. She will pour it into a tall glass, add ice and salt and stir vigorously until flat. Then she will take it out to him and say calmly, 'Drink this boy, it'll make things better.' He'll like that. She knows he will.

Leaving Davey hunched on the veranda, she paces about the lounge fretfully patting up cushions, straightening tablecloths, repositioning photo frames. What will she say when Mike gets back — dejected and frustrated as usual from his unproductive fields – and meets her at the back door, seeing in her distraught face straight away what she's been unable to avoid, what danger she's harbouring in their midst? He'd warned her. She couldn't say he hadn't. 'Just watch it,' he'd said to her in the car coming back from dropping Davey off after the half-term break, 'we don't want all hell breaking loose just because we're looking after a kid who wants to be a damn hero. Just don't go getting too involved.' Easier said than done. He should have known that there was no way she'd be able to avoid 'getting too involved'. Even if common sense dictated that Mike was right, that they should look after their own concerns, it was simply inconceivable that a son of the Bakers should be left wanting of their help, their comfort and sanctuary.

Now he's back here amongst them, their home, their livelihood, sitting outside, a living, breathing wreck, soiling their property with what he's been through, what he's bringing to them, passing on. There can be no guarantee they'll be immune from what follows, the reparations when it's discovered what he's gone and done. They are now accomplices, she is startled to realize, harbouring a criminal. She shudders when she thinks of the consequences; numbness lodges in her throat. This could bring them all down.

The situation around the farms is a fuck-up and deep down Mike's suffering beyond belief to see it all go to pieces. There is lead embedded in his bones, a hard weight that can only be the genuine hold of heartache.

The farm's been gazetted for redistribution. They'd got their papers from the Ministry and a few days later a blanket notice appeared in the government-sponsored newspaper, listing most farms in the district. He knew it was coming. He hadn't planned to tell Marsha – not with everything else she's had to deal with – but in the end she found out, having fetched the mail from town. Her reaction wasn't exactly emotional and he can't help wonder whether there's a part of her that wants done with the whole thing, now that Leigh's gone and Edenfields is lost.

Mike can't help but be struck by the twisted logic, that he, a skilled farmer, will be moved off – alive if he's lucky – and a government crony like the fat bitch who's taken Edenfields will move on. They won't redistribute fuck-all to the landless peasants. They won't care about the crops: the first thing they did at Edenfields was torch Joe's crop to the ground. All that's wanted is the trophy of owning a farm so they can gloat to the masses, proud to have booted a racist colonialist off his land even though colonial rule ended generations ago. The other day Marsha summed it up perfectly when she said that black blood spilt a hundred years ago still stains their hands. 'We'll lose seventy years of sweat and toil,' she predicted to friends over a dull braai.

What Mike refuses to tolerate is not the loss of the good money he earns, or the undeniably comfortable lifestyle they've carved themselves here, but that he'll be stopped from doing what he's been brought up to do: feeding people, helping to fill the country's bread basket. And why? It's not about correcting colonial imbalances – all that's just a red herring – but about nursing an ageing despot's addiction to power and tyranny. You don't need a degree in politics to see the picture clearly. And the masses are beginning to starve, drop dead like flies. Who's going to be blamed for that fuckup? he thinks. Well, this is their problem now: let them sort it out.

The farm's production has been all but halted. He has had to downscale everything by almost 80 per cent because a little paper stamped by the law courts says he must 'cease operational activities' in preparation for moving off. He's culled virtually all his livestock – cattle, pigs, sheep – sold them to get as much cash as he can. He's pulled everything from the lands to avoid the cost of irrigation, pest control, labour. The only crops he planted were those allowed by the woman at Edenfields. She'd come to him one day, driving up in her black Mercedes, tripping on the gravel in her high-heels, shouting to his face, 'I will allow each of you whites in my district to grow fifty hectares of any crop, providing you grow me fifty hectares of maize each. That is the deal. Take it or leave it.'

He hadn't tried to argue. He was stumped, shaken. He wasn't used to being told what to do – not on his own land, not by some black bitch in a stolen Merc. He had wanted to slap her fat face, she infuriated him so much. The urge surged through him in a blast of hatred. To think that here stood the cause of the murders, the destruction at Edenfields, a mere five feet away from him. He wanted to lunge out and punch her, throw her to the ground, kick her in the stomach till some organ ruptured and she fucking died the miserable death she deserved. Instead he nodded glumly at her instruction as she drove away, and afterwards almost collapsed on the bonnet of his truck, wheezing, a tight pain stretching across his chest. It was a symptom of repressed rage, Marsha told him. It happened quite frequently nowadays. The stress was getting to him.

He planted his fifty hectares of cotton – the easiest thing under the circumstances – in the fields near the house. He nurtured it, cared for it. It didn't take much of his time, but it was a good cash crop, enough to cover living expenses for a while. Life was now about short-term concerns. No matter how much it pained him to see the great farm lying virtually idle, he had to be a pragmatist. He had to weigh up his options, consider his future carefully. If the truth be told – and he knows many of his fellow farmers privately think along the same lines – he'd jump at the offer of compensation for the farm, no matter what family ties hold him to it. What they were living through was pure organized chaos. Simple as that. And when they start the fucking killings and burnings, then it's time to just pack up and leave. No time for sentimentality there. Just get out and be grateful you're still alive and in one piece.

He let her maize grow almost unattended on the far field by the old silos. He certainly wasn't going to go to any effort to contribute to her bank balance, no matter how desperate the country was for food. This was their man-made disaster, not his. But when she came over one day to inspect it, he was anxious. He wanted to defy her, but knew how dangerous it could be for them if she became angry. Instead she jumped and wailed with joy, immediately phoning someone up to arrange black-market deals, telling them how rich she was going to be. 'Rich farmer,' she shouted afterwards, 'I'm going to be rich rich farmer.'

He had stood there embarrassed and amazed. The maize crop was a ropy nest of tattered lime yellow leaves sagging across the dry dead earth. If this is what the so-called new farmers proudly called a maize crop then God help them all, he thought.

He kept out of her way. Access to Edenfields had been strictly forbidden. Several new signs at the entrance showed a skull and crossbones. She'd had the signs dug up from the power station down the road, transplanted. Apparently her own personal army – six or seven thugs – moped about the farmyard, washed themselves in the swimming pool, used the pond as a toilet, hacked down trees in the garden and made wood fires on the veranda to cook their meals. Night was when they sprung into action, striding down to the compound to interrogate the farm workers. Phineas, the Bakers' old cookboy, had reported it all to him in frightening detail.

He ought to be doing more to put things right, he knows that. But what? Everything he thought of would just add to the overwhelming mess of it all. He finds it's getting harder and harder to keep his head. In his heart, he knows Summerville is lost as well. Even the option of making himself a few connections in the right places, cutting deals with the cronies, keeping those who matter sweet with back-handers, is becoming more and more of a problem. When you start paying off one, three more pop up. His mind's swelling to bursting point just trying to keep track of it all. No, he's resigned to the fact that it's just a matter of time before another black Mercedes comes crawling up the road.

What worries him is what they'll do next. What will they do for a living if they can't farm? He has no other experience, no qualifications. He was born to inherit the farm, work it, live off it. They all had. In time they'll probably have to move on to Australia, New Zealand. He'll be forced to scratch out a living as a handy man, warehouse manager, something menial. Marsha can probably get a job as a secretary, personal assistant to some young yuppie executive. But what a prospect, after this.

And then there's always the chance, always the breath-catching notion that one day, one horrific night ... but no, he can't contemplate it, can't allow himself to be consumed by such nightmares that will only cripple him, paralyse him. They take precautions, sleep with guns by their beds. It's all they can do for now.

It has all happened so quickly. Edenfields was the first target, the guinea pig, but they're all to follow. A definite pattern is emerging across the country – for all the chaos there seems to be a precise, detailed plan of action. All the time they hear reports of other attacks in different districts. Farmers being killed, tortured, their houses being looted and trashed, the crop burnt to the ground. For him, the passage of time seemed to stop at 9 p.m. on a day two and a half months ago and ever since they've been living with the echoes of that night, waiting. He often wonders, and can't comprehend, just how it has all come to pass so fucking quickly. One week they'd all been content, the next chaos and death were upon them, sweeping them away.

He hopes for a sort of peace now, in the eye of the storm, a period of quiet, although with news of young Davey running away from school, threatening to do God-knows-what, things could take a turn for the worse again. On his way back to the house for lunch, Mike looks round disconsolately, his shoulders drooping, his step sluggish, lumbering over the hot dustiness. He is walking (fuel is so short) up from the cotton fields, looking at the decay. The fields are hard, sandy, arid. At least they're not like Edenfields: torched by thugs masquerading as liberators, left as nothing but charred, simmering wastelands. He can see those fields from the kopjes, a black deluge in the distance. Long stretches of fence between the two farms have been hacked down and stolen. Now those famous fields are an expanse of patchy desert lying in the baking heat, with weeds like ropes, leached, barren. It took a hundred years to make this land truly productive, and the strike of a match to return it to its desolation.

Even the gardens round the house, he notices, which were always so lush, immaculate, so talked about – famed enough to be featured in an edition of *Garden and Home* – have fallen dry and neglected. Flowerbeds are overgrown with tawny weeds, the lawn is brown, the celebrated bougainvilleas have gone drab and shabby. He's taken down the loudspeakers from the trees – the ones he'd lovingly, painstakingly installed when Marsha told him of her eccentric vision – because one night the cable had been cut, stolen. They'd woken up to find it gone, and his insides turned to ice. The thought of someone infiltrating their property, stalking about mere metres away from the house where they lay sleeping, unsleeping, groping at their property, taking it, made him feel sick. But Marsha didn't appear upset. 'Just take the bloody speakers down as well,' she'd said, dismissive when he'd tried to console her. 'They're pointless now anyway.'

It depresses and angers him, this decline, this slow disintegration of their way of life. It's now a silent place compared with what it had once been: joyfully musical, quaint, their own private paradise.

Marsha has lost her touch, her once unfailing green fingers.

Walking up the hill, Mike tries to count his blessings: we have our small patch of cotton, we have each other, we have the hills before us and in the evenings the sunset, the chanting of the workers calling the spirits to cleanse the earth, rid the lingering evil. When the thump of drums sounds in the distance, setting the day to rest with the evoking of spirit totems, he knows for certain he's an African. No one can deny him the same steady pulse in his veins, the heartbeat of the land.

The dogs meet him as he approaches the house and entering the back door he tugs off his gumboots, removes his floppy hat and sunglasses, squinting at Marsha who has come to meet him.

He knows at once something is up. It's the way she stands, contemplatively, her eyes slightly downcast. He walks through the house, emerges on to the veranda, sees the boy on the steps.

My God, he says to himself, looking down at the ailing figure with alternating waves of pity and awe. He's not angry, not really, even though whatever the boy's done has obviously been bloody foolish. He looks like he could have got himself killed, got himself into God-knows-what kind of trouble. He half wants to throttle him. But here he is. He's done it, he's done something. He's acted. He looks like a wreck to prove it: battle scarred. Something he himself is conspicuously missing. The presence of the kid, hardy and resilient, sick and suffering, floors him like an accusation and he has to take a deep breath to recover. 'Davey,' he says.

'Uncle Mike,' the boy replies weakly, turning his white, sweaty gaze from the steps.

'You okay?'

No answer, just a strange, unsure look Mike is unable to decipher. The kid certainly doesn't look relieved, if that's what he'd been expecting. But he can't tell. He turns, enters the house, goes to the bathroom to wash his hands for lunch.

Patting water on his cheeks, he looks at himself in the mirror. Against the dark room, the mirror shows a taut face red from the sun, dripping water. He breathes heavily. He's shocked to find his stomach tight, the beads of sweat quickly reappearing. It had been hot outside on the lands, blisteringly hot. His eyes are shot. Red spots flicker over the basin and taps and towel rack. But it's not the heat: it's rage. Red, seething rage. He's failed in what he should have done, betrayed his loyalty to his best friend Joe Baker. It shouldn't have been left up to a boy to set things right. Mike should've done it for him, done more to fight for justice. He's been a coward these last few months, a bloody coward. He goes out again, sits on the veranda blinking into the noonday light. Marsha hands him his lunchtime beer, cold, wet and frothy.

Davey is hugging his knees, grinding his teeth. Mike wants to ask some questions but is afraid of answers. The longer he stays quiet, the more certain he becomes of what's happened. It is as if Davey is talking to him in the silence, in a way he never would out loud, and he hopes Davey hears his responses. Together they exchange the shape of their predicament, the core of what hasn't yet been finished, and needs to be.

Marsha puts her hand on his shoulder, caresses him gently. He takes it, tries to rub it warm, looks up reassuringly. 'It's okay,' he mouths to her flatly, but sincerely. His gesture is simple, mild, but all that she needs to smile weakly and be able to cope with the startling effort needed to go inside alone to prepare lunch.

Davey comes inside but doesn't eat. Mike and Marsha force themselves, picking feebly at cold roast pork and potato salad: an attempt at normality. Now and then they mutter pleasantries – hot day, nice mayonnaise, could rain later on – but most of the time Marsha and Mike exchange pained, hopeless glances in silence while Davey struggles to sit up, his expression fixed, oblivious.

Afterwards Marsha leads him slowly to the bathroom. He walks as if on a tightrope, balancing himself against the walls of the passage, leaving grubby hand marks on the white paint. Wherever he's been for three days has left him smelling putrid. His clothes are dirty, his skin clammy and grimy, his hair smells of smoke, greasy and oily, grained with soil. They stand in the intimacy of the bathroom, and as if he were a helpless toddler, Marsha strips the clothes from his body garment by garment. They stick to him. She is able to master her distaste by imagining what he's been through; the way he has travelled this unfathomable distance, the things he's been exposed to.

He fails to respond to her, but is pliable. She lifts his arms and pulls the thickened sweaty shirt over his head. She is careful with her touch, aware her hands are cold, cautious not to transmit her anxiety as she slowly tugs down his shorts, gently peels off his underwear to leave him a naked figure, an old statue that's lost its marble whiteness but is nevertheless still a study in youthful, athletic beauty.

She turns the hot and cold taps on, positions him under the steaming fall of water and begins to lather his body with a soapy sponge. She works away at him as he stands, gently swaying under her control, and soon the fragrance of soap supersedes the odour of filth. She bathes the length of him, scrubbing him clean, and when she is kneeling beneath him, cleansing his legs and feet, dislodging the collected soils of his journey from between his toes, she feels his fingers press lazily into her hair, stroking her, kneading her scalp softly. Instantly she is suffused with warmth. She looks upwards at the slender stretch of legs, past the modest uncircumcised penis nestling in its sparse wet nest of black, up his chest, a gold expanse of smooth brown tan, and into his distant eyes, silent and grateful and infantile. Somewhere there, in this instant, she sees what she's longed to see: a momentary glimpse of them, of the Bakers.

She towels him off, happy he is fresh and more himself again. Now she can assess the extent of his injuries. From the medicine cabinet she takes out a bottle of antiseptic lotion and some cotton wool and begins to dab at his wounds. She covers the deeper cuts with plasters. A gouge in his right wrist needs proper bandaging. His body is badly bruised. His arms, hands and legs are covered with raw-looking blisters – burns? – which she bathes gently with calamine lotion. His hair, she realizes, has actually been singed in places. There is a worrying lump on his skull where it looks as if he's taken a blow. She thinks she ought to call up Doc Sam, but considers she'd better not risk breaking the news to anyone just yet. Perhaps tomorrow. She clothes him in shorts and a shirt from Mike's cupboard. His old stack of clothes she gives to Tobias. 'Burn these,' she says. She wants them obliterated. The old cookboy nods, puzzled, and takes the clothes away.

The shower seems to have had a soporific effect. As rain starts to scatter over the lawn outside and ruffle the pool, Davey drifts quickly into a deep sleep on the couch in the lounge. Occasionally he seems roused by the faint rumble of thunder echoing in the valley or pulled down further into sleep by the hypnotic drumming of the downpour, but for the rest of the afternoon, he sleeps.

After lunch Mike doesn't go back to the fields. He kills time, throwing a flat, gnawed rugby ball for the boisterous Staffies to chase, pull to pieces. He tinkers around the workshops, clanging away at a bent plough disc he's trying to salvage. Towards teatime he wipes his hands on an oily cloth, strips off his worn overalls, moves up towards the house. In the laundry room he bends over the sink and washes his hands with a strong lime-smelling detergent. In the kitchen he downs a glass of fridge-cold water. In the hallway he stops briefly at the long mirror to press a strand of hair into place and by the time he enters the lounge where the boy lies sprawled asleep across the couch, there is such a stiffness in his shoulders that after one glance he turns and walks into the office, leaving Marsha looking uncomfortable over the tea tray. He dials a number. The crackling line gives up a weak ringing pulse, the voice of a woman answers.

'Jenny, it's Mike. Is Gussie around?'

'No, Mike – he's down at the sties. What's up?'

He tries not to falter, not to pause. 'Nothing Jen, just please ask him to call me when he gets in.'

'Sure,' says Jenny Smit and rings off, concern traceable in her voice.

Mike sits back in his chair and he is hit by dread, like the dead weight of a stone falling from a height.

Every now and then throughout the afternoon Marsha enters the lounge to check up on Davey. A nagging paranoia grips her – a fear that she'll walk in there to find him passed away in his sleep, lost like his parents, gone to them. She can't help but think that he's fuelled with a strong desire to end his life, as if he were an old old man tired of it all. She stands over him at regular intervals, each time a quick stop in her heart before she detects signs of the slow breathing chest, exhalations of life from this desperately ailing thing.

At four o'clock she goes through to make tea, placing on the tray three good cups and saucers, polished silver spoons, a silver milk jug, a bowl of sugar, a neat plate of assorted biscuits, a tea strainer and a cosy. It is her attempt at restoring order to the day. She sits in the lounge, nursing the tea, waiting patiently for Mike to return from the workshops when she plans to whisper over the sleeper, once the tea has been poured and they are seated, 'You know Mike what we've got to do, don't you? You know there's no other way?'

The ritual of tea. The silver tea service – like so many things – takes her back to that day. Sometimes she thinks it's these small constant practices that prevent them all from becoming savages again. On this glorious afternoon, however, tea is her crowning glory, not her last resort. Marsha is sitting on a garden chair under the shade of the cool-smelling eucalyptus tree, watching Tobias struggle down the hill, precariously clasping a top-heavy tea tray, hoping he won't embarrass her by dropping it. Normally, in the shade, happily drugged by the notion of a siesta, she becomes lethargic, drawing close to sleep.

But not on this day. She is sitting straight-backed, rigid. A flamboyant photographer is moving around, shooting her 'sensational' creation from a hundred and one angles: the immaculate lawns flowing down the hill, the blazing flowerbeds topped by a riot of tall specimens, a profusion of colour. Carnations. Sweet peas. Marigolds. Pansies. Delphiniums. Candytufts. Zinnias. Dahlias. And her vigorous bougainvilleas, her particular speciality, displaying their flame-shaped blooms: bright purple, deep rose pink, carmine, fading apricot, light magenta, the sensationally rare white Alba.

She has to restrain the urge to follow the photographer about, pointing out her prized spots, her favourite areas. But she's familiar enough with the type to know he'd cock his head at her and defend his artistic licence. Rather a twit, she thought, the kind of bloke they'd all laugh over, mock at a braai. One of those, you know.

So instead she sits like a good Girl Guide while the woman from *Garden and Home* interviews her. Snooty, Marsha thinks, but impeccable taste in colour. Long slender fingers, beautifully manicured, hair graciously styled, tinted auburn, speaking with a hot potato in her mouth.

But it's Marsha's home ground, and so she talks, talks, talks about her precious, beloved, soon-to-be famous garden.

Still, she's uneasy. She is nervous about the interview – it's not everyday that *Garden and Home* wants you to be the main feature for the spring issue – but there's something more than that too. Something she can't place.

While being interviewed, she pours them all tea, offering a plate of her best chocolate almond cake, fat slices squatting like wrung sponges on a glinting silver plate. As she talks she wonders how her words will appear in print, how the garden will look burnished in gloss, spread across the page, exposed.

'Tell me, Mrs De Wet, can you share with us something quaint about the farm, some little historical anecdote perhaps?'

'Certainly.' She inhales to steady herself, and proceeds to tell the story of Sanja, who married the farm's founder, Petrus De Wet, Mike's grandfather. 'As a welcoming gesture to his new bride he planted hundreds of sunflowers all the way down this hill. Sanja, young, newly married and impressionable, descended from the wagon cart to a startling sea of yellow – a field of eternal summer was actually what she wrote in her diary. The farm was named after this episode – Sommerveld, but over the years that's mutated to Summerville.'

She exhales. They'll like that, she thinks in relief. Keep it going.

'That's a delightful story. Tell us about the secret of your success. I believe it's rather, how should we say, unconventional?'

Comfortable laughs all round, and Marsha gaily explains her invention, pointing to the several loudspeakers ingeniously concealed within the netted branches of trees all about the garden. 'I've found classical music to be the most potent fertilizer of all. They love Bach, Mozart. Hate Wagner. Beethoven's often too intense, but generally they're not very fussy.'

'Incredible.' Marsha doesn't know whether this is said in approval, disbelief or disdain. They all sit there solemnly while a Chopin nocturne runs softly about the mid-afternoon air, skipping, lamenting, somehow settling over the blooming bougainvilleas like a strange and curious potion.

'Very interesting,' the journalist remarks after the pause. The subject is closed.

She offers more cake. Impossibly, the journalist doesn't blemish her lipstick with even the tiniest trace of squishy icing, and says after a petite mouthful that she's entitling the article 'Classical Spectacular', and hopes Marsha won't mind being described as wonderfully eccentric. Marsha is much pleased – although she knows that Mike and Joe will raise their eyebrows, she also knows that she and Leigh will be able to laugh together, sharing the joke. The photographer curls his wrists around his zoom lens and prostrates himself along a hawthorn hedge, snapping some more pictures. More talking. Discussions on cuttings, soils, pruning.

Once they're gone she finds she's slightly at odds with herself, still a little ruffled. She tells Tobias to remove the tea tray and sits for a while longer under the tree a bit shaky, a bit dizzy. Perhaps it's just the excitement of the day, the climax to her weeks of research, preparation – indeed, the climax to her years of gardening, her gift. She's not by any means a gardening expert, doesn't do things by the book. Her methods are happy-go-lucky, hit and miss. Things just grow wondrously when she plants them. She has a knack. But determined not to sound foolish, she'd laboured over Tom Manson's *Garden Book*, done her homework on bougainvilleas, brushed up her formal and Latin names to appear proficient, knowledgeable. *Ardernii. Brasiliensis*. Gladys Hepburn. Killie Campbell. *Laterita. Sanderiana*. I've probably taken it all too seriously, she decides, shovelling my head full of all this tripe.

But it's not the Latin names of flowers making her dizzy. She knows there's something else, something vague and indefinite, overwhelming and immediate that's sitting on the edge of her conscience like a shadow, spreading.

She busies herself in the kitchen, trying to shrug it off. She works a bit at the computer on the farm accounts. Mike's in the fields, won't be back until dusk. She wants him close by, but for no special reason. She's lonely in the big house, inexplicably lonely. For a minute genuine dread descends on her, light like the wings of butterflies, but smothering her, impossible to survive. But what nonsense, she thinks, what rubbish. She can't concentrate on the numbers glaring at her from the pale grey screen. She turns the computer off, and wanders about the empty house.

Suddenly she thinks, I must phone Leigh. She doesn't have anything in particular she wants to say – she's saving her fifteen minutes of fame for the ladies' tennis afternoon – but for some reason the need becomes imperative. So she is there, flustered, picking up the receiver in the hallway, dialling the first few digits, then remembering: they're at the club braai. Her heart sinks, a low, plunging drop. She wants to be there, with them. She's missing something, she's passing up a precious, unrepeatable event for an absurd moment of vanity. What good is some splashy magazine article when she's facing the hollow drift of loneliness, knowing she's missed an afternoon with her best friend?

Then she hears the dogs bark, the gruff purr of the motorbike on the drive, Mike coming home. She goes out to meet him, shaking off her mood. As he removes his helmet, an impulse takes her and she leans over the bike handles and kisses him. Mike is taken aback, surprised by this uncommon outdoor intimacy. She relishes the clamminess of his cheeks, the prickly stubble he permits himself on Saturdays, a rest day from his usual self-discipline. She runs her hand through his thick crop of dark brown hair, ruffles it. She likes him looking rugged, sweaty, manly on his bike. A man of action, stamina. For church tomorrow he'll be a different person – clean-shaven, groomed, dapper, thoughtful in his navy blue suit – and she likes this duality in him.

He sighs a tired, satisfied sigh and she is instantly comforted. In his dry breath she finds a cure for her uneasiness. Now she knows all's well, all's peaceable with the world with her husband returned from his toil on the fields tired and moderately exalted by turns, as he should be from an honest day's work. At the back door he wipes his brow with his floppy Seed-Co hat, mops away the sweat-line. He moves to the bathroom and soon there she hears subdued plumbing noises, water from the tap, the quick trickle into the drain, and silently acknowledges this habit of his, making cleanliness a barrier between the rude outdoors and the private haven of home. It's important to her.

For a while, then, she manages to banish her disquiet. They talk, enjoying their evening sundowner out on the veranda, listening to the chanting over the hills, watching the sun slip. She tells him about the interview, the photographer. He laughs at the jokes she lays out for him. She listens as he tells her about the 2-week-old calf that had died in the morning from a suspected cobra bite. He speaks with a small sorrow in his voice, a professional regret. Both the death of an animal and the loss of a valuable asset weigh equally in his mind. Marsha tries to reconcile the two. There's a part of her that's angry with him, angry he didn't bother to call her to attend the calf, involve her in its suffering, as she's helped so many times before. But there are no pretences about Mike, there'll be no intended slight. He doesn't mince his words. He is plain, down-to-earth, and this is the aspect of him that makes her want to bask in his presence, grow by him. Sometimes, she thinks, despite the seventeen odd years she's spent out here, she's still too much at the mercy of her emotions. She's still got a lot to learn.

She tells him nothing about her strange thoughts, of course, but commiserates over the poor poisoned calf, smiles into his angular sunburnt face, the deep seriousness of his hazel eyes, and goes in to supervise Tobias preparing dinner.

But later, sitting in the lounge, watching the final round of an American PGA tournament, she brushes a strand of hair from her eyes, touching her forehead, and notices something odd. She's cold. She strokes her arms, looks across at Mike, strokes herself again, shivers all over, her hands like dry ice.

She continues to watch, dimly wondering who'll win, eager to share an interest in one of Mike's favourite sports. But for the most part she's trying to decide what piece of music she'll bathe the bougainvilleas in tomorrow. She looks over at the stereo cabinet where her collection of CDs is stacked – several hundred of them now, all arranged according to a strict chronology. She muses, breathes in and out a calm coldness. Perhaps Bach's third Brandenburg Concerto, or an early Haydn quartet? Or maybe, she thinks, contemplating her odd mood, I should go for something out of the usual, something reflective, sacred even? It'll be Sunday after all. Verdi's Requiem Mass?

Yes, yes … maybe.

They are both lying in bed awake. She doesn't want to alarm Mike. He's been under so much stress lately. All these niggling things going wrong with the farm, growing speculation about land redistribution. I'll just add to his worries, she thinks.

But she isn't well. She tries to warm her icy, torpid body,

wrapping herself tightly in the blanket and duvet, plugging the gaps to stop air getting under. She tries to lie still, but can't, unable to let go of herself. Sleep is a thousand miles away. Her mind is racing. Images stream in, out. There's so much to do tomorrow, but she can't think what. Half-formed thoughts cram, jostle for prominence. If this doesn't stop I'll make myself sick, she thinks. She raises her head from the pillow, looks across to see the time: 9:20. Putting her head back down, a quake of dizziness hits her. Her stomach wobbles as if she's on a rickety fairground ride. She is spinning in the bed, sitting up, trying to steady her head by clamping it between her hands. Mike stirs next to her, reaches out to pat her back, but she has fled to the bathroom.

The sound of the phone ringing is like a dagger pressed into her ear.

She has managed to lie down again, the startling sick taste wedged in the back of her throat. She has remained dismissive of Mike's calm insistance he should call Doc Sam. 'Just a bug, it's nothing.' Darkness again and they are lying, unsleeping.

The ringing startles her. She sits upright, her muscles knotted. Light blinds her, even the feeble dimness of the bedside lamp Mike has clumsily clicked on. Fight or flight. They see it in each other, in that quick first look. Mike gets up, stumbles down the passage. Marsha huddles back into the blankets, half listening, half withdrawing, desperate to rid these dreadful premonitions, forebodings. She can't make out what is being said through the door, down the passage, in the hallway, but a fear lies hard in the bottom of her stomach, and she looks straight up at the darkened circle patterns on the impossibly distant ceiling.

Mike rushes in, breathing heavily. 'Jesus, there's been an attack.'

She sits up, lunging herself forward. 'My God, where?'

He is fumbling at the cupboard, flapping at folded clothes. 'Where Mike?'

But she knows. Still, he makes himself say it. 'Edenfields.'

She lets out a short, stifled gasp. The bed turns in an instant; she is upright, blood washing in her ears, tunnelling her sight, as the first flash of her imagination is unleashed.

Mike is racing down the passage, she is groping after him, begging him not to go, pleading for him to take her too. Sitting in the driver's seat he looks confused, and she's tapping the window, handing him the keys. She's telling him he needs a weapon, but back in the gun room she's filled with dread, warning him to be careful, scared at the sight of the shotguns, rifles, pistols he's fumbling to load. He's yelling at her to stay inside, lock the door. She stays with her hand twitching the doorknob. Then he's off, screeching down the hill, and the dust is settling in his wake.

Suddenly it's quiet and all she can do is walk, up and down the still interior of the house, in and out of rooms, fidgeting with doorknobs and latches, staring at glassy family pictures all smiling and congenial. She looks for evidence of her existence in the tall mirror hung in an alcove by the dining room, but can't absorb what she sees: a stranger, itching to get away. She needs to be near the phone. She needs it to ring, and needs it not to ring. She wants news. No news is good news. She careens between the possibilities, battling to keep herself steady. She knows what's happened, and tries not to know, can't bring herself to accept the implications of the attack, the confirmation of her premonitions. Her stomach muscles are knotted, numbness has risen in her throat, she shakes unstoppably.

Time doesn't pass, and then it does, and gradually she finds herself empty. It's almost a state of grace. There is nothing she can do to alter what the world has suddenly done to her. Her surroundings fade away. She does not know how her mind processes such arbitrary shards of thought that come and come to her relentlessly now. She is unable to imagine what has happened, yet realizes that some massive and engulfing horror is close at hand. She looks within herself, searching for the ability to comprehend, but there are only chasms of lucidity that come, then go in the stream of nothing and everything. She has a dim notion of death and misery, but it fails to hold; an overwhelming need to acknowledge the sins of the past, but she is left repentant, guilty as ever.

Wandering about the house again, television on for company, she looks at photographs, the clear shape of a smile fixed upon a face, which something inside her touches and reads like Braille, as close and familiar as if these images were taken just minutes ago. Certain unique signatures – the turn of a lip, the glimmer of an eye – unlock exact, intimate memories.

And then, looking at the television, she suddenly sees things clearly. The pitiless scope of tragedy hits her: such a vast act so insignificant to the wider world, a small entry in the catalogue of brutality. Whose conscience will be stirred by this act in this place? Who will care when they rise happily in the morning, rubbing the invisible urban grime from their well-rested eyes, pottering about the kitchen with a strong cup of black Brazilian coffee, staring nonchalantly at the morning news when in three, four days' time a small news item may, may not flash upon the screen? They will look (and she can't bear this thought, is insulted by it) with plain indifference, perhaps a small pursing of their lips, before stepping into the humdrum metropolis to push along a living. What will they care for the Bakers of this world?

In the bathroom she stands swaying, desperately trying to overcome this sense of tumbling into death. Tears block her vision. She takes a couple of pills to kill the pain, and then there is a sound, and a while later, she is stumbling up the driveway where a hand penetrates the blur, a figure. It is Davey peering at her in the darkness, almost expressionless, bemused. At once she is fully alert, so she hears him clearly when he says, 'They've killed the dogs, Aunt Marsha, they've killed the dogs.'

She bundles a blanket around his shoulders once inside and Jack Hutchins makes them strong strong coffee, cup after cup. Jack tells her Mike is okay, that Edenfields isn't. He clearly can't bring himself to tell her what she knows, that Leigh and Joe are dead. He just stutters with shock, 'It's bad, my God it's bad.'

In an instant she pushes aside her own mounting sorrow to become a surrogate mother. She tries to think of what to say to Davey. He sits on the couch, still, and watching him she imagines she can see the truth sinking in, bit by bit, that his parents are dead, and when it does, she pictures the sharp fact hitting the reservoir of his heart, deep inside him, the water welling up, ready to spill. Then, as she knew it had to, a gentle steady weeping begins and she's happy for his sake that he's only a boy – a young, innocent child able to cry without restraint, to drain his heart. He doesn't shout and curse like an adult would. He isn't angry, yet. He just cries.

It makes it easier then for her to sit next to him, draw his head to her lap, stroke his hair. He's suddenly that child of six she once adopted as her own, who came to stay at Summerville when his mother was so ill. She used to read him Kipling and hoped, when he fell asleep under the warm caress of her hand, that his mind was filled with innocent, ageless stories of the elephant and the hippopotamus and the giraffe and the leopard. She liked to think of him dreaming, asleep across her lap, the quiet rhythm of his breathing a steady pulse for her own maternal longing.

But he doesn't sleep now. His head in her lap is heavy and this time he isn't lulled to rest by her warm hands because her hands, she remembers, are cold and have been for most of the day.

So she sits, sipping coffee, and he lies traumatized, crying out in fresh disbelief every now and then. Finally dawn comes, rising up under the curtains in the lounge, a bright doomsday sweep. She half expects things to disintegrate before her eyes; her coffee cup to fall to dust, the windows to shatter as the night dissolves into the sun. Nothing does, of course. Just another day. And eventually, stiff and strained, she eases herself out from under him and moves towards the hallway. She's concerned about Mike. She's beginning to imagine what he's found, what brutal sights he's had to witness, what savagery's surrounded him.

Then she hears a loud noise at the back door. Quickly, she goes through, to find three of the labourers holding a small buck, a foal, not big enough to be eaten. She knows at once it's been injured, probably caught in a snare, perhaps shot by a poacher. She looks it over methodically for a moment, sees in its glassy eyes the shimmer of mortality, the slate-stare of the victim, and withdraws with a start, backing away into the kitchen, suddenly powerless and unable to do what they're about to request of her.

'Madam, for you – you can touch it and make it better Madam.'

Now that Davey's come to her a second time she remembers the buck again. She had been unwilling to save it, to touch its wound, lessen its pain. The massacre at Edenfields stunned and pulverized her, rendering her abilities sterile. And thinking of it now she is filled with remorse. There is nothing she can do to rekindle her lost touch. It has been taken away from her. Or she's been absolved of it. Either way the buck was taken and deposited in an empty pen and she had tried her best to forget about it, and at the same time her garden began to lose its sheen, its freshness, gradually, so that now, two and a half months later, she looks out of the kitchen window waiting for the kettle to boil, and isn't dismayed any more. Perhaps this is how it's got to be. Perhaps there's something she's got to do before it's all put right again, a cleansing, a restitution.

Carrying the laden tray through to the lounge, she sits, looking at Davey asleep, his supple limbs at rest, an arm gracefully dangling from the edge of the couch. She would love to be able to cradle him. She moves closer, brings her head down to his, observing the level breathing in and out through his nose. She needs to make sure he's still alive so that she knows she is.

She sits fiddling with cups on the tray, the teapot, the strainer, planning to tell Mike what they both know needs to be done, but when he comes in he stands, looks down at Davey, breathes deeply and leaves at once. In this instant she knows a course of action has been embarked on. There's something he's planned, something he'll do to make them all safe from harm.

Mike waits for Gus Smit to phone back. In the interim he drinks his tea, eats his biscuits quietly. Marsha says little. The boy continues to sleep. There's really nothing to do except wait, think. On the TV is a live broadcast of a cricket match, and he has the dogs to scuffle with now the sudden rain shower has subsided. Later, when the sun begins to sink behind the hills, he leaves the boy and the lounge and moves on to the veranda. A sheet of rainwater droplets covers the weedy grass, a welling of freshness fills the air, a sweet replenishment. The dogs idle on the lawn, the odd mosquito buzzes.

It's time for their twilight ritual. The light falls and he sits in the wide wicker chair, a beer in hand, looking out, a certain chill through him tonight. Despite the wet weather, his anxiety about Davey and the sorry state of the farm, the faint thud of tribal drums will soon beat steadily into the coming night.

He's been sitting out here and hearing these sounds since he was a boy. His father sat him on his knee, made him listen, told him in playful, whisky-fumed breaths that it was the old toothless witch doctor stirring his mealie-meal pot, brewing his spirit-possessed beer. Later, as a boy Davey's age, he'd return from boarding school with a longing that no one else seemed to understand to hear those drums. And in the war, returning home from call-ups, even though it was too dangerous to sit out on the veranda for fear of guerrilla fire from the bushes, he nevertheless felt reassured by the roll of the drums at sunset, a signal that all was well and they'd avoided being attacked for another day.

Marsha gets herself a glass of wine and joins Mike outside. She, too, gravitates towards this nightly vigil, this massage of mind. Rising up far and wide into the air, spreading as if in a wave of incense, it is a daily purgative for her too. Especially, she hopes, today. The wailing and chanting will rise shortly, the drums will intensify in the distance. It has become a part of who they are, of this bond of two people by marriage.

She sips her wine, moves a hand across the fading light to touch Mike on the knee, seeking out the warmth of his skin and his resolve.

Mike sits quietly, an acid fear spilling in his stomach. He's never been quite so shaken by indecision. When Gus phones back what will he suggest? What risks will they decide are worth taking? A false move could bring the whole thing down on them, destroy seventy, eighty, ninety years of families' work across the whole country. What they do tonight has the potential to change everything in big, fundamental ways.

He needs the drums to thrash their rhythm of hope.

But tonight the sounds of faith from over the hills don't come. The air remains pregnant, heavy. They wait, and wait. There is a shrill of insects, the odd cricket buried in the dying lawn. They don't say anything. Marsha brings down her hand to Mike's thigh, but there is no warmth. Startled, she's about to say, 'Sod's bloody law Mike', but knows that would be tempting fate. At one point Mike sighs. A short, sharp, significant sigh. But no, they don't say anything to each other. After he's finished his beer, he'll get up and go inside to talk to the boy.

A hand seems to touch his face lightly, and he wakes. He's on the couch. He struggles to get up. Standing, he lurches towards the French doors. Aunt Marsha and Uncle Mike are sitting outside on the veranda, drinking their sundowners. Slowly he turns back into the room, and works his way through the house, out to the back.

A small way down a hill, after a patch of wet yellowed grass, there are workshops, a few pens, a few fowl runs, stables. Beyond that, the road winds through the farmyard gates. He follows the road. At the gates he pauses, suddenly exhausted. He sits on one of the mounds of rocks in front of the gateposts. To his left, a rusty orange plough disc mounted on a mouldy silver pole, crookedly upright in the mass of stacked rocks, reads Summerville Farm, in faded lean white letters.

And here he waits, a lone figure, silhouetted against the fading blue-black sky. Sometime soon they will discover the body at Edenfields. The quiet will draw them in and eventually they will go into the bedroom and see all of it, what he's gone and done, what they thought he'd never dare to do, what new vengeance he's driven like a stake into the hard, parched land.

They will see this. They will come. Just like the sinking of the sun behind him and the moonlight rising over his hands and arms and body, violence has this vicious cycle to it.

When he first went back to school, he'd had to sleep in the infirmary. Initially, they'd put him back in the dormitory, but he kept

turning the lights on. When night fell he grew dizzy, disorientated. Nausea spread from his stomach up across the back of his
throat. He couldn't even walk from the study room to eight o'clock
vespers along the darkened path to the chapel. His knees buckled;
once he had fallen, cutting himself badly.

After a few weeks he was able to go back to the dorm, provided
it was full of schoolmates. But still he wouldn't let himself sleep. He
fixed his stare on the pale gauze of his mosquito net, and listened.
After a few weeks, he noticed he'd acquired rather a good pair of
night eyes.

And so throughout the endless night, from lights out to the sal-
vaging break of day, he lay and pictured Edenfields: the only place
he wanted to be, the only thing he longed for, his world.

At first these images would lead to a gentle but uncontrollable
stream of tears that would leave his pillow sodden. Occasionally the
images would turn gruesome and he'd be gripped by panic attacks,
become quietly hysterical. Always, however, he endured in silence,
alone. He took no comfort from strangers. Instead, he pretended to
be healing, his mind at peace, cocooned in his mosquito net.

During the day he existed, groped along. Everyone was kind
and nice to him and he hated that. Aunt Marsha hung about, fuss-
ing over him. He just wanted her to go home, he wanted to be
alone. He withdrew into himself, spoke little. Not because he really
had any strong objection to conversation, but simply because he
couldn't seem to organize the words in his mind. Talk had become
pointless. And so for that matter had eating, sleeping, washing,
living.

He did eat and wash, though. He ate glumly, playing with his
food, moving it around his plate. He stood under the showers letting the hot water steam over him, holding a cake of soap, a bottle

of shampoo so that the other boys could assume he was all right. And he lived.

He was hounded every day by polite inquiries from the headmaster. He would turn a corner, descend the stairwell and there would be the head, making towards him. It happened with such regularity that he suspected his entire timetable had been circulated, and it was known exactly where he was every minute of the day.

'You okay Baker?'

'Yes sir.'

'Good. Good. Playing plenty of sport? Lots of cricket and exercise?'

'Sir.'

'Remember, play hard on the sports field and things will be fine.'

'Yes sir.'

'Good. Carry on.'

He wasn't stupid. He could read through the fake small talk the head's concern that he'd disrupt the entire school, break the nervy peace. His teachers were nice to him too: if he failed a test, he wasn't put on detention; if he didn't do his homework, he wasn't punished like his classmates. He hated being treated differently.

And then his friends. They just went on. They went home to their farms for the weekends as usual, went fishing, went hunting, brought back tales of seven pound bream, or the promise of spiced biltong as evidence of a kudu shot. They carried on caring for the school's animals – the two sheep, the three goats, the rabbits and chickens – and tended to the plot of crops they grew as part of the Agricultural Studies course. The rule they all followed was that nothing had happened, nothing at all. No one mentioned a thing. And perhaps that's how he wanted it, how he preferred to be treated, as if indeed nothing whatsoever had happened to him. As if he'd gone home for the holidays, had a great time on the farm, wild and carefree, and returned to school four weeks later like everyone else.

But he could feel his effect on people. He was walking, living evidence of everyone's worst nightmare. The other boys in the dormitory, each one the son of a farmer, now knew what the future possibly held. He realized that their sudden agitated exertions at school – working extra hours on the crops, being extra protective over the animals – were in a way an act of defiance directed at him, showing him they could keep going where he couldn't, pretending that it would not all soon be pointless. They were digging in their heels, to prove that by hard work and dogged resolve they weren't going to become him.

And their parents – likewise burying their heads in work, blindly increasing production like never before – he knew how they nevertheless talked in the car park on Fridays, speculating about when their own farms might be taken, invaded. They'd fall silent when they saw him, looking at him with sharp compassion, seeing in him, secretly living through him, their own future struggles.

To make matters worse Reverend Sanders started to call him into his small prefabricated office, mysteriously painted various shades of blue. The reverend would begin talking, gently, about the Scriptures, about the suffering of Christ. After a while Davey realized what the blue was – the reverend's attempt to paint the waves and the sky and the clouds. He couldn't make out why he'd gone to all this trouble. The room looked like the inside of a kids' playhouse, not a place where adults confronted reality.

'You do know that with the cleansing hands of God your troubles will be dissolved.' He looked at the reverend blankly. 'It may take time, but our Lord will prevail.'

He sat patiently, nodding, agreeing, searching for still birds in the blue sky. Reverend Sanders stroked his blue tie, brushed a crease from his pale blue shirt, looked very happy with himself and then proceeded to pray while Davey stared ahead at the wavy walls, imagining what drowning in salt water was like, how it stung the lungs, or how it felt to be gripped in the jaws of a shark and pulled deep underneath the surface.

No one was going to utter a few verses at him and make him forgive and forget. No one was going to buy him off with the promise of easy salvation. Christ hanging steadfast on the cross, dying slowly for the sin of mankind, wiping the slate clean with a sweaty, bloody brow, a greasy mane. Pictures of him never looked anything like a man who'd really had nails driven through his hands, or a crown of thorns levered on to his head, or a stake hammered deep, brutally into his inner self, his heart cleft in two where a bitter hardness had formed.

And so soon when Reverend Sanders threatened to have another of those little chats with him, he pleaded a busy schedule: cricket practices, chess matches, extra maths. He imagined the reverend stroking his tie, consulting Deuteronomy for answers, looking puzzled in the blue enclosure of his study. He couldn't bear that. All he wanted was to be left alone, drifting dead and gutted.

Pulled along by life, he began to fall apart. Flakes of himself fell off. It was as if he was being shredded from the inside, eroded and expunged. Helpless to stop himself splintering, he began to relish this descent into turmoil. He deserved to suffer; a part of him longed for pain, for the sound whipping Pa would have given him when he fucked up on the farm, when he terrorized the old women in the compound with chameleons and snakes, when he made one of the piccanins hop from one foot to the other as he stood about gleefully shooting them with a pellet gun. He would have relished the pain if it meant he'd at least feel something.

He took the money Aunt Marsha sent him and bribed the guards at the gate to buy him cigarettes. He locked himself in a stinking toilet cubicle, knowing full well that the smoke would spiral and spill into the bathroom. He didn't care if he was caught. He puffed away, sweaty and hot, filling his lungs and exhaling and looking down wearily at the grubby, slimy white-tiled floors. He bought a half-jack of cheap diesel-tasting brandy and sipped himself into a stupor. But it didn't change anything. He just hurled into the toilet when he couldn't hold it any longer, bitterly regretted it the next day in lessons.

He got hold of a weed drag off one of the groundsmen, rolled it, lit it and drew in deeply. He wanted the drug to swirl around this stiffness lodged in his chest, the rough, jagged stone of guilt and hate, and somehow dissolve it like a gas. Just as he'd wanted the alcohol to eat into it like an acid, the smoke to soften it like a vapour. For the first hour he just laughed his head off, on the floor of the bathroom, frozen against the wet walls of the showers. Then, sometime later, somehow naked and sweaty in a bed in the infirmary, he just cried and cried, heaving and sobbing into his pillow, seeing spinning patterns in flashy colours on the dull lime-green wall. Miss Robinson, the hostel matron, stroked his brow with a warm, smoke-stained hand, vowed to make him better, to get him some real help.

Real help. Those words were like a benediction. For some minutes he lay there giddy with hope, expecting at last an absolution, the sudden formulation of spirits in the room, his parents come to take him home to the farm just as if they were alive and he was ill with the flu and they'd come to fetch him and care for him. Ma's hand caressing his cheeks, comforting him. And Pa standing over him, looking down, faint concern etched in his eyes, and his grandfather's eyes, and all his forefathers', eager to see themselves in him, recovered and strengthened, carrying on the family tradition.

But when, sometime around noon, Reverend Sanders came calling, a blubber of blue by his side, a shark lurking about his bloody, wounded soul, he turned over, sunk again into the dark depths of despair.

He got into fights, told lies, broke rules. There was a rage in him that he couldn't control. He grew miserable, unruly, sulky, aggressive, unpleasant to everyone. People were beginning to lose patience with him. Sympathy, he quickly learnt, only went so far.

He would find himself treading the cold stone floors of the hostel late at night, sleepless and disturbed, confused and confounded by the quietness. Everything around seemed to be on the point of expiring and falling apart. The sickly green paint was peeling, cupboard doors were off their hinges, curtains were torn and hanging limply, pelmets and skirting boards were slowly being eaten by ants. Was he the only one to see it?

Not everything was at rest. The old boiler hummed and grumbled and occasionally, tired and disorientated, he half believed it was trying to pass on some secret message that he couldn't yet decode. And Miss Robinson – he used to creep down to her parlour, watch her through her half-opened door, a bottle of brandy in her hand, an ashtray in her lap, waving the butt of her cigarette in her stubby fingers as she murmured and complained senselessly to herself, lectured her absent nephews and nieces on their vices, life a blur in her brandy-soaked brain. In some ways he longed for her oblivious disregard, her seeming indifference to real life.

He also stumbled on a scandal. He heard noises from one of the male student teacher's rooms; muted groans, squeaking bedsprings, stifled ecstasy. He listened outside the door, then concealed himself a way down the corridor and waited like a spy. When the door edged open, the tip of a male face checked for safe passage, and then with a giggle and a last squeeze, Miss Moore emerged and fled into the dark. Miss Moore was a young art teacher, naturally attractive to him when he thought about her later, back in bed, fantasizing about her lithe, slim nakedness, the moist slickness between her legs which he could penetrate and plumb, spill himself into, leak his loathing into her like a tanker spewing its sludge. He could infect and pollute her. She'd be a sea to lap up his suffering. The idea began to obsess him. He'd wait for her smuggled arrival, sneak towards the door and press his ear to the thin wood, or try to catch a glimpse of the act through the tiny keyhole. He started to feel like a participator in a strange, obscene threesome, the half-witness they needed to make their affair exciting, elicit. In his mind, which beamed through the door, he came to possess the body which possessed her, as he'd reach down into his pyjama shorts.

But the affair seemed short-lived, a week or two of reckless fucking before Miss Moore grew tired of her escapades in hot, stuffy rooms, and so he was left again to hover about disconsolately, confronting the darkness that spread throughout the passageways. He took to huddling into windowsills, climbing atop cupboards and waiting, waiting in his imagination for the attackers to come so that this time he could jump down and start shooting, take the bastards unawares. He could have done that, could have saved them. Possibly. But he didn't. He sat in the rafters while Ma and Pa met their deaths, something stopping him: uncomprehending, paralysing fear.

As a farm boy he knew he'd failed in his duties. It was his job to act, it was in his blood to defend his family and their land. He should have been aware of the attack, heeded the warnings, gone out to meet the assailants head on. Perhaps he wasn't worthy after all. Perhaps he wasn't a true Baker, a rightful son of Edenfields' soil. During these long, tormenting nights he'd stand in the dark dorm, look down enviously at the other boys, know that they'd have acted, they'd have had the true farmer's spirit, their soft breath resolute even in deep sleep, their bones and muscles and limbs ready to spring into action.

He'd have given anything to be in their position. To have a chance at least, when the time came, to save his parents' lives, defend the farm. His had come and gone.

He began to pick petty fights, shun old mates conspicuously. He'd leave litter on the floor in the dorm so that the entire form was punished, leave the hot water running in the showers so the others would have to go cold. He came to detest the attention they gave to the crops and animals. Why should they be allowed the luxury of fooling themselves? He started breaking out of the dormitory building through a window in the video room, the mosquito gauze torn and rusted, and he'd wander round the property, stooping in the shadows around the towering maize stalks. He'd find himself overcome with a fury that beat inside him like a drum, whipping him into a frenzy he couldn't contain. He'd lash out with his hands, tearing the papery leaves, kick at the base of the stalks. He came across a rusted old machete and hacked at the crops until he was exhausted. If he'd had a jerry can of petrol, he'd have doused the entire acre, stood back and watched the blaze spread and streak, heard its crackle and roar. If he couldn't farm, why should anyone else?

His spitefulness was an extension of his stony grief. It grew harder, more angular, more ragged. A frustration brewed in him, a simmering violence he struggled to suppress. It had been easy in his grandfather's, his great-grandfather's day. They'd just lash out with the sjambok, strike down at one and all, vent a calm and mighty dominance over the blacks. They never had cause to suffer this building pressure, this worthlessness like he did.

And then it erupted. From within the midst of this blurry aimlessness one afternoon he suddenly found himself striding towards one of the cages in the quadrangle, snatching at the latch, delving in for a fistful of fur, small and brilliantly white. The other boys would fuss over the rabbits, let them crawl on their stomachs, lavish on them their care and attention. He hated their small noses twitching and searching the warm night air, living and breathing and existing. He yanked the creature by the ears and swung it from shoulder height, whipping it into the concrete floor, snapping its spine. It writhed, wriggled in his grasp, flinching. He pounded it again; it stopped moving.

He held it, a warm, flaccid bag of white, the heaviness of death such a lightness in his hands. The hard, rough weight wedged all this time in his chest had now, in an instant, become a glowing, pulsing, polished stone, a jewel. How he'd needed to kill, needed to inflict suffering. Such a pure, simple thing. Something inside him needed to snap, to flood, to find a release, to spill the tension. And he was relaxed, as if a certain small weight had been removed from his shoulders. He throbbed with sober gratification. In this act, he'd momentarily appeased everything within himself, lifted something of his lingering grief.

And so a little later he crossed the walkway, entered the phone room where he picked the ridiculously small lock, placed a call to Summerville and spoke to Aunt Marsha.

'I know what I'm going to do, I know how to deal with these people. I've got the solution. It's all okay now, it'll be all okay.'

In daylight Mike can get to Edenfields in twenty minutes. Tonight, with a truckload of farm workers, he's there in fifteen flat, and he's made one firm resolution: to shoot and kill the bastards. He doesn't care if he's taken down as well. He's going shoot and kill.

At once he notices an uneasy silence shrouding the complex, a disturbing stillness about the night. Not even the dogs bark. It disconcerts him. He'd have preferred an immediate confrontation, something physical to deal with, cast his anger upon – not this emptiness. He strides towards the house, the men following at a distance. The front door is locked, in darkness. He moves round the back, seeing at once, splayed around the courtyard, a carnage of dogs. His eyes jump between their bloodied bodies. Some whimper softly, some manage to pant. Most, he assumes, are dead.

He approaches the kitchen door and a figure moves out towards him. He stills himself, raises his rifle. The figure freezes, lifting its arms.

'Baas.' It is Phineas.

'Don't worry,' Mike says, lowering the gun. He enters the kitchen where the brightness of fluorescent lights takes some getting used to. Phineas stands small, wretched.

'What the hell's happened?'

Phineas tells him what he'd discovered – the dead dogs, the open back door as he'd come up to tell the Big Baas again about the rumours he'd heard at the shebeen, that the militia were threatening to attack a farm.

Mike inches towards the dining room. The pit of his stomach is tight and he realizes he is all of a sudden petrified. He's never been this afraid, not even on dangerous call-up missions during the bush war. His feet seem unnaturally heavy. He tries to steady his hands, to grip the rifle. The holster attached to his shoulder is lead heavy. But slowly, very slowly, he moves forward. 'Come with me,' he hisses to Phineas.

The light in the passage has been turned off, a tunnel of darkness. Mike doesn't like what he can't see and when he steps in a puddle of wetness on the floor, he freezes at once. 'What the hell's this?'

'Blood, baas. I turned the light off to make it go away.'

Mike breathes hard. 'Well, turn the bloody thing on again!'

Phineas brushes past him, and at one point almost slips. He gropes for the light switch in the corner. The sudden brightness half-blinds Mike to what lies below on the dark stone floor, momentarily making it appear like streaks of spilt water. Then: the glowing red, sparkling under the naked light. Things flash quickly in Mike's mind. The walls, the floor, the ceiling all seem to rove and turn. The bright bulb pierces his vision. A wave of nausea grips him. He breathes in, out, heavily.

But he carries on, moving slowly into the house, following the trail. He knows exactly where it leads: the main bedroom. All the while he points the rifle ahead, expecting to be confronted at any moment. Standing outside the opened bedroom door, a shiver, a tightness grips him; he loses his nerve altogether. He finds himself staring in at a small stretch of lamp-lit wall just below the ceiling at the far side of the room. His hands shake. His very bones seem to shake as well. He is about to turn away, retreat into the fresh air outside so that he can think things over, when he hears an odd sound: soft, sucking, chewing. He raises the rifle again, leans forward. His limbs are stiff, almost locked at the joints and he can feel the core of himself trying to retreat. But the sound persists and, eventually finding himself in the doorway, he is somehow drawn inside.

He squints. A body lies heaped, face down on the carpet beside the bed. The first thing he registers is disgust at the dog licking, gnawing at the butchered mass of meat, bones sticking from the split scalp down to the lower back. There's not a patch of skin, but a wide stretch of rutted red, pink. He can't take in the whole of what he's seeing, but discerns the oblong shape of a head, the pap of brain spilling from the cracked skull, and acknowledges the shape of male legs – Joe's legs. Jesus. His heartbeat pounds in his head. He can't move his eyes; they stay wide, staring, fixed. The blood drenches the carpet, drips from the cream bedspread, its rich smell thick in the stuffy room.

The dog still sits, licking and licking with its pink wet tongue at the wet pink flesh. Mike moves forward quickly and, with all the energy and anger he can muster, violently kicks it away. It yelps as it goes flying into the corner. When it tries to stand, confused, he sees its rump and hind shank have been hacked at badly. It hobbles forward, back towards the meat of his master, slave to the scent of blood. With his foot he pushes it whining and growling out into the passage and shoots it in the neck. Dark dog blood splatters the light cream walls. The tremor falls to silence.

He turns, flees. He isn't thinking. His mind has seized up. He moves rapidly down the passage, into the dining room, out again, back up the passage. He comes across the bathroom, enters it, slaps at the taps for water. He splashes his face, wets his hair. He heaves, retching dry air. He throws more water over his face and stands back to realize he's urinating, but he can't stop. The piss steadily darkens his grey veldskoens. He lets it wane, then walks back down the passage, into the dining room, the kitchen, out into the hot night to shout at the men still moving about the garden. He doesn't have the faintest clue what he's saying. The men stand, nervous and unsure. He shouts louder, but the right words don't come.

So the men don't do anything. They just stand, looking at him. He makes his way back to the house. He's got to find Leigh and Davey. He's got to find them and save them, take them away from here. He walks back inside, searches the dark rooms, knocks into things, falling, fumbling. He calls out repeatedly, 'Leigh', 'Dave'. No answer. He enters the lounge; the doors leading on to the veranda lie open. He goes through, sees a body, Leigh's body, sprawled naked, legs grotesquely apart, her blood-red nightdress up over her head from which an axe sticks out, wedged in her skull. He turns, flees through the lounge, down the passage, into the hallway, back outside.

'Davey Davey Davey,' he calls, again and again. He moves about frantically, petrified he'll come across another grizzly sight, another body – a mutilated teenage boy. He issues instructions to the men to search the surrounding lands. He could've run away, tried to flee … or his body could have been dumped in a ditch, in the vlei.

Half an hour raking through the gardens, the workshops, the sties, coups and barns can't find him. Where can he be? They call out his name. No reply. Only a still, quiet night, stripping Mike's nerves bare. The more silence, the more fear. It is piteously dark. He forgot to bring torches, and the spread from the security lamps dotted about the garden is pathetic. Venturing round the back of a bush or probing the deep shadows of a dark spot under trees is terrifying. The possibility of a whole new world of horrors has been opened up.

Farm labourers throng the garden, singing and making violent threats to the absent attackers. They are hysterical with anger, the shock spread wide across their faces, spitting and stamping the ground, wailing and ululating. He tries to organize them into search parties, but it isn't easy, nobody can understand anyone else. His mind falls numb, shell-shocked. He can't think what procedure he ought to follow, what he ought to do. His days of call-ups, organizing searches, dealing with death during the war, fail him. He ends up shouting and insulting them, annoyed they won't stop their frenzied wailing to help in the search. 'We've got to find the young baas David,' he repeats over and over. 'We've got to find him!' When words fail to motivate them, he loses his temper, firing a shot into the air. Some of the men think he's gone mad and they run off. Others are at least jolted into action. They search further afield.

Back outside the kitchen, in the courtyard, he decides to shoot the ailing dogs. At least this is a way to end some misery, pass the time until he can figure out what to do. The Bakers had eight dogs. He somehow knows he needs to account for them all. He knows he needs to do this. One lies already dead in the passage where he shot it. The other seven are here, heaped about him.

And so, mindless and blighted, he starts his mission of mercy. He goes to each of the seven dogs, one by one, assesses its condition, and if by some miracle life still teeters from its hacked, bloodied torso, he takes aim from above and blasts a rifle bullet through its neck. But the gun is far too powerful, it rips through everything, penetrating the neck with ridiculous ease. The ground erupts and chips of concrete are flung into the air. In the end there are bits of shot-up dog everywhere: all about the courtyard, spread over the concrete, spattered red and meaty against the white walls, dripping even from the windowpanes of the kitchen. Eventually he stops, drenched in the sight of blood and flesh, knowing that it'll be stamped into his consciousness, shape his thoughts, for ever. He wonders whether there's such a thing as instant madness.

His mind is a fuzz of speckled red shades. He roves the courtyard, muttering and murmuring. Things, simple things, he all of a sudden finds staggeringly difficult to control. His right hand holds the rifle, but its weight is absent, removed. One leg aches with pins and needles.

Eventually he finds himself outside the kitchen door again. He begins to lower himself to the floor, wanting to lie down, when the headlights of a car pierce the road, speeding up the hill. Several men get out and come towards him. He knows them, knows them well, but somehow can't put a name to any of them just yet. He only recognizes shapes, the odd feature. Resting against the wall by the kitchen, breathing heavily, panting, exhausted, he hears voices, swearing, fresh anger and fear. One of the men is Terry, one Gus, one maybe Dirk. Another truck pulls up. More men get out, approach.

'Don't go in there,' he shouts, moving his body across the kitchen door. 'Don't bloody go in there, don't. I swear, don't go in.'

Terry, it would seem, is trying to reason with him. 'Now come Mike, take it easy.'

But he doesn't want them afflicted like he is, doesn't want to subject them to an eternal haunting. 'No, don't go in,' he repeats, spreading his arms across the doorway. 'Horrible, horrible things. Horrible I swear – you don't want to go in there.'

'Now listen Mike, the first thing you've got to do is put that gun down. Can you hear me? Put the gun down!'

At last he registers the instruction, lowers the rifle, and breaks down into a convulsion of tears. At once Terry is next to him, holding him up, saying to one of the others, 'Jesus Christ, take him away, he's well and truly out of his mind.'

Several of them are standing amongst the dogs, shaking their heads, swearing. Then: a horrified shout from around the front. They all rush off. Someone has seen Leigh on the veranda.

The arrival of the other men steadies Mike's mind and he is conscious enough to press upon them all the need to know what has become of Davey, and despite their shock at the sight of Leigh on the veranda, they are at once active again about the property. The boy has quickly become a beacon of hope. If he's been spared, if he's alive and hiding somewhere, then there might just be a God.

Once again the gardens and surrounding lands provide nothing and eventually they enter the house – which they'd been avoiding on Mike's stern command – slowly searching its interior, and eventually discover the trap door to the bathroom ceiling lying open. They gather around and Mike insists he be allowed to climb up via the basin to probe this cavity of hope. The inside of the roof is hot, dank. A metre or two away from the trap door stands a cumbersome geyser. He flashes Terry's torch, shuffles round on the rafters, finds himself staring at a bare-chested figure, kneeling awkwardly, clutching a spanner in his hand.

'Davey,' he says calmly, relieved. 'It's okay Davey – you're safe now. We've all come to help.'

The boy is sweating heavily. He has a streak of grease across his chest. His hair is ruffled, wet. 'I think I fixed it Uncle Mike,' he says quietly, raising the spanner.

'The geyser? You've fixed the geyser?'

'Yes, I think it's working now. I think there was a short in the mains. I reconnected the wires.'

'That's good of you, son. I'm sure you've done a great job.'

They coax him down, wrap a towel round his shoulders, whisk him outside, trying to shield him from the pools of blood, signs of the massacre. Outside, unavoidably, he sees the dogs and immediately begins to cry. As they reach the car, Mike clutches him to his chest. They stand together.

Then he says, 'Someone take him to Summerville for God's sake. Marsha will look after him.'

Relief turns to anguish, then to anger and finally a stifled, numb sense of bitter shock. They walk about stunned, sit unbelieving and silent in their trucks without purpose, stare out at the violent blur of darkness.

Gus is supportive. He stays with him, talking to him in a calm, pragmatic voice, telling him over and over that he's done all he can, that he couldn't do any more. He thinks of practical things to say, makes suggestions as to what they could be doing. He keeps Mike from brooding, keeps him from these bouts of hysteria. 'Just keep a grip on it my man, just keep a grip,' he says firmly, when at one point Mike announces flatly that he wants to hunt down and kill the motherfuckers who did this, each and every one of them if it's the last thing he does.

And then: reality, sobriety, the chilling understanding that this could have happened to any one of them, to any one of their families. Mike thinks of Marsha. He just hopes by now that Jack Hutchins is there, a presence at least. He realizes that some terrifying thing has come amongst them.

Mike hangs around disorientated, not knowing what to do. One of them has phoned the local police station, but there is no reply. The line rings, rings, rings. Sometime later they try again, and are told the police have no transport, no fuel to get there. 'It will have to wait until morning. Otherwise, you yourself must come and fetch us.' Two of them speed off, cursing.

No one goes inside the house again. Only Mike has seen what lies within and the state he'd been in when they arrived must've said it all. But each of them walking about shocked and stupefied pictures in his mind what has befallen Joe and Leigh. They shudder. They have seen something of human nature tonight, its defilement, its rank barbarity.

It is going on 2 a.m. when Bert and Dougie arrive back with the policeman. One policeman: apparently another could not be spared. This one is tall and lanky, and clutches a tatty clipboard.

'What has happened here?' he asks, seeing the dead dogs. 'Someone has killed these dogs.' He shakes his head, looks at the bodies more closely. 'These dogs – they've been shot. All these bullet shells. Who shot them?'

Mike comes forward. 'I did.'

The policeman lets out a short exclamation. 'You mean to say you killed these dogs, you shot them?'

'Yes, I put them out of their misery. They'd been hacked up badly.'

'Are you going to compensate the owner of this property? You cannot just do this.'

'These dogs belonged to the farm, to the Baker family, and they'd been attacked so I put them out of their misery, that was all.'

'So what right have you got to go shooting someone else's dogs? You are responsible. You cannot just come on to someone else's property and kill their animals. It is against the law. Do you not know the law? This here farm, this property – it is not yours to do with as you want. It is not for you to come here and shoot someone's animals. Would I come on to your property and start shooting your animals? Your sheep, goats, horses, cattle? Would I come and break the law by you? Well, it is not like that. It is not how we do things. It is not the way.'

After his lecture he makes a cursory inspection of the house. When he sees the Bakers' bodies, there is a thin, but sincere change in his demeanour. He is clearly shocked, as if he hadn't expected it to be as grim, as brutal. After a while he sighs, and sounds genuinely distraught. 'Ah, this is not good,' he says, repeatedly, shaking his head, 'this is not good at all.' He says he has known the Bakers for years.

Outside again, within earshot of the labourers, he says, matter-of-factly, 'It is unfortunate, but these armed robberies happen. It is now unfortunately quite common.'

He speaks for the remainder of his stay to the workers. He tells them that this was an armed robbery. 'It is very bad for this to happen, but the baas and the madam have been very careless to allow armed robbers to come into their house.' The labourers stand about stiff and unsettled, not daring to say anything, agreeing reluctantly with the policeman that there had been no sign of trouble for the Big Baas Baker and that, yes, it must have been armed robbers, thugs.

When the policeman leaves, Mike is forced to go with him, charged with trespassing, improper use of a firearm and wanton destruction and defacement of property belonging to a third party. He is booked and temporarily locked in a cell, a tiny windowless box of concrete. He can't sit because the floor is fouled with a stinking dankness, crawling with lice. So he stands for the remainder of the night, part of the next morning, shaking and sobbing, an unbearable dryness at the back of his throat. He finds he can't see Joe's face clearly any more. Something discolours it, fragments it. It appears in his mind out of focus, blurred. All he can see is the dog, sucking, gnawing. An animal feeding. As for Leigh, he can't seem to see her face at all. It is permanently covered, as if by a sack.

Finally Dougie and Terry negotiate his release – an astronomically large sum of cash for bail, no receipt issued. He is a bit roughed up, clearly exhausted. They all are by now.

'Is Marsha okay?' he asks, 'and the boy?'

'They're fine,' Dougie assures him, 'everyone's fine.'

'Then we've got to go back to Edenfields.' He sees the danger, the clear pattern: one day you are removed, the next your land is taken over. Lock, stock and barrel. During the unending night he'd become convinced they were going to keep him locked up so they could take Summerville too. He'd been hoping and praying that Marsha would've had the sense to take Davey and go into town, stay the night with Pastor Fellows or Doc Sam.

But now he knows that Edenfields is the prime target, the one they're after first. He's got to get back there, try his hardest to safeguard it.

They drive off, speeding towards the farm. A short way down the hill from the house they pass a white lorry, stopped alongside the workshops, by the tobacco barns, surrounded by a bunch of surly looking youths in ragged clothes. There are fifteen, twenty of them. They are dancing, shouting war songs, brandishing banners, waving lighted torches. As their truck passes by, the youths lunge towards it, hammer on the roof, chase after them, feign killing motions.

'Fucking hell,' says Terry.

Parked outside the house is a large black Mercedes with tinted windows. Three police Land rovers litter the garden. Outside the back door, Gus and Richie are standing in front of a highly animated, stern-looking woman.

They get out, approach the gathering. Five or six policemen stand behind her, straight-faced as she waves her hands about, instructing them in her loud, obstinate voice. She is threatening, rabid with intent.

'Who are you?' she demands, seeing them.

'I'm Michael De Wet, I'm the immediate neighbour to this farm.'

She looks him up and down, her lips puckering, sneering. A policeman speaks to her, whispers in her ear.

'You, you were here last night trespassing on this land,' she starts.

'No. I came here after I had been informed of an attack on the owners of the farm.'

'I am the owner of this farm,' she shouts. 'You were trespassing on my farm, what gave you the right to come here? This is my farm, my land.' She pulls out a brown envelope from her handbag, waves it at them. 'Read this – this is an official document stating that as of the eighth of this month this is my farm. The eighth – two week ago. These people who were staying here, they were trespassing as well. They were not supposed to be here. They were meant to be off. You do not know the arrangements. Their time was up. I have been more than patient with them. I have been more than fair. It is now unfortunate that they are dead, but it is not my concern. This is my land and they chose to be on someone else's land illegally. If they are attacked by robbers or thieves it is their bad fortune. I was being good to these people by giving them an extra week to move off and now see what has happened to them. Have you seen the mess inside this house? It is disgusting. It is a big problem for me now because I was intending to stay here from today – but there is such a mess I cannot. It has delayed my plans, it has ruined my schedule.'

Phineas is led from the low shadows of the garden by a policeman and made to kneel in front of the woman. Mike can see he's in a daze, just like himself, overwhelmed.

'Have you finished getting rid of those dogs?' she asks.

'Yes madam,' he says, tears suddenly streaming down his cheeks.

'Well get inside and start cleaning that mess in there, you work for me now!'

She turns to them. 'And you – you must leave at once before I have you removed. I do not have time for this. I am a busy woman. I have important things to do.'

She flaps round in her handbag as her mobile phone rings, laughing at the voice of a friend.

The men leave. They don't try to argue, don't try to negotiate. They climb slowly into the truck and just drive away. Mike sits shell-shocked, mutters about sudden pains in his chest. Dougie breathes deeply. They don't speak. They don't swear or react angrily when they drive past the militia swarming the lands, past a battery of searing flames on each side of the narrow, winding road, burning black the wheat crop, Joe Baker's prized fields.

News has spread across the district and life seems to have come to a standstill. The farms all lie still. Terry drops Dougie off first, then Richard Brighton, then Gus, crisscrossing the network of farms before eventually reaching Summerville. On each farm the tractors lie fat and clumsy, the combine harvesters stand abandoned like small islands on the fields. The farm workers huddle round in groups by the farm store or on the dusty soccer fields beside the compounds. The old women chant and wail. The elderly men, many who have no doubt worked for and known the Big Baas Baker at the grand old Edenfields Estate for years and years, sit on the stoeps melancholy, meditating, brooding on the spiritual world.

Finally Terry's truck crawls up to the farmhouse at Summerville and Mike stumbles out, childlike, into Marsha's arms.

It is three days before they can track down where the Bakers' bodies have been taken and five days before they are released in recycled black body bags. The names of two entirely different people are still scribbled on old labels. One says: 'road fatality'. The other: 'shebeen dispute'.

'You can't do that,' says Mike, standing in the cold, grubby tiled room at the police mortuary with the funeral parlour man he's hired all the way from the city. 'It's not right. These people deserve to be properly handled.'

The policeman labouring over the paperwork sighs, then scribbles the Bakers' names on fresh labels, writing 'armed robbery' on each, sticking them over the old ones, not knowing which name goes with which bag. They put the bags into two coffins, slamming the lids.

The funeral parlour man objects strongly. 'You should know that this is of extreme concern,' he says, 'to disrespect the dead. Especially in our culture, the true African way.'

'Have you paid a deposit for the bags?' the policeman asks. 'We need them back by Friday.'

Mike and the funeral parlour man nod.

'Then sign here.'

When he goes into the house again Mike can't find Davey and instead fetches himself another beer from the fridge. As he sits down the phone rings.

'I'll get it,' he tells Marsha.

Back outside he drinks his second beer quietly, chatting occasionally to the dogs, and eventually telling Marsha they ought to go inside because the worshipping isn't coming – not on this night of nights – and anyway he's being nabbed on the ankles by mosquitoes. 'Yes,' she says, 'so am I.' They move inside, as if on any other night, to the soft light of the lounge, a warm, homely room, where they'll sit in front of the TV and watch sport or game shows or British sitcoms until it's time to eat dinner.

So they go in and sit for a while, trying not to think about Davey Baker outside somewhere, waiting for the trouble he may have brought to them.

After his third beer, the tension and worry and anger Mike felt at seeing the boy on the veranda steps has faded into heavy resolve. When Marsha tells him it's about ten minutes to dinner, he takes a walk outside, the dogs curious and oblivious by his heels as he moves down towards the gate, and he sees the figure of the boy sitting upright on the mounds of rocks. Suddenly he's struck by the physical presence of Davey, the broadness in his shoulders, the gawkiness ready to topple over into strength and masculinity. He watches the shape of the sitting boy transform into the imposing outline of a man, a sentry at the gate, defending them all.

'Come Davey,' he says, approaching. He puts a hand to his shoulder, to touch this strange new being. 'It's dinner.'

Surprisingly Davey speaks. 'Do you know what I've done Uncle Mike?'

'Yes boy.'

'I did it.'

'You did.'

'I shot her, like I said I would. I shot her.'

'Yes.'

'I couldn't help it – it's all I've been thinking of, all I've wanted to do. I just had to.'

'Come in, now. It's dinner.'


He tells Uncle Mike he'll be there in a few minutes. Alone again, he looks round him, blinking into the dusk light, and suddenly kicks hard and angrily at the dusty, stony ground. Yes, he'd done what he set out to do – he'd made a plan, he had given himself a second chance. It was going to be like the adventure stories he used to enjoy reading: he'd be the young hero on whose shoulders everyone's future depended. He'd been chosen for this task, this dangerous mission, and he'd see it through right to the very end no matter what hardship befell him. He'd planned everything so well. He'd packed his provisions, he'd crept out of the hostel, scampered across the gardens, made his way down towards the playing fields, squeezed behind the water reservoir, climbed the rubble of the fallen wall. He'd waited in the bushes for the train to arrive, he'd endured the journey, done the deed.

So why didn't it help? Why couldn't he look the memory of Ma and Pa in the face? What does he have to do to make it go away, to cleanse himself of guilt and regret? Even now, nearly three months later, and after all he's been through, all he's achieved, the pain still strikes his chest, the back of his neck, his stomach, his skull. And it is real pain, a true deep agony. Every blow struck across Ma and Pa's bodies is a secret unhealed wound across his. He experiences everything, even the tensing of their flesh before the blow, the tight squeeze of their eyelids.

He sits, miserable, at the dinner table. Aunt Marsha serves the chicken casserole Tobias has made and she and Uncle Mike sit in silence, watching him, eating slowly, trying not to finish before him. He picks away minutely at a drumstick, flaking off slithers of white flesh, sloppily steering half a potato across his plate, back again in a sea of gravy.

Eventually Aunt Marsha says, 'You can leave what you don't want Davey.'

A while later he sits in the lounge while the others half watch a stupid sitcom followed by a daft action series. Aunt Marsha makes coffee at around 8:00, and then says she's off for a bath. Uncle Mike and he sit for another forty minutes until eventually Mike waves at him to break his empty stare and says, 'Why don't you go to bed boy?'

Drowsy and obedient, he plods off down the passage to the spare room Aunt Marsha has made up. He strips off his clothing, pulls on a pair of sleeping shorts left out for him and slips into the coolness of sheets.

The light stays on: a glow stuck like a wad of fireflies to the ceiling, radiating warmth, security, assurance, a fixed reality. He lies on his stomach, his hands tucked beneath him, staring at the colourful patterns that make up the curtains. He can't make out what the patterns are meant to be – something distinctly ethnic like zebra print, earthenware pots. At least they are something to focus on for a minute or two, before his memories take over.

It is the school holidays and every night before sleeping he says into the darkness of the room, 'Half past four, half past four.' Nothing answers but the thought of what bliss the morning will be, a mystical vision of the earth at daybreak, the presence of prize beasts in shadowed bushes, the vlei, the veldt, and so he falls asleep facing the digital flash of the alarm clock.

He wakes with an urgency of exhilaration, looking over to check the clock. It pulses weakly, its dim numbers reading 4:29. He is filled with a sense of triumph. His ability to outwit the clock proves his brilliance, independence, superiority. The moment the string of beeps begins to sound he taps the alarm button and lunges from bed with a resolve he knows only boys who grow up on farms possess, galvanized by the thick whiff of sun-baked soils, the off-sweetness of the vlei, the rich pungency of rotting animal hide already in his lungs.

He is fully awake before his bare feet touch the thin mat beside his bed, so the upwards stretch of his arms and swivel of his naked torso is mainly for show. He dresses rapidly, pulling on underpants, shorts, a scruffy old shirt, socks so that his large hunting boots will fit comfortably.

It's not as cold as winter, but certainly cool after the warm tomb of his bed. Outside on the open plains with the sun not yet up, the earth not yet heated, he knows a chill will tighten his flesh, making his finger tremble against the icy metal of the trigger.

He does not put on his boots yet. Gripping them tightly he tiptoes out of his room. He doesn't want to wake Ma and Pa, asleep down the passage. They don't know about his early morning adventures.

The red stone floor shines under the light that stays on all night over the passage. He slides in his socks silently towards the wide arch leading to the dining room. He thinks of Phineas scrubbing and scrubbing at soiled socks, blackened from their travels over floor polish and dirt.

In the kitchen he eases the small camouflage flask from the back of the fridge. He'd filled it the night before. Strapping it over his shoulder, he moves hurriedly to the adjacent storeroom where the tall gun cabinets stand. He hears the dogs in the courtyard, rousing, readying themselves. Perching on a concrete sink, he struggles with his boots before sliding off and moving over to bring down a gun. The steel is icy, enthralling, giving him a sudden thrill. Every night he sneaks the gun cabinet keys from the office drawer while Ma soaks in the bath and Pa snoozes in his armchair, nursing his rum and lemonade, and dashes to unlock the thick padlock so that overnight the gun waits for him: its black shaft, its hard wooden butt.

He loads the gun, holding it carefully in the crook of his arm. He eases open the kitchen door. Outside it is still night. He looks up to see the stars sunk in blue sky, the trees standing black and still. He searches for signs of day, the faint grey tint to the concrete slabs of the courtyard and the walls, and is left wondering whether he has again risen too early. What will he do when he finds himself tensed and ready and the guinea fowls still asleep in the scrub, ignoring their deaths?

The dogs greet him ecstatically, their tails whipping the air, their wet noses pressing, wrinkling against his legs. This is the most dangerous part of the whole operation and he's quick to quieten them. He leads them down from the house, jogging. Once out of the yard, past the gate, they bolt into the wild, yelping recklessly.

With the open land stretching before them and the risky part behind them, he allows himself to imagine Ma and Pa tossing in their bed, muttering about those bloody dogs again, before being pulled back into sleep.

He indulges the animals, throwing sticks and stones for them, allowing them to charge up and down the hill's dark stretch of road before sending them back to the house. They cannot come because they'll disturb the game, much as he would enjoy their company. They trot miserably back up the hill and then sit on their haunches, a row of silhouettes, facing him stoically as he disappears beyond a curve in the descending road.

And so he's off walking, pacing himself along the winding road. He draws contentment from the heavy weight of the gun on his hip, the gritty crunch of his hard boots on the gravel. The slight wetness under his armpits and the stale smell of sleep on his body make him realize that he is indisputably happy. Walking the scored soils of Edenfields, free and unrestricted, he's happy.

Soon the sheen of trees quickens in the distance – over the hills – and then a green shimmer sticks to a blade of grass, and when a shaft of muted pink appears on the tip of the horizon and depth suddenly appears in the crevice of a stone, he knows that daybreak is imminent.

He must hurry to his spot before the fowl wake up.

He veers off the road, moves swiftly through the narrow, dark tunnel of foliage. He seldom emerges unscathed – the thorn needles, the claws of a clutching branch, grope at his bare skin. But he is used to cuts and grazes now, even embraces them. They used to send him crying off to Ma; now, if the pain really is biting, he'll swear sharply before scooping the blood away with a finger or licking at it if he can. He knows he is hardening with age. Now it's good to fight against the pain, to focus on a clear hurt and conquer it.

Today, though, he emerges unscathed, and in an open area, having left the cultivated part of the farm well behind, he stops, scouting for promising locations. He must be able to conceal himself low so that he can wait for the birds to wake and fly down from the trees, or move out from under the scrub into the open grasses where they will bask in the sun, seeking warmth. That's when he'll take pot shots at them, taking advantage of their slowness and panic, hoping to bag four, perhaps five if he's lucky, so that afterwards he can sell them to the workers, make another easy killing. The action won't last more than a few seconds, but it's for this momentary ecstasy he comes striding five miles into the hostile wilderness, into this foreign place, infiltrating the territory of sleeping things so that he can plunder the land with his gun. He gets great satisfaction from knowing that for this finite time he'll hold the absolute attention of every living thing. Beasts larger and mightier than him will startle and cower, raise their ears to his presence. It's not for the fowls he's come, or not only. He's here for them all.

And so he picks out his place in the pulsing veldt, squats and slides forward on to his belly until he is lying snug against the sharp tufts of grass, the coarseness of the earth. He sets his sights and surveys the shadowy tract of land in front of him. The long grass is still pale, a fresh film of dew on a spider's web suggests it is still too early and he resigns himself yet again to waiting. A chill has settled on the ground and he suddenly finds himself uncomfortable, the position he's lying in absurd. He rests the gun respectfully against the trunk of a tree and sits up.

These days he feels a growing need to take stock, to think through things he's begun to make out, but hasn't quite found a place for yet. The early morning allows his mind the space to turn them over, search for where they fit. He thinks of Ma's overattentiveness, Pa's perceptiveness. He thinks of the farm, of fishing in the dam. Often he thinks of Katie Hutchins, who he's suddenly found attractive, alluring. He saw her briefly a few weeks ago when she came to play hockey at his school. During the term her chest had grown fine and shapely. He imagines her breasts soft, manipulable, cupped in his hands, and he finds he cannot condemn himself for thinking these vivid thoughts, cannot think that sex is wrong or sinful, or be repelled by the thoughts of lying tangled, trapped in Katie's tanned flesh.

But with the glimmering of light down on the vlei and a tint of beige awakening in the hollow of a tree, he pulls himself together and retakes his position. He takes his early morning bird blasting seriously. Katie and her slender thighs can wait for later. He nestles down again, hugging the gun. With his mind alert, his fingers readied, he urges the guinea fowl awake with a quiet 'Come on, come on.' There's no sign of a flourish yet, but he waits patiently, stilling every muscle in his body, like a snake spread out in the litter of leaves. Now that daylight has broken he will stay like this for up to twenty minutes if he has to.

The birds remain concealed and he waits and waits, composed even when a thin trail of sweat dribbles down his temple. Only once the sun has burnt to nothingness the small rosy clouds floating in the sky and started to reheat the red earth does he detect a faint rustle in the bush. He tests his sights again, squinting down the black barrel, resting his finger squat against the cold trigger.

*

But something unexpected happens: a noise off to the right. Not a bird noise, but deep, guttural. Instantly his attention shifts, listening. It comes again – a groan from a mammal. Yes, certainly a mammal, carnivore, possibly a leopard, a lion even. At once he scrambles to his feet so that he can flee if charged; the guinea fowl are startled into the air, wings beating like his own pulse, but he keeps the gun pointed at the mesh of vlei from where the sound came. His heart is in his throat, pounding away with exhilaration, terror. Again the soft noise probes the air, closer, a hushed groan, the sound of a sniff before feasting.

He remains poised, unblinking. What beast stands ahead of him? The natural power of the bush floods him, the fear something unseen can instil so suddenly. He thought he knew his place amongst it all – its acceptance of him and he of it – but now he feels far, far out of his depth.

As the noise pushes forward again from the wilderness, he flinches and falls backwards, the gun awkwardly twisting in his arm. He scrambles clumsily to recover. Stay on your feet. The golden rule: stay on your feet at all times. His breathing quickens. His pulse is racing. Yet inside he's calm, almost as if he's grasped something incomprehensible: the definition of infinity, the implication of eternity. Pa would be relaxed. When Pa hunts you can sense the control, the patience, and now, through the tall grass and scrub ten metres in front of him, a brown mammal breaks out into the openness.

He raises the gun at once, fires. A boom. A shudder against him. The animal recoils, disappearing in a startled flash. He takes aim again, but it's pointless. It has gone, whatever it was. Some small buck.

Did he get it cleanly? He's not sure. He ought to track it down and finish it off. Pa's always telling him about hunting rules. And besides the hide, the meat would be good pocket money. He'll skin it, salt it, hang strips of its meat on hooks to dry in the sun. It'll make good biltong. Then next time they're in town, he could buy some new tackle at Fisherman's Corner in the shopping village. But he can't really be bothered. He looks round. The fowls have long flown off. That animal has spoilt the morning's hunt. Stuff it, he mutters. No matter. He'll return to the house, slip the gun into the cabinet, climb back into bed so that he can be innocently awoken by Ma in an hour or two for breakfast.

He follows the same route back through the foliage, on to the gravel road. The light over the savannah now glistens on the dewy red soil. Ant mounds tower, shine. He's looking all the time for things to compensate for the lost fowl — birds, rabbits, a sluggish snake — but there's nothing. Everything seems to have fled from him. Oh well, tomorrow. He walks briskly up the winding road and begins to tire. Everyday he resolves to eat a biscuit for energy before he sets off, but everyday forgets. He sips at the cold water from his flask.

Soon, beyond the tall bush, the vast blanket of fields appears on each side of him. He can hear the sprinklers ticking away, scattering water, and as he moves further up the road, he begins to smell the rich sweetness of wet earth. He breathes in deeply. There isn't a smell more welcoming in the world. It's an Edenfields smell, unlike any other. Pa is bound to be around somewhere and he's cautious to avoid being seen with the gun, even though he knows that first thing in the morning he's never on the fields but far off checking on the sties, on the births and fatalities overnight.

He waves to the workers as he passes them. They're always happy to see him and he knows it's because one day he'll be the Big Baas at Edenfields and they'll all want to get jobs for their kids. They're sucking up to him. He often wonders what it'll be like to run Edenfields completely, absolutely. Would he change things? Would he dare? Pa always does things so thoroughly. He seems to know just what to plant each season and in what proportions so that not a hectare is underplanted. This year there's more paprika, more barley, less hypericum, less citrus, the usual stockpile of tobacco. Last year was the opposite – how does he always get it right? And he works like a horse as well, from sunrise to sunset. Ma always used to say that if the cotton crop comes out smelling of stale sweat it's because it's germinated in Pa's armpits and if the mealies taste extra salty it's because they've been watered by the sweat from Pa's brow.

He's often overwhelmed with what the future holds. Will he be able to live up to it all? They've won so many posh-sounding trophies recently. They are Pork Producer of the Year and last season they won the big one – Tobacco Grower of the Year. And they are always being mentioned in editions of *Commercial Farmer's Monthly*. Just a few months ago there was an article praising Pa's methods of cultivating wheat stocks.

He makes his way up through the green sod-smelling fields and enters the vicinity of the farmyard, striding past the crow-infested orchard, the moss-meshed reservoir, up towards the lawns in front of the house. He wonders vaguely where the dogs are. They're normally leaping about him as he returns. He skulks across the courtyard, enters the house from the back door leading into the storeroom. Suddenly he stops in his tracks. Ma is a few metres in front of him, rinsing something in the sink.

He backs out the door, moves out of sight. Why is she up? He cannot let her see the gun. He'll be in big trouble if she does. Go back to bed, he urges her, it's far too early for you to be up. He peers around the door again and sees that she's moved off into the kitchen. She's baby-talking to the dogs, looks to be making a cup of coffee. Soon she'll be off back to bed.

But she isn't. Stubbornly she stays, fiddling with knives and a whisk, clanking a pan about the stove. Go back to bed. Don't always be so bloody impossible! He hears an egg shell crack, the inevitable sizzle of the splattering fat. She's frying an egg and this can only mean one thing – Pa is still somewhere in the house. She always fries an egg for him first thing in the morning. But why, why isn't he down at the sties? If he sees him with the gun, there will be shit – serious shit! With Ma he stands the chance of sweet-talking his way out of trouble, with Pa he's stuffed.

He creeps round the house, veers down the hill, comes up the other side. Their bedroom curtains are drawn. Steam is curling, billowing against their bathroom window. Pa must be showering. He stands next to the drain where the water runs, trickling slowly. Got to act quick. He moves stealthily around to the veranda where he hopes the door to the lounge has been opened. It has. He sneaks in, holding the gun parallel to his body so that it may just go unnoticed if he were spotted. Slowly he inches into the passage, listening, trying to place Ma and Pa within the house. He imagines the egg spitting loudly in the kitchen and Ma poised over it, spooning hot oil. He hears the shower drum above him, pictures Pa standing underneath, singing, humming. If he's quick he should be able to make it. He plans to dash into his bedroom, hide the gun underneath his bed, but as he makes off down the passage he catches a glimpse of Ma coming through the dining room arch. Christ! At once he rushes into the nearest door – a bathroom – closing it quietly behind him.

Ma strolls past. He knows the sound of her slippered footsteps over the stone floor. Above him somewhere he hears the geyser mumble and suddenly a muted squeak, as the water is being turned off. He sighs. What to do, what to do? He looks around and up, suddenly noticing the trap door in the ceiling. Perfect. He balances precariously on the basin, pushes up on the hatch, shifting it inwards. Dust falls in a cloud and he shuts his eyes tightly. When the dust eventually settles, he looks up again, manoeuvring the hatch further into the ceiling. He bends, picks up the gun and slides it into the rafters before pulling the trap door closed and climbing down. He wipes his grimy hands on his shirt. He takes off his hunting boots, stands them behind the door. He throws his cap and shirt into the laundry basket so that now he looks as he ought to: bare-chested in his shorts, as if he's just stumbled out of bed.

He opens the door and scampers quickly down the passage, entering his bedroom. He gets under the bedcovers where it's warm and inviting and he is relieved. He's done it. He's safe. Soon he finds himself drifting off and when he awakes – too hot for sleep – it's almost half past eight and Phineas is holding an earthenware cup of strong-smelling coffee beneath his nose. The old man's smiling face greets him; chipped teeth, crooked jaw, sunken cheeks, wiry stubble. He hobbles round the room in his khaki uniform, his short crispy hair shining in the faint stream of sunlight through the curtains like twisty bits of grey glistened steel. Davey peels away the sheets and bedspread and lies for a while, lazing in a pool of blissful calm. Phineas is quick to draw back the curtains. The sunlight comes flooding in. The heat spreads to him, rising over the surface of the rumpled sheets at his feet.

Things are going according to plan and Mike is relieved. He said he'd give Gus a call by around 9:00 once everything was settled round the house and the boy was in bed. Now it's ten minutes to and suddenly time and numbers are important. Gus is thirty kilometres away, it takes twenty minutes to get from here to Edenfields, they'll need at least two hours to do the job, three of them to carry it off.

Mike reasons that if he phones Gus before 9:00, it'll put him on edge. He sits and waits. Time slows maliciously. He would like another beer – the desire hits him startlingly – but he knows that tonight of all nights he should keep himself as clear-minded as possible. On other nights, it's different. It's astonishing, his absolute lack of guilt in sitting up late in front of the TV, sipping iced scotch and lemonade until at some stage he finds a neutral, even agreeable, aspect to his hopelessness. When one has nothing to do, drinking is perfectly acceptable. No responsibilities, nothing to contribute. Of course, it was different when every morning as the light broke through the bedroom window he'd wake to the absorbing prospect of production, to the fulfilment of farming. He used to stay out all day, come home utterly exhausted, and the tiredness from sheer hard work was something he lived for then. It exalted him, made an honest man of him. He didn't have the time to watch sport on the TV during the day, drink a few beers at lunchtime, nurse a few brandies in the afternoons, hit the sundowners in the evening, the scotch later on.

Tonight, however, he's keeping himself as sober as a judge (give or take the three beers he's already had) and for a strange few minutes while he waits to phone Gus, his blood surges again with purpose, with strength and intent. He's got a chance to do something at last: something for Joe, something to put matters right at Edenfields. Sensations he's almost forgotten about in the past few months – will, reason, control – flow through him.

He knows Joe would have done no less for him. More. Joe'd do his utmost – probably to the degree of reckless stupidity – to protect Marsha and Mike, the farm, the heritage between the two families. He probably wouldn't have been so pacified and controlled as Mike's been, so able to check that short temper he'd had since they were kids together, but he'd do what needed to be done all right. Maybe Mike should've been more proactive, more outspoken and condemning of what's been going on, but where would that get them? Booted off the farm a few months earlier, butchered for speaking the truth? He remembers thinking, a few years back, that Joe would one day speak his mind once too often. He'd been vocal on almost every agricultural policy that came out, criticized the control on prices, duty on imports, tax on exports, and had even voiced his dissent to the provincial governor in public once. Not the best thing to do.

But that's democracy, Mike supposes. And Joe had always been a stickler for fairness; you had to hand it to him. Out of all of them, he'd been most concerned about the welfare of his workers, set up rural schools in the district, assisted them with medical treatment, even gave them a small dividend of the profits after a bumper season. Talk about the fucking irony of it all.

Well, it's now up to him, in some small, perhaps redundant way, to pay homage to all that. Just like when they were kids and they'd watch each other's backs to try to avoid a lashing with the steel-spiked belts their fathers carried around like their religion. (My God, he thinks, those were the days: rugby tackling the calves into the dust, swimming and pissing in the forbidden reservoirs, ambushing the tractor driver, snakes in their sisters' beds, shooting the piccanins from a tree with stones from a catapult.) Yet, try as they did to worm their way out of it, the lashings did come and together they'd bear the pain, the sjambok tearing their backsides, bringing blood and agony, and all the while making them tougher, into the men they'd both become.

At 9:00 exactly he gets on the phone. Gus seems to snatch at the receiver.

'Yes,' he says.

'Are you ready?'

'Let's do it,' says Gus. The line goes dead.

And now Mike knows there can be no second thoughts, no turning back.

Thirty kilometres away Gus Smit says to Jen, 'Listen, I'm just going over to Summerville, Mike suspects there may be a situation brewing.' Instantly he knows he shouldn't have put it like that, absolutely the worst thing to say to a bloody woman. But he has always been tactless, try as he might. He sighs at her anxious expression. 'Don't worry.'

'Gus.'

'It's just a precaution. Remember what we all agreed on. Better safe than sorry. We're all in this together.'

'My God, what if it turns nasty?'

'It's not going to. Don't get all carried away. Now just try to relax. Stay here. I'm taking Dirk with me – call Annie to come up and stay with you and I'll put an extra guard on the gate.' He walks into the hallway where his worn veldskoens, black jacket and powerful torch stand, waiting.

She follows him, suddenly realizing. 'You knew about this didn't you? You've known the whole afternoon, ever since Mike phoned earlier on.'

'Let's not start with that – I didn't want you to worry.'

'Jesus Gus, I'm part of this too. I need to know. I'm worse off in the dark.'

'I'm sorry,' he says, fetching a shotgun from the gun room and loading it. He turns, she is shaking her head, her chest heaving gently.

'I hate that sight – above all I hate that sight,' she says.

He stares down at the long black gun-shaft, dimly realizing its implications. He makes a move to touch her on the arm. She backs away. It's because he's now an extension of it, of its obscene killing power, the ability to change beyond redemption. He makes his way out of the back door, his manner now stiff.

'It's Davey Baker isn't it? Gus – don't ignore me,' she says, chasing after him, 'it's Davey Baker isn't it? He's back. He's gone and done something.'

'I don't know, so there's no point overreacting. Just stay indoors.' He moves towards one of the farm trucks, opens the door. She tugs at his arm. He tenses, before turning to face her.

'Don't let that boy bring us all down. We can't all become extensions of his eternal grief.'

Gus looks at her for a moment, curious at her callousness. 'Just stay inside,' he says and then drives off at speed.


Down the road at the manager's cottage, Dirk Strydom moves over his young wife Annie, moving deeply inside her, thrusting and moaning. They have been married for five weeks. Sex doesn't bring shame any more. The action is unconditionally sanctioned.

He comes in a glorious shudder, her clawing his back, slapping his buttocks, eking him out, an absolute ecstasy. For a while he pauses there, hanging over her, luxuriating in the waning grip he has inside of her now, waiting for the inevitable, fleshy softening so that in a few moments he'll simply flop out, expelled from the vortex of warmth, and fall back in a fit of satisfaction. They'll laugh, giggle, embrace these moments after.

There's a quiet knock at the door. Gus reckons he knows what he's disturbing and is sorry, embarrassed. The knock immediately arouses Dirk's suspicions – the prospect of danger now so common he's constantly alive to its signals and procedures. A knock at the door this time of night means one thing. He pulls away from Annie, pulls on a pair of shorts.

He talks in a muted drone at the door down the short passage. Annie cuddles the sheets to her bosom. She hasn't been a farmwife for long enough to be a victim of its paranoia. She is not suspicious or perturbed when Dirk comes back into the room to dress for the outdoors, and she is wholly pacified when, kissing her hand, he says, 'Be back soon, love you,' and smiles. She will lie back when he's gone, nurse the warmth of his seed now deep in her body, dream of raising children under the healthy African sun, basking in the glory of it all, the natural beauty.

Back at Summerville Mike is ready, waiting. Gus and Dirk can't get there soon enough for him. Every minute makes him edgier. He goes over his provisions again. They'd each agreed to bring a torch and a loaded gun, and wear dark clothing. He'd also collected a twenty-litre jerry can of petrol, a box of matches, the shovels. It's all here, stacked in the driveway.

Suddenly he is struck by the magnitude of the task ahead. Christ, there's actually no way three of them will handle it. What if something goes wrong and one of them is needed to make a diversion or keep a watch out? What then? The more he thinks of the whole plan, the more he's certain they're undermanned. Impulsively he phones up Terry Richards, tells him the situation, says they're all meeting at his place and will go from here.

'Fine,' says Terry, 'see you shortly.'

With this alteration of plans Mike knows they could be biting off more than they can chew. They run the risk of having all and sundry know about it.

There is safety in numbers. Blood will have blood. Too many chefs spoil the broth. Which is it?

Jesus, he suddenly thinks, laughing to himself a nervous, cautious laugh. It's probably all of them.

In the kitchen Davey finds Ma baking bread, pushing a large chalky rolling pin through a thick wad of dough. There's nothing better than hot fresh bread. He can't wait to eat it with soft butter. Ma normally makes him a loaf a day, but even that's not enough to quell his appetite. He stands for a minute or so, watching her slap, knead the dough round vigorously. She seems to give off puffs of flour.

'Stop smoking,' he says.

She turns and smiles. 'Morning sunshine. Sleep well? Just shove the kettle on if you want coffee – it needs some water.'

He lifts the water jug, stomps through to the scullery, where Phineas is rinsing dishes in the sink. 'Quick, quick,' he says, 'water.' Davey throws him the jug and Phineas fills it from the tap, smiling cheerfully. Back in the kitchen, he fills up the kettle. One of the dogs stirs itself from the cool tiled floor and moves to him, pressing its muzzle to his lap. He pats her. She's a soppy bitch, more so than the others. 'Yes, yes,' he says playfully. 'Who's a pretty girl? Who's a pretty girl?' He walks through the back and the other seven dogs come trailing after him. The sun's warm on his naked chest. The sky is the most perfect spread of blue. He yawns, stretches, this time for real. He throws a stone for the dogs and they go charging off down the hill, barking and yelping.

'Coffee's ready,' Ma calls.

Back in his bedroom, in a small ritual he performs daily, he stands briefly by the window and looks across the lands that spread beneath the farmhouse, down the hill and out, out to the horizon. Oupa Baker got it just right: nice, comforting sunlight heating the bedrooms in the morning, shade cooling them in the afternoon. And that reminds him – he'd better get on to this blasted holiday history assignment. Before school broke up, they'd been given a project to work on, a 2000-word essay on the history of their family and home. Two thousand words! Bloody hell – it isn't going to be easy. He knows the vague story, he'll have to speak to Ma to get all the exact details.

He turns from the window, runs his hand through his hair. It's greasy and still a bit dusty. He sniffs his armpits. Better go for a shower, he thinks. There's a chance they'll go to the sports club later on and Katie Hutchins could well be there. Can't be stinking like a dog.

For a while afterwards he sits in front of the TV skipping channels until Phineas comes through to call him for breakfast. It's fatty and oily – just how he likes it – a slap-together of bacon, eggs, sausage, tomato, toast. But there's no black pudding and he mutters to Ma, who is still busying herself in the kitchen, baking and preparing food. Beneath him at the breakfast table, all eight dogs sit patiently, drooling and whining softly. When he's finished Phineas hands him eight chunks of stale bread soaked in the cooling oil of the frying pan and he leads the dogs outside and commands them to sit before giving each their share.

It's too early to go fishing. For a few minutes he plays with the dogs on the lawn and then decides he can't put off the chore of bathing them all any longer. It's got to be done. He calls Phineas and Delight, and together they tackle the difficult, frustrating task. The standing family joke is that they call Delight, No Lights, and the sight of the lanky, brainless garden boy chasing after eight sopping wet hounds causes much amusement. Phineas takes charge, issuing stern instructions. There is a great deal of wild leaping and wet licking, soapy water shaken and flung about – the dogs enjoy themselves, and he does too. Afterwards he sprays and smears fly repellent over their ears and shouts at them when they immediately try to wipe it off by rolling on the lawn.

Later he and the dogs trail off down to the swimming pool for what he calls morning swimmies. He doesn't allow the dogs in today – not after their nice bath and dose of fly repellent – and instead enjoys teasing them, provoking them by splashing and patting the water. They go ballistic, yelping and balancing at the edge of the pool and at the last moment, just before he is about to be pounced on, he sternly warns them not to jump.

He takes a particular interest in the pool. It's his baby. He has a vision of a sparkling blue expanse of water, crystal clear, shimmering with traces of golden sunlight piercing the surface, just as he always sees in adverts on the TV for pool chemicals. Of course, he wouldn't object to the sexy lady with her white bikini and tanned body lounging about either. But when he gets back to the farm at long weekends and holidays, he's always cross to find the pool a murky blue-green – not quite rank green thank God, but certainly not sparkling blue either. He tackles Ma about it, accuses Pa of allowing the muddy dogs in every day at lunch. They laugh it off and promise to obey his instructions. These holidays he's determined to bloody get the pool right. He's already told Delight to dose it full of every chemical he can find in the pump-house.

When he comes back up to the house he finds Ma sitting on the veranda next to the tea tray. She cuts him a slice of freshly baked carrot cake. It's still warm, almost melts in his mouth. But then she spoils everything by saying, 'That reminds me mister, your school report arrived yesterday.'

He knew this was coming sometime. His immediate reaction is to sigh and feign sulking. But Ma won't be so easily put off.

'From the looks of things you need to start doing some serious work. You know you'll get nowhere in life without a good education. Your English and French are appalling for a start.'

'What good is French going to do me? I'm not going to live in bloody France am I?'

'That's not the point. It's about application – trying your hardest. That's why we send you to the best and, I hasten to add, the most expensive boarding school in the country.'

There is a noise coming from the lounge and all the dogs go scampering in. It's Pa, who emerges looking hot, red-faced, sweaty.

'Hi Pa,' he says.

'Son.'

'Want some tea?' Ma asks.

'Far too hot. I'll get a Coke. Come with me boy, I've got something to show you.'

He's relieved to be taken away from Ma's nagging. He and Pa drive in one of the trucks down through the fields. It's become so hot that almost at once his thighs begin to sweat on the imitation leather seats. Overhead the sky is perfectly clear and in the distance the tops of the hills look fuzzy, as if slightly out of focus. Pa drives very slowly, carefully overseeing the work on the fields as they go along. He stops regularly to shout at the workers if he sees that something is lagging behind or not being done properly. One stern word from Pa and the labourers leap into action, scurrying round at ten times the pace they'd normally be working.

'You should clone yourself Pa,' he offers, 'like Dolly the sheep.'

They pull up alongside one of the fields, and walk some distance into it. Pa bends down to brush back a stalk of the crop. It's wheat. The field spreads, a blend of beaten gold on all sides of them. The tufted bristles press against his legs.

'You see this, boy?'

He kneels down to look at the base of the stalk Pa is showing him. It is coated in a fine yellowish-white powder. 'Yes.'

'This here is a very dangerous fungus. The scientific term is Septoria Leaf Blotch. It's caused from using a bad batch of pesticides. George noticed it. We're bloody lucky we caught it while it's still this colour. If it turns from this into a light green you can kiss the whole field, maybe even the whole crop goodbye. It spreads within days. Now listen carefully – you treat it with a cocktail of benomyl, copper hydroxide and mancozeb. Got that?'

'Benomyl, copper hydroxide and mancozeb.'

'Right – remember it. You can't trust anyone these days boy. Not even your good old pesticide supplier. First thing on Monday morning they're going to get what for from me. As it is we've saved this field and it looks as if she's going to be a real goody.'

He looks over the field again and smiles. 'Looks real good Pa.'

Pa looks at him sternly. 'Farming's all about detection boy. You're a detective, right, you see things early, make plans, solve problems before someone – well, your crops – get killed. There're killers lurking around every farm and your task is to save the crops. Simple.'

'Yes Pa.'

They smile at each other. He doesn't often see Pa smile during the day. He's always so focused, taking everything so seriously. Just like a detective.

'Tell you what boy – why don't you take over this field. I'll leave it in your hands for the next four weeks or so until you go back to school. I won't interfere at all – promise. She can be your baby entirely.'

'Serious Pa?'

'It's about time you took on a field of your own.'

This is just what he's been wanting for a long time now: responsibility. Something tangible he can do to prove his worth to Pa, to at last make him see that he can do his bit on the farm, help out, contribute. Even though four weeks is precious little time in the overall life of a wheat field, it's still a start.

More significantly, he is beginning to sense something different in Pa's approach to him. He seems to be dealing with him more on level terms, as a partner, as a man. He discusses ideas, plans with him, shows him the ropes more thoroughly than before when he used to get the feeling Pa answered just to shut him up, to stopper his boyish inquisitiveness. He realizes now this is an important step, this new-found communication, understanding.

'Thanks.'

On the way back in the truck there are more concessions when Pa inexplicably reaches out his hand and pats him playfully on the head. He smiles again – twice in one day – before slowing down the truck and leaning out of the window to yell angrily at one of the labourers who's standing with his hands on his hips, not working.

Before they reach the farmhouse they stop to pick up the farm foreman, George. Davey gets out, jumps in the back and watches through the dusty caked window as Pa and George talk gravely about various aspects of the farm. Back to being left out: for a while he's glum again. But he knows Pa and George have an understanding, a unique way of communicating. And anyway, Pa always says George is second in command on the farm. The one thing you need is a foreman you can count on, he's told him many times before. Find yourself a good foreman and the farm runs itself. He's always found it odd, the way Pa treats George, even though he's only an old black.

By the time they get back to the house, he's got an hour or so to go fishing before lunch. He's allowed to take one of the trucks. He brings along a couple of dogs and has two piccanins load his tackle box, the worms, two rods, a wide-brimmed sun umbrella and a cooler bag on the back before they speed away. Ma's always telling him not to drive so fast but he enjoys skidding and kicking up dust sheets as he goes. The scruffy piccanins hang on for dear life and when they arrive at Broadlands he teases them: 'One day,' he says, pointing a finger, 'you're going fucking flying my friends. Just wait and see!' It's a small mission in life to throw one of them off the back with his reckless driving, but so far he hasn't succeeded and instead they just smile and say, 'No baas, no chance.'

Normally they would take the small six-footer out far into the dam, but today they don't have enough time, so instead they nestle down on rocks by the shore and cast out. Somewhere, usually lurking about the rocks, are a few large crocodiles that Pa brought in to deter the poachers, and he always looks out for them. At the time he'd argued bitterly with Pa, claiming that they'd eat all the best fish, but now he rather likes the idea that he has crocodiles in his dam, on his home. How many people can say they have their own crocodiles? He sits under the umbrella, delves into his cooler bag for one of the three beers he's had the piccanins smuggle out of the storeroom. The deal is, smuggle me three beers and take a Coke each for yourselves. They're more than happy and whenever Ma or Pa wonders why the beers go down so quickly, he blames Phineas. 'Strange,' Ma remarked the other day, sarcastically, 'he doesn't seem to steal nearly so many during term time.' Does she know? Probably – she's shrewder than you sometimes think.

They fish and exchange banter and drink and at some wonderfully idle point he's once again filled with the warmth of perfect contentment. He banishes the thought of the essay he's got to do, Ma's nagging about his poor grades. They can't reach him here, doing what his father and grandfather did. This is the life and there's nothing he'd exchange for it – nothing. You can offer him all the money in the world, a fleet of twenty sports cars, a night with ten of the sexiest women – but he'd always choose Edenfields, just as it is.

They chuck horse pellets into the water as a lure. The brown-green water close to the rocks is clear for a couple of feet down and as the grey pellets sink, pulled down slowly by the dim current of the water, a fish or two glides in to snap them up.

'Bass,' he says, excitedly. 'Come here you fuckin' fish.' He drops his line close to the slowly sinking bait that has quickly flaked into small particles and waits, but there are no takers.

Marsha is restless in the house. She's had her bath, shared out the chicken bones to the dogs, given the cockatiel a fresh bowl of water. She finds herself walking up and down the passage. She tiptoes towards the closed room where she knows Davey lies, awake with his thoughts. She's about to knock, open the door, go to him, but her hand, uplifted to the door handle, falls away slowly. She sighs, resigns herself to her weakness and turns to enter the hallway.

Outside Mike is standing, talking quietly to the dogs, kicking the chewed rugby ball. There's something fragile about him, as if he's a boy doing manly things for the first time, undertaking an awkward rite of passage. But then she sees the jerry can and the gun stacked by the truck. Everything looks so organized, so pragmatic, as if he's simply off with the guys for a weekend of hunting and letting his hair down. It's a strange combination. She half imagines herself waiting to kiss him goodbye, wishing him a good time, warning him not to get up to too much mischief without her.

He doesn't see her and she doesn't want him to see her watching him like this. He'll only see in her a reflection of his own fear. Some bloody hunting trip, she thinks. She shelters behind a pillar, still watching, aware of the licence granted by the night. She doesn't know what to make of it, but breathes out, as if trying to expel her concerns, and is startled to see a slight puff of mist drift into the air, as though it was one of those crisp, dark winter's mornings and she was on her way to inspect a calf its mother had pushed out into life during the night. Yes that's it, and oddly that's what Mike reminds her of too: a calf lying on its side, new to the ways of the world, embarking on something unknown and terrifying, covered in its thin sheen of blood and shit and slimy blue afterbirth, glinting under the naked night-light.

She goes inside, climbs restlessly into bed and pretends to read the new Margaret Atwood. But her eyes merely move over a haze of print while her mind floats a million miles away. She can still sense Mike outside, trying to bolt these parts of himself together. Only so many things in this world, she believes, can be achieved through human willpower; only so many tasks can be done by the courage of man and she knows that he will struggle against his conscience during the course of the night, that at times he'll be moving faster than his moral compass and be left wondering why a man like himself, a simple, honest man, has been landed with such an ordeal. It will be a test.

And she knows she herself won't be free from the demon that will follow them from now on, drag at their heels like a stubborn dog. She wonders whether anything will ever be the same again after tonight. She feels something definitive settling in the air, warm stifling air locked in and slowly circling round the bedroom. She tells herself she's exaggerating the situation. Perhaps Mike's task will be done as quietly as their everyday work round the farm: watering the terminal violets on the kitchen windowsill, feeding the orphaned piglets with a warm milk bottle.

She forces herself to focus on the page of her book: in reality the chances of Adelia having had a lover were nil. The town was too small, its morals were too provincial, she had far to fall. She wasn't a fool. Also she had no money of her own.

*

But it's pointless. She just can't concentrate. She finds herself staring straight ahead at the wall, with no idea how much time has passed. Then the phone rings. It's Jen Smit. Inquiring, all-knowing Jen Smit.

'Do you think he's actually gone and done it?' she asks, immediately.

'I don't know,' says Marsha, trying to avoid answering the question directly, but not pretending she doesn't know who Jen's talking about. 'He won't say.'

'But it bloody well looks that way, doesn't it?'

'Could be.'

'Hell.'

Marsha finds herself a little riled by Jen's annoyance, as though her own inconvenience was the main consequence of Davey's ordeal. 'Let's not jump to conclusions.'

'No, but let's be prepared as well. We can't afford to take any risks ourselves, not with all this chaos going on.'

'No.'

'When they discover what's happened, if it's happened, they'll go ape, that's for sure.'

'Yes.'

'They'll tear us all down.'

'I know.'

'So much for courage, the boy's gone and put us all in jeopardy now.'

'He's only done what they've all been thinking about doing.'

The line goes quiet for a while. 'Yes,' says Jen eventually, 'I suppose.'

As Jen puts the phone down, next to her poor Annie bursts into tears again. She's been crying on and off for the last half an hour.

'Now, now, love,' Jen says comfortingly, abandoning her caustic manner. 'They'll be okay.'

'Why didn't he tell me where he was going? Why does everything around here have to be like this, so bloody nerve-racking?'

'Nobody said being married to a farmer was going to be a bed of roses, love. I know.'

Outside, at last Mike sees signs of Gus and Dirk's arrival: the sharp flicker of headlamps through the dense bush. He readies himself. The truck drives up through the gateposts, jolting over humps and rocks, and pulls up alongside him. They all nod to each other – they keep the evening's business terse, to the point.

'Right,' Gus says, 'let's do this.'

Mike makes his way to the stack of shovels. Dirk hovers round, nervously eager. Suddenly, as Mike's about to load two of the shovels into the back of the truck, a thought strikes him. He pauses.

'What's up?' asks Gus.

'What if we're spotted and my registration number's traced?' The others haven't thought of this.

'Good point,' says Dirk. They all hesitate. The danger has suddenly become palpable, a dark figureless shadow, smothering their thrill, unnerving them, changing the complexion of things.

'We'll cover up the number plates with tape,' suggests Gus.

'And if we're stopped by patrols? How do we explain it?'

'It'll only add suspicion.'

Mike can't help but sigh. He just wants to get the whole damn thing over and done with. 'Right then, we'll just go, and not get spotted. No problem.'

'Now take it easy there,' says Gus, 'we've got to think of ourselves as well. Let's not lose our heads over this. We're trying to fix a problem, not make one.'

Mike shakes his head free of uncertainty and moves on with the shovels. They continue loading the back of the truck.

'What are we going to cover this lot with?' asks Dirk.

Mike thinks for a moment, goes down to the workshops and comes back with a navy blue canvas boat cover. They fold it up, pile it in the back. Jesus, Mike thinks, this is turning out to be a bloody mission. Once the truck is packed, Dirk and Gus clamber into the front, ready to go. Mike looks back up the drive.

'What are we waiting for?' asks Gus.

'Terry's coming too.'

Gus doesn't like surprises. 'Fucking hell, you never said anything about anyone else. It was supposed to be the three of us, no risks.'

With a deep breath, Mike patiently explains his reasoning. Gus accepts it reluctantly, sighing and saying, 'Oh well', but Mike can sense he feels he's losing his grip of the situation. The last thing they need is a breakdown of trust, Gus looking out for himself rather than the group.

'So,' says Dirk, 'how are we all going to fit?'

Another bloody good point, Mike realizes. The truck's a single cab.

'One of us will have to go in the back.'

'For Christ's sake we'll be seen.'

'We can crouch down, under the canvas.'

'What! No thanks.'

'Jesus!'

Just as Mike begins to think that they've made a mess of the job, that already nothing's going their way, Terry drives up, miraculously in his twin cab. 'We'll go in Terry's truck,' Mike says. 'Christ – it's got tinted windows, it's black – what could be better?'

They all pack out laughing with relief, although they know they shouldn't, really. They've had a break: they're back on track.

*

Soon they are driving through corridors of tall netted vlei, lit a startling khaki by the headlamps. Insects swirl in front of them, disappear behind them. The odd bend in the road shows up red animal eyes every now and then: wild boars, bucks, stray goats. At one point they swerve to avoid a python bloated like a bag from its feeding, its shallow clear eyes threatening and primeval. They drive on, cautious, slow.

Their biggest fear is that they'll be stopped at a road patrol. This, of course, never used to be a problem. Now movement is meant to be restricted, things have changed. Nevertheless, tonight the road is clear. In fact, the quietness is unnerving – they hardly see another human being, even when passing by the various compounds. There are a few bonfires, flames reddening the night sky, but the figures sitting round them seem inactive, stifled.

Gus remarks, 'Something must have happened.'

'Ja,' replies Terry, squinting out to see what's not there, trying to gauge the unknown.

The absence of the drums has already made Mike suspect that something unusual is up, and Marsha, he acknowledges to himself, would have registered it ages ago. But it's not enough to make them turn round now, not on this vague intuition.

They move on through the dark network of roads. Eventually they will enter the boundary to Edenfields Estate through the wide stone gates, and about seven kilometres on start to ascend an undulating hill, following the narrow winding road that will lead them directly to the farmhouse. A long while before, when they are still several kilometres from the boundary, they will kill their lights and creep upwards as slow as possible, a cat stalking the darkness. They will have to do this to avoid being spotted.

2

The ground is hard, gritty, a touch damp. The stiff, rotting smell of decay is rife, and the tall slithers of grass make him sneeze, irritating his eyes. It's not an ideal start, but he sits patiently in the bushes for an hour, leaning against the boundary wall, looking over at the tangle of railway track. He thinks that he'll get to Edenfields by dawn, take them by surprise, and by six he'll have reclaimed the farm. Then it'll be done. In the meantime, the hum of a mosquito annoys him but he can't see to kill it, so there is nothing to do but wait quietly in the dark.

Finally it comes: a distant thudding, then a pleasing shake of the ground. He leaps to his feet, fastens his satchel to his back, charges forward. But he isn't alone. Blacks appear from every direction, startling him. He didn't anticipate this; the commotion disorientates him. He'd pictured solitude, inconspicuousness, travelling alone through the African night. He's not sure he can bear the prospect of being hunched up against unknown bodies. He can't bear strangers. From strangers come killers.

But there is no option. He can't abort his mission at this stage. He can't give up. He knows he has to overcome his weaknesses if he's going to succeed. He's considered this in advance: he'll have to toughen his resolve, neutralize his reactions. He just has to do it. He decides to run further up the line, where the train will come to rest. This way he'll be one of the first to attempt the jump, secure himself a safe, tolerable place to sit. He runs a good hundred metres while the train churns on, finally coming to a halt. He scrambles to get on board, which is easier than he thought – the carriage is low, only a few feet above ground. He hops up, moves towards the front.

The blacks jostle for places; mainly nannies, carrying parcels and babies strapped to their backs.

'Stay down, you be seen.'

He cowers low against the railings, huddling into a corner. The trailer is one of those used for transporting livestock. It's pen-shaped, smelling faintly of pig shit.

A man leans forward and grins at him.

'Why, why you on this train?'

A drunk. All he needs.

'I'm running away from school.'

'Ah, my friend. School is shit! Shit shit shit!'

'Ja.'

The man scratches in a scruffy bag, producing a brown container of brew. He proffers it. It's greasy, sick-looking and smells vile.

'What is it?'

'This – this is very special beer, my brother he make out in township. Very very good.'

'What's in it?'

'This beer it has everything. That's why it is so special. I tell you: it has skin of a goat, gut of a mombie, the wheel of a bicycle and, and an old car battery.'

'A car battery!'

'Yes, yes. That is great secret. Old car battery. Give it good kick.'

He doesn't dare take a sip, and hands it straight back, unsure whether the man is playing with him. His manner is hard to gauge. His eyes are blurry, bloodshot. He doesn't know whether this apparent friendliness is mere drunken talk or not. Hard to tell with these people. But to quell the nervousness that's suddenly taken root, he wants to keep talking. He asks where the man is going, about his family. His answers are slurred, long-winded, cryptic.

The train stays still for a long time. There doesn't appear to be any danger of being caught. There aren't any patrols, the roam of flashlights seeking them out. Just the odd echoing clang when carriages are hooked up, cargo being loaded by the stationmasters further up the track. Finally the train begins to roll, quickly picking up speed. He remains hunched against the railings. The air is cold and unpleasant, burrowing into his back, and he regrets not thinking to find himself a post more in the middle of the trailer. Those already huddled there are obviously experienced travellers.

He takes out his compass from the satchel, points it. Almost exactly due south. Perfect. It's all under way: he's escaped. There can be no stopping him.

After a while the shacks of the townships and the floodlit factories leaking twirls of smoke disappear altogether, overwhelmed by a wide expanse of colourless bush, stark flatlands, then the shape of blackened hills in the distance. There is an immense outpouring of vacant land: even in darkness the existence of an endless, impenetrable terrain is at once exciting and terrifying. There are infinite dangers, dead ends and wrong turns. The prospect of becoming lost, swallowed up in the mayhem almost overwhelms him, even on the train. Success lies in following his path, in executing his plan with absolute precision. He grips the railings, and looks out into the night.

Opposite him, far too close, the drunk snores, sputtering noxious fumes. Although the rhythmic thud of the train is drawing him, too, into sleep, he dare not let himself drift off. He doesn't trust his fellow passengers; he must remain alert to their actions. Plus he could miss the stop altogether and then what? He keeps track of the time, flashing the light on his watch, but the hands barely move. After two hours, he has a dim headache from the constant noise and wind, his backside is numb and his hand is rigid from clutching on to the railings. He ought to let go, but by holding on he is secure in his spot, separated from the herd of people, squashed and common and smelling. He wonders how often they hitch an illegal ride on this Midnight Express.

'You, where you get off?'

A seamy man wearing a black woollen cap and a brown canvas jacket has manoeuvred his way towards his end of the pen. He crouches close by, so close that an acrid smell of stale sweat and smoke repels him. At once his heart skips a beat, his whole body tenses and he instinctively retreats further into his corner. Six months ago he would have sat at ease, even here, and dismissed this approach. He tries to remember his old fearlessness as a farm boy, used to the outside, used to dealing with blacks.

'Where, where you get off?'

The man speaks impatiently, an undertone of hostility, so he tells him.

'Then you pay. Fifty thousand.'

'Fifty thousand!'

'You pay to me. I organize this train. It is my trailer.'

The drunk has woken. A terse conversation takes place, most of which he can't translate, before the drunk duly hands over his fare. The man gives him a steely glare, but momentarily turns his attention to other passengers.

The drunk leans over. 'Better you pay too. There is no free ride.'

He objects to this injustice. 'But he's here just as illegally as everyone else. He's not a train official.'

'No but he run this trailer. He says who can ride or no. So you must pay or else big trouble.'

Reluctantly he takes out the wad of money he's brought with him, peels out the required sum and hands it over the next time he's asked. Not a further word is exchanged, but he is left with a cheated, chilly resentment.

Half an hour later, the train begins to slow. Finally it stops, but the area, dimly lit by security lights attached to tall wooden poles, doesn't look like the coal mine where he intends to disembark.

'What place is this?'

'Where you want to go?'

'Astra Mine.'

The drunk considers this for a minute, then gesticulates for him to follow.

'But is this the place or not?'

'This is as close as you go. The only other stop is right before border. If you are caught at border you be locked in jail for ever. Better you come now. We are close to the mine.'

'How close? The train's supposed to go right to the mine – I've seen it there before.'

'Close, close, come. We no have time to waste.'

He is apprehensive, but follows anyway. He was so sure that this train – heading south from the city – would eventually end up at the coal mine. He's seen the train in the district so often, with Astra Mine's logo printed on the cargo carriages, but this man would know better than him. He doesn't like his plans going wrong, not after he'd believed it would all be so easy once he reached the mine and just had to walk a few ks down the central district road and then wind his way up to the farm.

He shuffles to the edge of the trailer and jumps off, running quickly after the drunk into the bushes.

'Stay low. If officials catch you here they beat you up bad bad. It is not like city – here they do what they want.'

He cowers down, panic-stricken. Yet somehow he knows he's in good, experienced hands. He wonders how all these people get away with it, but as he looks round he can't see another soul. It's quiet, desolate, eerie. Never before has he seen such a crowd disperse into nothingness so quickly and he draws some reassurance from the fact everyone seems to have got off. It seems he's done the right thing. The drunk and he wait in the bushes until the train eventually pulls away again. It's quite nippy, so he reaches into his satchel for his jacket. The mosquitoes dive in his ears. He bats at them, ineffectually. He checks the time: 2:30. But that seems wrong. It normally takes far longer by road to reach the district, at least four hours.

'Are you sure we're close to the mine?'

'Yes, we close close. It only about eighty kilometres away.'

'What! Eighty ks!'

'Yes, not far.'

Despair claims him. Eighty ks seems an impossible distance. He struggles to run five ks at cross-country. Now, between him and his district lie eighty kilometres of rank wilderness. Who knows what they contain? Anything could happen. Any disaster. He has prepared himself for a degree of hardship – the train, the walk, the final part of the mission – but his mind hasn't grappled with the idea of covering such vast distances of unknown, unfriendly country.

The drunk starts to wander off down the track, and he follows. The drunk doesn't object. Although he doesn't know the first thing about this man, he seems friendly enough, humming traditional songs in a husky, dry voice, and he assumes he'll be safer with him than without him, at least until morning.

They walk for a good fifteen minutes, eventually reaching what looks to be the local shebeen. It's an iron corrugated shack with one naked light bulb fixed up to the corner of the roof. The air is dusty, thick with the clouding smoke of what is certainly weed. Strong weed: even at ten metres the smell goes straight to his head and he covers his face with his jacket sleeve. A crowd hangs round, mostly men, some women, talking loudly. Beside the shack there are two rusty petrol drums in which a man dips containers and cups, serving his customers with great dexterity, never spilling a drop. From somewhere there is the hissing babble of a radio, strains of local music.

All these strangers in the dark. His panic rises, and he steps back a little, into the shadows. The drunk seems to know everyone and quickly finds a spot, greeting all and sundry. Even in his alarm, he is strangely disappointed, hurt by this act of disloyalty, so crudely abandoned for beer and women. Well, so be it. He's not comfortable venturing into this crowd. He'd rather be by himself, carrying on alone if need be.

He moves round the back, trying to slink out of sight. A small distance away he sees a thin cow tethered with a rope to a tree, making a loud din, moaning and mooing as two men chop chunks of meat from its rump with a dagger and drop them into a big black sizzling pot, steaming over a wood fire. The startling stench of frying flesh rushes him and an instant dryness lurches into the back of his throat, forcing him to block his nose to stop himself from gagging. Suddenly the wilderness seems to be closing all round him. He doesn't want to see such disgusting things; he wants to keep his mind clean, focused on what he needs to do.

He hurries on into the darkness. Night-time or not, the sooner he gets to grips with his mission, the sooner it will all be over. He walks round aimlessly for a while, unsure which way to go. About a hundred metres down the narrow dirt road he sees the outline of a few buildings. One has a light bulb glowing over a small stoep. He approaches cautiously, crouching along the line of the vlei. He stops short of the first building and surveys the area. It looks like the centre of a small settlement, a growth point perhaps, with two or three stores.

There isn't a soul in sight, so he sits on the edge of the stoep. The concrete is cold and hard. There are ants everywhere. The light flickers annoyingly, as if about to fuse. He knows sleep won't come easily out here, and beyond sleep there is only a dry, stale lingering. But he'll have to wait till daybreak to get his bearings.

His throat is dry. As soon as the store opens in the morning, he'll buy himself a nice cold Coke. He looks about, studying his surroundings. A few metres away a skull with horns lies half buried in the soil. Stark white: the dark horns curving neatly, those of a billy goat. He wonders where the rest of its bones have ended up. They've probably been ground up for medicine or used to crush wheat or mealie cobs.

He tries to rest a bit, but spends most of the time fighting off ants and mosquitoes. At some point, though, he drifts off. He can't be sure whether he actually sleeps or not, but eventually when he looks up there are weak signs of daybreak, the reassuring thrum of the sun in the sky.

In daylight the place seems even more of a ghost town. Light underscores the forsakenness of the few squat buildings: litter and orange peel strewn about, trodden-on beer cartons, an old car frame overgrown with grass, an immense unravelling of dust. He walks round a bit. A faded red Coca-Cola sign hangs above the shop's door saying Cheap-Cheap Store. His thirst intensifies, but the store doors are locked with a chain and thick tarnished padlock.

He tries to imagine what purpose the other buildings serve. He peers in through the windows but some are broken and boarded up, others have iron bars across them and torn curtains – all he can see is his own shadowy grey reflection. He can see through one: inside it's dark, stacked with heavy furniture, a rack of clothes, a table littered with pots, pans and cooking utensils. It looks to have been abandoned. Round the back, stacked outside the door, is a huge collection of small brown bottles and other junk: lots of dirty clothes and boxes. The smell is powerful, and disturbingly famil-iar – not garbage, more like piggeries, of expired sows or dead piglets dumped and awaiting incineration. He leaves investigation for the swarms of flies.

He makes his way back to the store, but it hasn't opened. Why would it? He waits for twenty minutes more. The sun broadens as a force over the hot land, and he really needs to get going. But he also needs someone to show him where the main road is. He remembers Pa's lessons in hunting and scouting: always know your exact bearings at all times. So he waits, drawing circles in the dust with a stick. Then he stands and stretches, keen to keep his energy up. He begins to make circuits of the building. After nine laps, coming back to the road, he sees a figure making its way in his direction. Soon he recognizes who it is: the drunk. He is relieved.

'Hello. Do you know when this store opens?'

'It open soon soon. Where you been?'

'I've been here all night.'

'That is very very stupid, boy. I been worried where you go. I been worried about you all the time. It is not safe to stay by yourself.

Very bad things happen to you. You should have stayed at beer hall with me. All of us we stay together during night at beer hall. We look after you. We safe there.'

In the daylight, he can see the drunk's face, underneath his wiry beard, is badly scarred. It has deep pink gouges that have hardly healed. He must be recovering from an injury of some sort, some horrible ordeal. He isn't drunk now, but looks moody and angry. He shakes his head, waving a stubby finger.

'They find you and beat you. Always they take you in the night and beat you. It very very bad.'

Outside the store he starts to fiddle in his pockets, producing a small key-ring.

'This store – it's yours?'

'Yes, Cheap-Cheap Store, best in area. Cheap-Cheap.'

He goes in. It's stuffy, musty, stale. It makes him want to back away in disgust. But the storekeeper is welcoming, spreading his arms to display his wares. There isn't much. The shelves are virtually empty. There is a small stock of soap, boxes of matches, jars of Vaseline, a selection of chewing gum, a few spiky combs, tubes of hair gels.

Then he pulls out a packet of dried kapenta from underneath the counter and holds it up proudly.

'I give you special. You have money? I give you good good price.'

'No. Do you have any Cokes?'

'Cokes?'

'Or any drinks?'

'No no. No drinks in store. No drinks for eight months or more.'

'Eight months!'

'But I have kapenta for good price. Only food in store.'

It's true. Looking around he can't see a scrap of food anywhere on the shelves. Not a blackened banana or a shrivelled orange. Not even sugary sweets or salted peanuts. Nothing.

'You pay me now. Good price.'

'No. I only wanted a drink.'

'Ah – no drink. Now, do you want kapenta or no? You have good money?'

'No. I only wanted a drink.'

'Then if you no want kapenta, you go! You go now! You no waste my time.'

The sudden change in tone frightens him, raises his guard, but he needs to know where the main road is.

'It is that way. Now you go. Go. Go. White bastard boy.'

The shopkeeper waves his hand angrily in the direction of the door. He moves out quickly, suddenly very aware that the man may grow aggressive, so angry is he at not selling the packet of dried crushed fish. Outside he looks for the main road, which is easy to see now he knows where to look for it, flush behind a copse of unruly thorn bushes. He runs towards it.

His plan is simple: check south on the compass and then keep walking until a car comes by to give him a lift. It probably won't take him all that long, after all.

But no cars come. He walks for a good hour, plodding along the grey track, singing rock songs under his breath to while away the time. An old bus flies past about half an hour later and an orange peel is tossed at him, but no cars. The sun is up, beating away. He is surrounded by a natural frieze of greens and browns, various shades of bush, then kopjes and outcrops standing hard and brazen in the distance. Soon his feet begin to tire. He tries to concentrate as much as possible on his purpose, hoping time will pass quickly. He sees the task with such clarity; so much rests on his shoulders and his alone. He is motivated, settles down into a rhythm. A car has to come belting by any second – it has to – and then he'll get a lift, be at the farm by ten. What's a few hours' delay? He is optimistic.

He walks on. Another hour. He's walked for two and a half hours, perhaps three. Now the mid-morning sun is becoming unbearable. His head is pounding: foolishly, he hasn't brought a hat. He drapes his jacket over his head but it is too thick and hot. For a while he ties his shirt like a bandanna, but realizes his bare back will soon start to burn. The idea of making a hat from grass occurs to him, but he doesn't have the energy to stop walking. The road seems endless, a hazy mirage, shale and stony in colour, accumulating in the distance. The tarmac is a liquid grey, sizzling hot.

He encounters no wildlife. The trees have leaves, despite the heat the bush is luscious and fallow, but there isn't a single sign of life – not a bird or a baboon, not even a fly or stick insect darting about the vlei. There isn't even the hint of a breeze. Everything seems stagnant, drooping and idle, retreated from the unbending waves of heat.

Eventually, coming round yet another curve in the road, he sees the blazing shape of a small building in the distance. At last: there's the chance of a garage, a store, a drink, so that he can save the water in his bottle. At the sight of the buildings his legs weaken with relief and he almost staggers, but struggles on, seeing the buildings get closer and closer. Almost at the clearing, he falters and falls. The gravel looked even, but it's lined with hard rocks, knife-edged stones. He looks up to see a large group of people has appeared, staring at him in questioning silence.

He is embarrassed. He didn't think it possible to be absolutely dog-tired and embarrassed at the same time. He gets up quickly, sees that his knee is cut. The blood wells up, but the cut isn't deep.

His feet have gone numb and he hobbles towards the nearest building as if walking on stumps. The numbness gives way to the jabbing pain of pins and needles. He sits down, undoes his laces, loosening the shoes, and rubs his feet. The sun thumps down. The gravel is sharp and hot. The small crowd continues to watch him in silence. He is pretty close to tears.

But he is determined. He gets up quickly and limps towards the building. It's not a store at all. It's empty. The ceiling has been removed to reveal the roof's coating of asbestos. Daylight streams through in beams. The lights, the sockets, the switches, the windowpanes: everything has been stripped. On the concrete floor chalk markings look like boundaries for games.

Outside he walks further down the dusty gravel patch. There is another building, even more dilapidated, but when he approaches he sees it's a large room with a few women sitting on beaded mats, braiding each other's hair. From outside he had heard them talking loudly, but they fall silent as he enters.

'Hey, is there a store round here?'

He asks the question in the local dialect, but they just look at him, staring blankly. He walks out, angry at the unwelcoming attitude of these people, their cold, blank regard of him. He'd expected them to be helpful and friendly, or at least approachable, like the blacks on the farm, always eager to be of assistance, obliging by nature. These people seem different altogether, making him wonder whether he's in the right part of the country at all. But he must be. He's gone south the whole way. He can't have stuffed up that badly and landed in an entirely different area, it's just not possible.

He tries to shake off his doubts and walks on. A little further into the clearing he sees an old man sitting on the mound of a crisp earthy ant hill, shaded by a tree. He wears a dark blue suit, with a striped tie, a shirt threadbare at the collar. He is hunched over a walking stick singing what sounds like a gospel song. His eyes are shut. His face seems serenely focused.

'Hey, you.'

The old man stirs, lifts his head. His wide-rimmed glasses are bottle tops: thick, distorting. He squints through them.

'Yes my son.'

The old man's cut-glass accent surprises him and he is forced to change his approach.

'Sorry. I was just wondering whether you could help me please?'

'It would be my pleasure son, what do you require?'

'I want to know if there's any store round here? I've been walking for hours.'

'No I am sorry to say the store was closed some months ago. But if you are thirsty I would be happy to give you a drink of water. I have some at my home.'

He isn't sure. Water around these areas probably isn't safe to drink. And he has brought his own water in a drinking bottle. But somehow, perhaps because the old man speaks so sincerely, he finds he is unable to refuse.

'Some water would be great, thanks.'

'Well then you must come with me. You may find it a slow journey but my legs are not as youthful as yours my friend.'

They walk a short way through the growth point before turning up a narrow overgrown path. The man battles over the dongas, but after a while they come to a circular clearing, a kraal where a dozen or so mud huts stand. There is no one in sight. No livestock either: no goats, chickens, cattle. To one side a patchy field has been cleared where a few vegetables, rows of shrivelled maize grow.

They bypass the kraal and carry on up the narrow path to a ledge sticking out the side of a small kopje.

'Here is my home.'

It's a square shack made of concrete slabs, bigger than the mud huts in the kraal, but still nonsensically small. The tin roof has rusted, patched up with some tatty sheets of black plastic and a few old maize bags, weighted down with rocks.

'Do you not think it is most beautiful, the location of my home?'

He is unsure how to reply. It's a small hovel stuck in the middle of nowhere. But, looking beyond the bushes, the view is attractive. Green hills dense with trees weave through the fawn landscape, far into the surrounding countryside.

'It's a very nice place for a house.'

'I have a belief I will share with you and that is I believe the beauty of one's surroundings reflects the purity of one's soul. Every man should endeavour to search for such a location as I am fortunate to have here. It is very peaceful and spiritual to me.'

'Ja, I guess that's true.'

The old man beams with happiness and shows him to a stool outside the door of the shack.

'I enjoy sitting here in the early mornings and evenings. It is most inspiring.'

He sits down. The stool is hard, but accommodating. The man opens the door, goes inside. It is dark and cluttered, yet not un-inviting. He can see the outline of a narrow bed with several crosses of different materials and sizes fixed above it, across the room a shelf packed with utensils, and then jammed into every nook piles and piles of books. The old man emerges carrying two enamel cups and a clay jug.

'I will drink with you young man. I am quite parched myself.'

The old man puts the cups down on another stool and pours the water. It looks clear enough, but he decides to risk the question.

'Where does this water come from? Do you have a tap behind your house?'

'No, no my friend. There are no taps here. This water comes from a well in the next village. It is only twenty kilometres away.'

'Twenty ks!'

'Yes we are blessed to have any water at all. Most blessed. We are looked after well in these parts.'

He doesn't know what to say. Is this old man mad? Imagine having to travel twenty ks to get a jug of water! It just seems ridiculous. He shifts uncomfortably on the hard stool, now hurting his backside, thinking of something to say.

'Well, how long have you been living here?' he asks.

The old man rubs the wiry stubble on his chin. 'Let me see. I have been here now for almost eighteen years. You see, I used to be a headmaster in my day – at a mission school out in the reserve. I was, one may say, a respected man. People used to come from far and wide to seek my advice and counsel. Then I retired here, my home village. I have my lovely home and my view. But my advice is not so much sought out any more, I'm afraid to say. The younger people of today have strange views. Still, I pass the days reading my books. Do you know Dickens and Jane Austen?'

'Not really.'

'Yes, wonderful – I can get quite lost in those worlds. My worst fear is that my eyes will fail me. It would be a most dreadful thing. But I have kept you from drinking your water – please be my guest.'

He looks at the yellow cup, at the clear water and sips it slowly. It tastes fresh enough. He's desperately thirsty and his instinct is to drink quickly, in one gulp. But he knows that would be wrong, especially as it's so hard to come by. He doesn't want to waste it. He thinks about the distance he walked and wonders whether it's even as much as twenty ks. He reckons it must be.

'But of course,' the old man reflects, 'it may be that I will soon be too busy to read.'

'Oh?'

'Yes, I am keen to try my hand at another venture.' The old man smiles broadly, revealing a row of rotten teeth. 'Do not look so surprised. There is still much I am capable of doing, despite my age.'

'What sort of venture?'

'I believe I am in line for a handsome plot of land one of these days. I will put the few remaining years the good Lord has given me to good use. I will farm, and make a living selling crops. That is an honourable profession; one I've wanted to do for some time.'

'Here? You have a plot here?'

The old man breaks into a hearty laugh. 'No no, my friend. That would not be too successful. The land here is not very suitable you see. No, I would locate to more arable soils. For many many years we have been promised good land, and now, finally, it seems our faith and loyalty are being repaid. We have waited patiently. It hasn't always been an easy wait. There have been times when I've become frustrated, I admit that, when it seemed we'd been forgotten about out here. Hard years of drought and little food too. Yes, hard, hard times. But I've always believed that the word will be kept, and that is happening now. It will only be a matter of time now until I will be able to live on my promised land.'

He sits awkwardly for a while after the old man has spoken. He's not angered or embittered. In fact, the more he sits and the more the reality sinks in, the calmer he becomes. If anything, he's a bit sorry for this old man's delusions. He suddenly appears a bit pathetic, not like the clever man he'd thought he was when he'd first heard his posh accent and saw his piles and piles of old English books. What good has reading all that fancy stuff done him, being a headmaster and all, if he still believes he's just going to be handed a piece of land and told to farm? The poor guy's clearly not seen what's going on. He's damn well not getting a slice of Edenfields, that's for sure. He'll see to that.

'And you young man, what has brought you to such an obscure location?'

'Well, I'm sort of on the run,' he says. But he has no intention of telling the old man anything now; his pity has turned to impatience. He stands, looks down coldly at the crippled figure, suddenly a bit repulsed to have drunk water from a tin cup, a clay jug, a well twenty fucking ks away. The man's just a stupid peasant, like millions of others, making the best of what hasn't been given to him. He thinks: if I came back in a year's time, he'd still be here sitting outside his shack, looking at his view, reading his books, stupidly waiting to become a farmer. 'In fact, I have to go now. Thanks a lot for the water.'

The old man looks up, surprised at his sudden urgency, as if he'd wanted him to stay longer, talk to him more. 'It is a pleasure. I have enjoyed your company. Good luck.'

'Thanks a lot.'

He walks back through the small path in some haste, regretting the time he's now wasted. He reaches the main road again and carries on. At some point a car simply has to come by and stop for him: it has to. He realizes that if he'd suffered from the sun earlier on, he is in for a hard time now. Soon it is blisteringly hot, especially along the tarmac. He tries to stay as close to the line of vlei as possible, not only to avoid the heat rising in a firm flourish off the road, but because occasionally a passage of trees offers shade.

It isn't long before he is sweating profusely. His throat is intensely, painfully dry. He allows himself a few sips of water from his bottle every hundred steps; it's the logical thing to do to keep him focused. But the water is warm, offering little refreshment and tasting faintly of chemicals. The plastic bottle is so hot it's begun to soften. He permits himself two jam biscuits from the box he's brought, figuring that the sweet, sugary jam is a good supplier of energy. But still he quickly begins to tire. After an hour, each step is heavier than the last. Each step is almost unbearable.

He sees no one else. Still no animals or birds. The land seems flushed of everything, eerily as though it's waiting for him to pass. But really he knows that, like on the farms, the land, the wildlife have retreated from the onslaught, the killings, the attacks, the invasions. It's all an extension of her doing, and so much rests on his shoulders now to bring that right, conquer the villain and her henchmen.

He struggles on. His breath is heavy and laboured. His brow drips. His hair, his scalp are drenched. His eyes have taken severe strain – the reflection off the tarmac is relentlessly intense, the sun in a mirror – and they begin to water and become irritated. His crotch is itchy, his shorts are damp with sweat. His toes are cramped and sore. Pain shoots up his back. Occasionally he becomes giddy, seeing a galaxy of faint yellow red specks that fade after a moment, leaving a slight chill.

Doubts buzz through his head. It doesn't seem like the landscape he's passed through so many times by car. There's something about it – the grassland looks thicker, more weed-strangled, more obtrusive. The fan-shaped ridges of the hills are far harsher, shinier too, deposits of ochre clay stacked like the bases of ruins of temples, overgrown with tawny vegetation. The jutting rocks are gaunt and black. Normally, they're softer: whites, greys, blues and silvers. Surely by now there should be something he recognizes, something familiar? But there is nothing. He doesn't know how he'd handle it if he was on the wrong road and this whole journey was taking him further from his target. He thinks of the forbidding distance he's travelled, the sun, the effort – all this effort has to add up to something.

He tries to get a grip on his mind. He can't allow himself to go to pieces like that. Even if he is on the wrong road, the worst thing is to go nowhere at all. And if he's picked up by a car, as he must be soon, he'll be taken to his destination, or at least to the right path.

Eventually, another hour later, he hears the sound he's been waiting for – a car coming up behind him. A shudder of excitement peels through him, both hope and desperation. He turns: the car's a clapped-out green Peugeot, its exhaust shot, and it appears to be moving incredibly slowly. As it gets nearer, he begins waving his arms up and down. This could be his one chance, his quick salvation. It's the first car all day, God knows when there'll be another. He waves more frantically, knowing that it just has to stop for him. No one could possibly leave someone stranded on the side of the road, in the boiling sun. Is it slowing down? It seems to be. He begins to reach out for the door handle, then sees just how packed it is with blacks, and, anyway, it's going far too fast – it has no intention of stopping. It's not going to stop! In a flash the old Peugeot passes by, rattling on.

'No, no, stop! Please fucking stop!'

He screams, stamping his feet, but to no avail. The car is soon a small blob in the swelter. One car all day, and now it's gone.

Suddenly he breaks down; the dam gives way and he's crying a flood of tears, his chest heaving, his breath impossible to catch. It never occurred to him that someone would drive by without picking him up – that someone would leave him there. He cries and cries, frantic, hysterical. It's becoming so hard. How can it be that nothing is working as planned, nothing at all?

He stops and bends over, his tiredness and disappointment falling down through him until it seems that there's nothing left in the top half of his body. He's been drained, thoroughly leached of energy and will. He takes a few steps, but his legs buckle. He collapses to the hard dirt and sits, panting away the dizziness. Get up, he hears himself saying. Get up and go on. He knows the longer he sits here, weakened and despairing, the harder it'll be for him to get up and start off again. A sudden flash of Pa's physical strength waves up through him. He's got to draw on that, be strong and endure the hardship.

With a short spurt of determination, he pulls himself up and trudges along, slowly. He has to stop every 100 metres for a small break, a minute sip of water, enough to wet his tongue, sluice round his mouth for as long as he can. It is no refreshment: he would kill, simply kill, for an ice-cold Coke. The thought of his fridge at home brings tears back to his eyes.

He lumbers on, determined to master his emotions. He tries to concentrate his mind on things more physical. For a while he counts the steps he takes, matching them against the white stripes on the road. He catalogues the different types of trees, tallying up an indigenous and exotic table in his mind. Three-quarters of an hour later there is a blurry shape sticking out into the road ahead which arouses a splinter of interest. Closer by, he sees it's a buffalo carcass, half heaped in the bushes. He's immensely relieved to see evidence of another creature, even a dead one. Things at last seem a bit real, a bit worldly. It provides him with an excuse to stop for a while, examine the strangeness. The beast's hide is dry and its stomach a huge gaping hole, picked almost clean by scavengers.

He notices something odd: a small round paraffin tin standing by the buffalo's hind legs. He looks in, sees rotting meat piled to the top. Then, the buffalo quivers. He staggers back in panic, a quick snatch in his heart. He can't believe what he's seen, but it moves again. A shudder. He stoops down, peers in. A small child, clutching a dagger, is hunched up inside the bloodied, bone-shelled carcass, chopping and scraping off flakes of meat. He sees the white vapour of eyes glaring at him, a small hand resting on the squishy plexus of skin.

Behind him comes a sudden noise in the grass – he sees more children hiding behind bush. They aren't wearing any shirts; they have bony chests, bloated stomachs, snotty noses. They don't look at all distressed or appalled, but mischievous, as if they're just kids caught in the act. He mutters for directions to the district, but at the sound of his tired, husky voice they flee with a giggle into the deep cover of bush, startling him with a sudden frenzy of throwing small stones and clomps of dried mud. He ducks and moves off, trying to swallow this small panic, to calm his heartbeat.

It takes him a while to talk himself down and recover his rhythm. He longs for this day to end, this savage drift of time. He longs for this hell he's going through to dissolve. The more he walks, the greater his belief becomes that he's on the wrong road. By car he's used to seeing many more growth points. They seem to appear every few minutes, around every other corner, these little buds promising villages. Now there's just a seemingly endless stretch of road leading nowhere, to an infinite dead end. He thinks through each stage of his journey, retakes each decision, but concludes again that if he got on the train going south, he simply has to have ended up somewhere within the district. He has to! He takes out the compass again, points it down the road: exactly south. He'd checked his direction on the train, when he first got on to the main road. He couldn't have missed some gradual swing of direction.

To console his misery, he decides to eat another two jam biscuits. He has begun to believe that his despondency is a result of a lack of sustenance to the brain. The jam has gone all gooey, sticking to the plastic tray; when he levers out a biscuit, it goes all over his fingers, a warm, syrupy squelch.

'Shit, shit, shit!'

He screams out in rage, every fibre in him seeming to stretch and strain. He begins to throw the packet into the bush, but stops himself just in time. He eats the biscuit moodily, licks his fingers and wipes them on his shirt, but the stickiness remains. Such a small annoyance, yet his mind rages. He carries on walking, fighting back a new wave of tears.

The next thing he's aware of is the sound of a car engine. He must have lost track of time. He hasn't been watching his surroundings; the sun still beats down, maybe from a slightly lower angle. But now a car, as though summoned finally by his will, out of his dreams! Such ecstasy. He turns to see a metallic blue twin-cab truck belting towards him. But will it stop? He waves his hand furiously, he half staggers into the middle of the road, knowing it can't possibly go by this time without stopping. But it's going way too fast. He glares at it, breathlessly, his eyes registering this monstrous cruelty, his heart beating against such an act of utter selfishness. As it streams by, he glimpses a white couple, two God-sent saints, and waves even more vigorously, begging even for a turn of the head, even to meet someone's eye. The truck passes, but about fifty metres up the road it comes to a screeching halt and immediately starts reversing. As tired as he is, he is able to hobble and half jog towards it, the purest joy flashing inside him, the belief that his life has just been saved, that it's all going to be okay now, finally okay!

He finds himself on the passenger side, where a youngish woman sits, smoking. He assumes she'll roll down the window, but she doesn't. She just sits, looking ahead. The sun reflects off the fine dust sheet of a windscreen, and he can't make out her expression. For a moment he doesn't know quite how to react – is he meant to get in? He stands, stuck, his mind still swallowing the glorious idea of a truck in front of him. Then the driver waves his hand, signalling him to move around to the other side. He shuffles round the bonnet and tries to say hi, but not a sound comes out.

'Yeah mate, need a lift?'

'Please.'

'Yeah, of course, hop in.'

'Thanks, thanks a lot.'

Never has he meant those words more sincerely. He's on the verge of crying with gratitude. The driver seems to be in his early thirties with long blond hair kept in by a well-worn Yamaha cap, his face acne-scarred, unshaven, with a thick moustache. Opening the door, he hears some sharp exchange between the couple. The woman doesn't look around as he collapses on to the warm plastic of the back seat.

'Hello,' he says to her.

'Hi.' She continues to look straight ahead.

Now he's in the truck, the blessed truck, there's no way he's getting out. As he closes the door, a wet slobbering mouth takes him by surprise, licking his arms. It's a brinjal-coloured terrier.

'That's Jinx.'

She has a slender soppy face, her breath hot and stinking. He tries to nudge her over a bit, but she won't budge. Instead she climbs on to his lap, licks at his face.

'Jinx!'

The man yells and the dog hastily retreats to the other side of the seat, her tail between her legs. He wipes away the slobber with his shirt.

'I'm Garth by the way.'

'I'm Davey.'

'This is my wife Tara.'

Tara turns her head slightly – perhaps she's looking at him in the rear-view mirror. It's difficult to tell behind her sunglasses.

After a moment they get going. Garth drives at tremendous speed and it is a great great thing to sit still in the truck watching the countryside go streaming by. He is immensely relieved, extremely happy. He rolls the window down a bit and rejoices in the cool, fresh air hitting his face. It is sheer bliss to be there in a nice comfortable seat, resting his aching, blistered feet. It is strange, almost bewildering to think that just a few minutes ago he was in such desperate trouble, in such low spirits. Now he is uplifted to near delirium. His fatigue begins to close over him; his limbs seem heavy enough to sink through the seat, through to the bottom of the truck and to brush the road flying by below. He smiles, pats Jinx playfully on the head, his goodwill and happiness extending to every conceivable thing.

Moving at this speed, he realizes that this is the right road after all. The landscape he knows so intimately resolves into view, so different from a moving vehicle. As he remembered, small growth points start appearing every now and then: it was just a matter of time before he reached the next one. He'd have been okay, he'd have made it. The relief floods through him like the sea.

'Hey I don't suppose you want a drink do you? It's a beast of a day.'

'Ja, thanks, that would be great.'

'Honey, get us a drink.'

Tara remains still for a moment, before slowly reaching down into the cooler bag at her feet.

'We've only got beers,' Garth says.

'That's just great. Thanks a lot.'

Tara passes a brown bottle back to him. She moves at a different pace from Garth. He wonders for a moment if she's drugged, before his attention is consumed by the ice-cold bottle in his hand – a true, deep pleasure to touch. It suddenly strikes him: this is the drink of men, a reward after a hard day's work on the farm. He deserves it! He presses it to his face, rubs it against his thighs. The cold mingles gloriously with the sting of sunburn. He is so thirsty he tries not to down the beer in just a few gulps, but he can't help himself. When he's finished he pretends he's still sipping, not to appear rude.

Occasionally Jinx creeps forward and starts licking his arm. At first he tries to push her muzzle discreetly away, but in the end he just lets her do as she wants. Every few minutes Garth yells at her, until Tara says quietly, 'Don't yell at the dog, please. I've got a headache.'

'Oh Christ!'

They carry on driving. He's offered another beer and again knocks it back quickly. His thirst doesn't seem to be diminishing.

'Where you heading Davey?'

He tells him the name of the district.

'Oh yeah. Things a bit of a fuck-up there now aren't they?'

'A bit.'

'I tell you, I'm glad I'm no bloody farmer all right.'

'Ja.'

'Jesus, and that attack a few months ago?'

'Ja.'

'That's one fucking story all right. Poor damn bastards.'

'Ja.'

'Know them?'

'Ja, I knew them.'

Garth shakes his head and mutters to himself. He sits there look-ing out of the window, patting Jinx for comfort as she slobbers and pants. Fortunately as Garth's about to speak again, Tara interrupts him.

'Do you have to talk about this? It's too disgusting.'

'Well then, don't listen honey.'

Tara turns her head slightly in Garth's direction and stays silent.

Just then a fast-moving bulge of blackness streaks across the road in front of them. Garth slams on brakes, swerves. There is the sharp squeal of tyres, an instant cloud of smoke and dust, the smell of brake fluid.

'Christ!' Garth shouts.

He looks up to see a big black boar plunge into the bush on the other side of the road, its head cocked, its wild red eyes glaring at him, straight at him, before its bulk is claimed by the dense scrub. A surge of shock rings through him. He sits back.

They travel for another forty minutes in silence. The sun is well on its descent now, the bright white already mellowed into gold, and beginning to change to orange. He thinks about how long it would have taken him to walk this distance. It would have taken days – days – if he'd managed it at all. Now he is perfectly orientated, knows exactly where he is. He's not far from the district at all, not by truck at least.

But soon they start to slow down. Up ahead is a garage he vaguely remembers having seen before, although Pa had never stopped there – it's a rundown old place, isolated in the bush. Propped against two vermilion petrol pumps, chalkboards say 'No Petrol, No Diesel'. He must be travelling with the owners.

They pull off the road and drive round the back. They enter a scrapyard: the bodies of old broken-down cars are packed closely together, rich in red rust, presiding over a vast array of engine bits, spare parts, and old tyres stacked ten high on top of each other. Further away a water reservoir towers on a metal tripod, and to the side there's a small dingy house hemmed in by overgrown grass.

He isn't sure what to do. Should he ask Garth to drive him the rest of the way to the farm? How much further is that? He can't quite remember – not far, but after his last misjudgement, he's loath to just say thanks very much and walk. Maybe Garth is just dropping Tara off because of her headache? They pull up outside the house and Jinx starts leaping and barking. Tara gets out and stalks towards the back door looking like she's about to topple over on her high heel stilts. Garth and he get out as well and stretch.

'Thanks a lot for the lift, I really appreciate it.'

'Yeah, no sweat. Sorry I can't take you further but we kind of have to watch the petrol you know.'

'Sure.'

'Even a fucking garage owner struggles with petrol, can you believe it?'

'Ja, it sucks.'

'I'll phone round and try to hitch you a lift first thing in the morning.'

'Well ...'

'It's no sweat. You can't go on. Seriously. It's just a fuck-up around these places at night, especially for a white guy.'

'Okay, if you're sure it's no problem.'

'Course not. I'm sure you've heard the stories of what they do to those poor fuckers they catch.'

When he got into the truck, he had thought he would be in the district by nightfall at the latest. Now his thinking seems to have slowed down; he can't seem to work out what to do. Should he walk there? Nightfall is a couple of hours away and he pretty much knows where he is now. But Garth is right, that probably isn't wise. It might be better to get a good night's rest and then carry on first thing in the morning. So what if his mission's completed one day later?

Garth leads him towards the house. Outside the back door a massive collection of empty booze bottles is stacked in rows. The kitchen is tiny; the sink piled high with dirty dishes, pots and pans. There's a fatty, cooking oil smell to the place.

In the lounge, Garth moves a stack of old car and motorbike magazines off a chair for him, and then disappears down the small passage into the back of the house, after Tara. He hears stern words, but can't make out what they're saying. The door opens and he hears another exasperated 'Jesus Christ!' But when Garth comes back into the room, he seems happy enough.

'Drink?'

'Thanks.'

All they have is beer or vodka. No mixers. He has a beer.

The evening falls, then the night. Soon Garth and he are outside on the veranda lighting the gas braai. There's no sign of Tara.

'Don't mind her. She's pregnant you know, moans about these damn headaches all day long. Gets a bit much after a while.'

They cook some boerewors and small rump steaks. Garth dumps Tara's on a plate for her to have later, oblivious to the scatter of flies that suddenly dart about busily. Garth and he sit and eat, and drink. Garth talks telling him about how he came to take over running the garage after his old man had a stroke, how he and Tara used to go regularly to the mine club for beer fests and braais, about the wild parties they've had over the years, the punch-ups and dramas, the scandals of all and sundry.

'But we don't go much any more,' he says, sounding a bit down. 'Most of those mining guys have moved on. It just doesn't pay any more. Not with all the fucking hassles you've got to put up with.'

'Ja, I guess.'

'It's a pity you know. I swear that place has got the cheapest booze in the country.'

He doesn't say much himself. He's tired. He just eats his food happily, drinks his beer. Garth certainly knows how to down beers all right: he drinks at least three to his one. He hopes Garth won't get too drunk and forget to arrange his lift into the district. He just wants to get going again, eager for morning to come, a fresh start to his mission.

But Garth talks more and more, drinks more and more. Slurred, pointing his finger, sucking the top of the beer bottle between statements, he eventually veers on to the farm issue again, slates the government.

'But I tell you one thing – one thing that I know for fucking certain – and that is, those bloody farmer bastards, they have it good.

They've had it real good for years. You know that? They've been creaming the cash, living the high life. Don't tell me they don't fucking understand that one day it's all going to be pulled away from under their feet. Hey? Don't tell me they don't know it. And you know, not one of those bastards ever stops at my garage – not one. You never see one of those guys at the mine club for a drink. Oh no, they're far too bloody good for us miner guys and mechanics.'

He doesn't bother responding: they're only words. And the man is clearly pissed. He just sits, sipping his bitter beer in silence.

'And I tell you another thing. It's people like me who're going to be bloody laughing in a few years' time. We're the ones who're going to be spared all this bullshit. I'm going to get to keep my garage, I'm going to have a job. The bloody farmers aren't are they? I'm not going to be fucking attacked and chopped into pieces for my land, that's for damn sure.'

When they've finished eating, Jinx is allowed to lick the plates, slobbering at the juices of the meat. Perhaps that's how the dishes get done all the time.

The mosquitoes have begun to bite so they go inside. He's longing to go to bed, but Garth wants to show him something and leads him down a passage into a locked room. He flicks on the light revealing a huge shining motorbike standing on a blue mat in the middle of an entirely empty, very clean room. The walls are clinical white, the tiled floor shimmering and smooth with polish. The bike's a Harley.

'Cool.'

'She's my baby. My pride and joy. I live for this machine.'

'Do you ride her often?'

'This beauty? No fucking way. She's too precious to drive around here.'

Garth strokes the gleaming silver handlebars, looking at him. He wonders whether he's supposed to respond, say something more about how fantastic the bike is. But he doesn't. It's just a bike in the middle of an empty room, a bit weird, a bit pointless. They move back into the lounge. Garth puts on a CD of some bizarre sounding music, loud. Black Sabbath.

'Bloody great stuff,' Garth yells.

He's heard of Black Sabbath, but they're before his time. The music sounds distorted and overloaded. Garth moves his head backwards and forwards, singing along, a beer in hand, playing air guitar.

He sits on the sofa and after a while becomes horribly nauseous. Even the dim light in the lounge seems too bright; the music hammers down the beginnings of any thought he has. He inhales, blows into his cheeks. Probably the sun more than anything. He touches his arms: they're clammy and hot, sore to the touch. The back of his neck is worse. He is severely, stupidly sunburnt – he decides to make this beer his last one. His stomach's heavy, his throat dry and he sits up on the edge of the sofa, ready to rush outside to throw up.

Suddenly Tara comes charging out of the bedroom in a skimpy nightie, looking sleepy eyed and wasted. She stamps her feet and screams at Garth to turn the music down. She's holding a bottle of vodka in her hand, half full. She starts to sway, gripping on to the back of a chair. Garth completely ignores her. She stamps her feet again, shakes her head. She goes close up to his face and starts screaming. Garth shouts back, suddenly throwing a punch, striking her across the jaw. She keels over behind the chair, the vodka bottle slides from her hand, goes rolling across the floor. Garth glares threateningly at her, but then turns away, pumping up the volume much louder than before.

He can't stomach this. He knows he's going to throw up any second. He gets up, grabs his satchel and makes for the kitchen. The door handle is locked and there is no key in sight. He begins to panic. He's trapped.

He's about to heave. He looks round for something to throw up in. He's hot and sweaty. He needs air. He takes a deep breath, bolting everything in place for another moment, and goes back into the lounge. Tara's crawling round on the floor, searching for her bottle. Garth's playing his air guitar while Jinx barks wildly, leaping up at him as he eggs her on.

'Come on Jinxy, jump jump.'

They don't seem to notice him so he moves over to the lounge door and frees himself into the cool night air, moving quickly through the yard.

He stands outside for a minute, breathing heavily, slowly, the deep black air a soothing tonic, like a tall glass of iced water. But he wants to get as far away as he can from this house. He runs past the workshops and garage until he's back on the open road. He stops to throw up into the bush. Too much beer. Too much sun. But it's the shock of it all that really upsets him. The cruelty, the frank violence between two people, man and wife. At some point when he's retching, he starts crying. He just can't seem to stop himself. His eyes blur with tears, his breath is laboured, the taste of vomit vile and vitriolic in his throat.

He can't see much and waits for the tears to clear, and his night eyes to light the cover of blackness about him. He stares out, trying to think which way to go. The road looks different in the moonlight. He doesn't like the dark at all, but it's a thousand times better than going back to Garth and Tara. With the district not that far off now, he decides to risk walking it during the night. At least he won't have the sun to contend with – it's probably the way he should have done it in the first place. He heads up the road, back past the garage on his left and keeps on walking. It's quiet, except for occasional low moans deep in the vlei. The presence of beasts in the dark wilderness fills him with a strange, nostalgic comfort, making him realize that he is close to home. It's cool and not unpleasant, but the mosquitoes become a constant irritation. They feed constantly, biting his ankles the most. For a while he reaches down from time to time to slap them away, but it's impossible to do that and walk. So he lets them have their way. He'll scratch at their bites when he's done.

. He walks for some time, maybe an hour or so, but then begins to tire again. His adrenalin has faded, and the weight of the day settles back on his limbs, plus the beer that's still in his system. Soon his eyes start to droop, getting heavier and heavier, his body responding to the magnetic atmosphere of the night, the strange creaks and lowing that spread out across the wide open land, pulling his mind to sleep, even though his legs are still moving. He seems suspended in the dark, the road moving like a treadmill beneath him while the surroundings remain vacant, impenetrable, constant. The stars in the sky don't change. He is a boy walking across Africa.

So he compensates, formulating an imaginary landscape around him. He is walking on a sandy white beach. A blue sea is breaking over him, washing up against his legs. Palm trees litter the shore giving shade, and a jungle of tropical greenery spreads inland. He is berated by a parrot, shimmying up a branch: red, green, blue. The water is clear aquamarine. Brightly coloured fish skim coral reefs.

His fantasy takes him further. Kneeling in the water, a short distance away, is a gorgeous tanned woman playing and splashing about. She has long wavy blonde hair, slender legs. She wears only a see-through T-shirt drenched by the sea, clinging tightly to her firm breasts and body. He strides towards her, and when he finally gets to her, she peels away her top, takes his tired head to her wet naked breasts. He fondles them, licks at them, makes love to her in the water. She opens her moist inviting legs so he could place his hard, throbbing cock there and fuck her.

He's aroused himself greatly and rubs himself through his shorts as he walks, his being pinned to his body at the top of his head and his cock. Occasionally he stumbles and finds he has to open his eyes, steer himself back on track, before taking leave again. Then he finds himself lying in the dusty verge by the side of the road.

He knows he has to stop: it is senseless to continue as he is. He gazes round trying to find a tree to lie under but can't make one out. He crawls into the bush, quietly tumbles down into the spiky grass. He drags his satchel under his head and rests against it, lying on his back. He fiddles at his shorts, frees his penis. He comes quickly. A shuddering orgasm. An unbelievable relief. A clean sheet of peace. A fall through the sky into a lightness soft and indescribable.

He lurches forward, shaking away the grogginess, jolting awake his mind. For a few seconds he is confused about the repellent nakedness of his surroundings, the darkness. The grass is uncomfortable, the earth hard and cold. A mosquito vibrates in his ear. He doesn't know how long he's been asleep, but when he pulls his shorts up, the semen is still a damp, sticky patch on his stomach, flaked in his crotch. He sits up, stares through a speckle of red flashing dots. He stands and swaggers a few steps into the bush to urinate. He is full, a bit bloated, but is soon relieved.

A rush of blood to his head makes him dizzy. He sits down again at the side of the road, staring ahead blankly. He dimly recalls that the district is not far off now and that he should try to reach it before the sun rises, but for the moment he's forgotten why. He wants nothing more than to sink into the ground, to become planted, like a tree, stretching his roots into the cool earth and breathing in the still air.

He is still exhausted, despite his short sleep. He aches all over. The pain of sunburn lies in a tight ring round his neck so that each time he moves his shoulders or turns his head sharply, the fierce sting makes him wince. He lies back, rests his head once again on his satchel, assuming his clouded mind will soon clear. Memories of a blow – a knife, was it, a bottle? – float through his mind. Something painful that he wonders whether he should make a greater effort to recall, before he lets it float away into the night. He stares up with swimming eyes, registering the waning moonlight overhead, a scattering of chaste, distant stars. The endless buzz of the mosquitoes in his ear seems just as distant. He wonders for a while what the mosquitoes eat when there's nobody around.

After a while he becomes aware of a faint sound, a low grumble. He stirs himself, raises his head, looks about but can't make out anything around him. He might well be blindfolded – blinded, even. Maybe he's surrounded right now by people silently laughing at him in broad daylight. Maybe he's in the dormitory, and the guys are playing a trick on him. Maybe he's in the attic. Why would he be in the attic?

He lies still; every effort to move brings another ache. A short while later the sound becomes more distinctive: a straining, a chug- ging. There is a blur somewhere in the distance of his mind, a mass of white, some massive creature lolling towards him with two bright staring eyes. Then he brings it into focus: it's a lorry, a white lorry. It's moving slowly, roaring all the while. The lorry looks familiar, a moving slab of horror, but chances are there are lots like it. On the back a bunch of men stand stamping their feet in unison, shouting, jeering, ululating.

Suddenly he finds he's running through thick bush. An impulse from underneath the dream has got him up and moving, fast, away from the road. Something is following him, he can sense it. He trips over tree stumps, falls into ditches. The foliage is thick and thorny, difficult to penetrate. But he runs and runs, hurling his body forward in a way that strangely seems effortless, the sudden surge of energy unfathomable.

Then a great hard weight comes down on his back and he's lying again on the dank ground, dazed. He squirms and fights, but a heavy body straddles him, gripping his hands behind his back, pushing his face into the ground. He tastes a mouthful of gritty soil, a clump of grass, and tries desperately not to inhale or swallow. He starts coughing anyway: it gets up his nose and he gasps for air, unable to breathe. He ought to try to struggle free, but finds himself surrendering. His body is deadened, paralysed. He allows himself to be yanked up, aware only of the sharp pain shooting through his shoulders and the roughness of thick rope chaffing his skin, binding his wrists as he is dragged ahead.

The back of the truck is uncomfortable; the ruts and grooves jab at his bones. He is not conscious of making a protest, of trying to plead or beg, but the pressure of a hard boot pegging him down at the neck prevents him from crying out at all. There is the sensation of motion under him, the shrilling strain of the engine, and then the boot is released. He is lying on his side and can only seem to stare straight ahead into sheets of white gloss, ripped by rust. He can make out several figures clad in combat fatigues, but can't count them precisely. A scud of beer is passed round, spilt carelessly. How he'd die for a sip, a dribble! There is smoke in the air, the smack of marijuana and exhaust fumes. A chorus of cheering starts up, and the stamping of boots sending a hammer of shocks reverberating through his muscles, into the nerve centre of his being.

The idea half enters his mind that he should attempt to jump from the truck, but he can't connect the idea with any muscles, and the ability to act. He pictures the spin of the wheels, the brutal tangle of rough metal pipes underneath the chassis. He doesn't have the courage.

A moment later he is yanked by the collar and kicked hard in the head with a boot. His vision fractures, but there isn't much pain, as though he's wearing a helmet. Sometime later he is aroused by a stream of liquid splashing over his face. Briefly, he relishes the warm relief the shower brings to his tight, sunburnt face. A taste: the putrid acidity startles him. He strains to look up at the giant figure standing over him, an arc of urine jetting from his exposed midriff, the long pipe of a penis. Mild disgust fills him, but he is only able to lie there helplessly until it is finally over and he can once again be allowed to drift off, high above the plains, into the calmness of clouds.

Now he is lying on his back, propped up against the stump of a tree. Lights flicker not far in front of him – a fire? – and a high-pitched screech drills into his ears, boring at his brain. Ahead there's a gathering of some large beasts, their wobbly bulk shifting now and then, beige and grey in the darkness. A herd of elephants most likely, though he can't quite see their features, the flap of palm-leaf ears or the slow swing of their trunks, and he can't begin to wonder what he's done to deserve the glorious, safe company of elephants.

There is a dull thud at his brow and the instant he tries to move his neck, to turn away, severe pain rips through him. His feet and

legs are numb, beyond his power to move. He keeps very still, staring ahead mesmerized and mystified by the stationary elephants.
Strewn everywhere is a great collection of grass and branches
they've cleverly gathered and are about to consume in a feast of
their slow, meticulous munching.

A while later there is a firm wetness down his legs; his bladder
has failed. Afterwards there's a great release in his stomach, as if
someone had been sitting on him and has now got up. He lies
unmoving, dozing and not dozing, conscious always of a tension, a
threat, constantly skirting about the fringes of his perception. He
goes through short phases of being startlingly afraid, then utterly
calmed. And then he emerges into a state where he simply needs to
vomit. He collapses on to his side, afraid he's going to choke, but
nothing comes. The nausea eases, slouches back into his stomach.

Later the elephants have gone, replaced by a string of thatched
huts. They stand in a crescent, a scar against the darkness. A crowd
of still, subdued people is gathered in the foreground behind the
struggling glow of a bonfire surrounded by stones. The huts and
the people are not far away – the firelight flickers over his feet – yet
somehow he senses this isn't his drama. He's a bystander, in the
shadows.

To the far left he can make out the shape of a vehicle in the
darkness; a white vehicle, a truck.

A man is kneeling in front of the simmering pit, and four figures – tall, bony – slowly circle him, moving with the same rhythm.
The man has his head bowed, but is somehow familiar. He knows
his shape. He can't see clearly, but the man appears to lift his head
slightly and cast a stony glance in his direction, to hold his gaze for
a moment. Where does he know him from? How is it possible that
the two of them have met before? A white boy and a black man in

the midst of this vast, malicious wilderness, this canvas of chaos?

The beatings start: clubs made from thick, mangled branches. To the man's stomach, to the back. He tries to close his eyes, turn his head away, but the sight keeps swimming in front of his vision. The blurred bobbing of a head, a spray of wetness in the air. The rhythm of the blows shudders through him – the dull thud, quick snap of bones, rupture of tendons, muscles, organs. Perhaps he has his eyes closed now, but the blows continue inside his head. Now the man has collapsed, disappeared almost – vanished as the need for the others to beat him slowly vanishes. Again, though, the air pulses, the crowd sways and ripples as a small boy is brought forward. In front of the crowd the boy is stripped naked, his few clothes fed one by one to the fire. Do they need more fuel? No. One of the figures pulls a glinting stick – a knife – from his khaki jacket and lowers it to the boy's waist, to his genitals, under the scrotum. He holds it there for a moment. Then, the yanking and cutting; only momentary, as clinical as filleting fish, a few seconds. Then this butcher holds the hacked organ to his own crotch and waves it at the crowd. He laughs a loud, raucous laugh. The man who'd been beaten is dragged out of the ground, clasped by the head, his mouth forced open, the slither of boyhood stuffed down his gullet while the boy himself is dragged back limply and dropped in dirt.

The crowd is frozen; this is directed at them. It could be them. The child and the man he recognizes have gone. Can either of them have survived? He can't see them – there are a couple of people lying down round the fringe of the fire, maybe they are there? Near one of the figures – a fat woman, wearing a dress – he glimpses a rabbit – a white rabbit. He smiles, dreamily. A rabbit! It's crawling over the woman's body, its head, its nose twitching at the great split across her stomach. He wants the rabbit to come to him – tries to click for it with his tongue, and although he can only be making the smallest of sounds, the rabbit responds, leaves the dead woman and tentatively hops towards him. After a few moments it reaches him – he smells the sweet distinctive mixture of soft fur and blood as it reclines timidly in his hands. He wonders where it has come from, wonders whether he's conjured it up, a friend in this hallucination of the end of the world.

For a while, an empty space. The rabbit is gone. Are the people gone too? The fire is still there, bright, brighter. The night is still there. It seems married to the mayhem. The hooded clouds, the trees cloaked in black. The world seeps and droops.

Then the four figures re-emerge, perhaps just seconds later, through the centre of the crowd, moving slowly. They are closer to him now than they have ever been – maybe now they have come for him. Maybe now it's his turn. Panic lurches up in his throat, but it's a mere instinctive reaction, merely his body. In fact, he is not surprised. He deserves it. For being a traitor and a coward he deserves what he gets, this bleak and public end. For being a failure too. He is young, but he's had his chances. He tried to accomplish his mission, to reach his destination, to do something to repent for his weakness, do the right thing. But he failed. He knows that in real life, the hero never really saves the day.

So they come towards him, slowly. They speak and the words drift past him. They hold blazing torches, leafy branches lit in the bonfire, and he half expects them to strike the ground and propel a current of blue lightning through his spine that will send him spiralling into a deep bottomless abyss. Instead, there is a chemical smell – not what he thought – something from another world. It is the sudden rich stench of petrol, and even before a great explosion of tin somewhere beside him, he knows that perhaps time is on his side. Around him the world ignites, explodes into flame. God, how Pa could do with that petrol on the farm: such a needless waste! And then, in an instant, a spreading orange wave rises overhead, followed by deep black rages of belching smoke.

The village is instantly ablaze. People run about crazed and hysterical. The fire burns the dusty soil, sodden with petrol, spreading to every hut. He smells something close to him, and when he threads his hands through his hair, he finds it's being singed, burning his fingers. He pulls his shirt over his head to keep away the brutal heat. Dry thatch explodes above him and he has to be quick to avoid the falling debris. He crawls on his stomach, but in every direction a great battery of flames roars. The noise is unbelievable. Somewhere the first of the huts collapses, sending a spiral column of dust and thatch high in the sky. The air above is an intense glowing red. Heat blows towards him in smoking gusts, momentarily blinding him. He finds a passage that he can run through. More of the huts burn and buckle. The manure in the mud walls combusts amazingly, shooting up fireballs and burning bits of straw. He inches through the flames and hobbles out through a closing gap.

It's only when he's on the outside looking in that he grasps how hot it had been inside. He touches his skin: it's sizzling. The fine hair on his arms has crinkled into nothing. The only thing to do is stand and watch. Bodies and figures brush past him, blank, bewildered faces. All sound is a muffled roar, a shell to the ear. Everything burns, burns, burns.

He has lost all perception of time, and stumbles round endlessly in the tumult of smoke, plumes of an afterlife, but eventually he surfaces from this haze to see that the sky has caught up the red; the day breaking. The fire burns away as the sun rises, showing the remains of the village. The occasional shell of a hut remains, those reinforced with poles, but the only thing standing to any great height is the grey waft of smoke.

He looks round. For a while he wanders round the crater, this vast wasteland. There are no people – perhaps he imagined them. Everything is soaked black, simply black. He comes across a pen, the wire still so hot it's glowing red. He squints in hoping not to find the carcasses of dead animals, but there they are. Bodies of goats, piled up. Their torsos charred crisp, the flesh occasionally a hard glistening red beneath the burns. The smell unnerves him; the smell of flesh burnt alive. It somehow smells differently to the smell of dead burning flesh.

He reels away, retreating into the bush, but it's too thick and he has to stop, deep in the claustrophobic vlei. He is raw all over, smeared in fine black soot. His clothes are filthy, heavy with grime, reeking of fire. His hair and face are sticky, his legs, his pants damp. He needs water, but when he reaches behind for his satchel, it has gone. He looks at his wrist: his watch has gone. He searches his pockets: the money too. He leans back against the trunk of a tree and shuts his eyes away from the spiral of grey black clouds floating towards infinity.

**3**

Mike, Gus, Dirk and Terry approach Edenfields. Two kilometres away from the boundary gate, they cut their lights, and drive slowly. Each man rests his gun on the doorframe, covering his sector of the night. They've agreed in principle to use firepower if necessary, though strictly as a last resort. They know the course of the road, luckily. Mike knows it best. They stop just inside the wide stone gates, built like columns to announce the beginning of Edenfields. The danger sign with its skull and cross-bones glares at them, quietly preposterous, intimidating. Mike and Terry swap over so that now Mike's driving; an acknowledgement that from now on he's in charge, that everything's his call. They're all tense, nervous, on edge, but when Terry jokes, 'It's just like taking pot shots at baboons in the night,' they relax for a second or two. They wind along the road carefully; there is just the faintest glow of moonlight to guide them. Even so, they may as well be walking blindfolded through a thorn bush.

They poke their heads out of the windows, listen hard. It's important they are on the lookout for animals, adversaries. Without the headlamps, they won't be able to see red eyes. They won't be able to detect the militia, more than likely armed. They know if they hit a large animal now, grazing in the scrub at the side of the road, the damage could jeopardize their whole mission. It's dicey, but it would be even more dangerous – impossible, in fact – during the day.

They crawl on. Each man is responsible for his quarter. Terry takes the front view, left-hand side, Mike the front right, Dirk and

Gus behind them. After years of working on a farm, in a team of men, each instinctively shoulders his share of the burden, proud to be silently depended on, with words reserved for the essential, the critical: left bend, about ten metres ahead. Clear straight. Getting too close left side.

After a while, Mike can see enough to drive properly. His eyes have adjusted quickly, and the moonlight seems to have brightened. Nevertheless, they still take precautions: they drive at a snail's pace, barely twenty kilometres an hour, and every half a kilometre or so they stop completely, turn off the engine while Terry gets out and quickly circles the truck to make sure they aren't being followed or observed from a distance. It's like being back on patrol.

They make slow but steady progress. At the speed they are going it will take them another forty minutes before they begin the ascent up the hill to the farmhouse.

Normally Mike would chafe at the slowness, and although tonight it prolongs the anxiety, he finds some reassurance in the meticulousness of their mission, this measured pilgrimage to a venerated place, a great farm in a great district in a great country in Africa. Marsha might call it a crusade. She might say that they're going to rid the world of evils, of demons – to help restore a world where the good prevail, and the villain is defeated.

Well, that's all rather story-bookish, Mike reckons, a bit of Marsha the romantic. But he realizes there's some truth in it too – at last they've chosen to act for the better good. They're breaking the stalemate, bloody doing something about the problem instead of standing by and allowing the situation to tear them down, the corrupt to reign, the proper order of things to be overridden.

Of course, that's not how this country is any more. Bad things happen to good people, and, anyway, Mike assumes that the other guys probably aren't actually thinking much about the larger implications of what they're doing. Perhaps, unlike him, they haven't realized that by doing this, undertaking this task, a line has been crossed, a new beginning has been attempted. It's an act of defiance, revolution.

But it's dark and they must concentrate.

As they progress Gus isn't just keeping an eye on his side of the road. He's thinking about the implications and he's a bit pissed off. In fact, he's growing more and more uneasy. He doesn't say anything, but the further they advance, the more he's not comfortable with Terry in the truck. Mike should've checked things through with him beforehand. He shouldn't just have casually added risks to the equation.

And Terry is a risk. He makes Gus nervous. He's too impulsive. He's too headstrong. He has a habit of dominating situations. And he has a dark past. Gus knows what Terry did during the bush war. Terry makes an open secret of it: that he was a member of the elite killing corps, the infamous sniper brigade, responsible for countless killings and unsavoury deaths. He recalls the many stories, the widely rumoured antics, the reputations that followed these guys around. How they'd close in on villages, massacre the entire lot, women, children, babies.

Gus isn't so sure Terry's reformed either. He's a bloodluster, and that's dangerous. When all this shit had first started, when the Bakers were killed, Terry had raved on about how they ought to get out there and kill a few Kaffirs, make them pay. They'd all dismissed him – it was something uttered when they were all in shock, angry and hateful of everything. Now he's not so sure.

And that's not what this is about. Gus believes that in this case and in this case only, they have the right to fight the aggressor, physically fight and defend themselves against murderers and attackers. In this instance they have just cause to take matters into their own hands. Divine cause. He's a man of solid faith. He believes in righteousness. Terry sullies that, adds blood to the wine.

He isn't comfortable knowing that the justice Davey Baker suffered could degenerate into yet another act of needless violence. He'll keep quiet, but he knows he needs to keep an eye on Terry.


About halfway to the rise they are alarmed to come across a gaping crevice in the road. The whole track has been partly corroded away. Even with everything that's gone on, they wouldn't have expected this in a million years: on a farm, everyone knows that good roads lead straight to the bank.

'Jesus, all we bloody need,' says Gus.

They get out. It's basically a crater in front of them, a massive donga, and it clearly hasn't been helped by the afternoon rains. A couple of steps away it looks impassable, a slosh of mud, loose sand, but when they get closer they can see a way through. They're relieved, but puzzled as well. It doesn't look like something caused purely by neglect or the weather. They don't want to risk shining their torches, so they kneel down to squint into the crater. It looks man made — the gravel seems to have been hacked at. It's been done intentionally.

'What the hell is this bitch up to?' Dirk is the first to ask. 'Surely she has to get on and off her blinking land?'

It unnerves Mike, Terry, Gus: this is how you stop a convoy. It means someone's waiting for them, anticipating them. Maybe. They look at one another.

'What do you think?' Mike asks.

Terry shakes his head. Gus says, 'Don't know.'

'Should we call it off?'

They sigh, contemplate, weigh it up. No one wants to make the decision. Gus is about to suggest that things are becoming a little too complicated for his liking, a little too unnerving, but Terry says, 'It could've been dug weeks ago.'

Dirk agrees with him. Gus says, 'I'm just not sure.'

Finally Mike says, 'Let's go on, we're just wasting time.'

They all agree. Mike gets back into the truck, shifts into four-wheel drive. The other men navigate, guide him. The truck ploughs headfirst into the donga. He accelerates, the tyres briefly slip and squeal in the mud, but soon grip and pull the vehicle up, out the other side. It was never really going to be a problem, not practically anyway. What they can't work out is its meaning, and whether their increased alertness makes them safer, or more in danger.

'Let's just keep an extra sharp look out,' Gus says.

For his part, Terry thinks this is all a bit late in the day and definitely bloody amateurish. He'd been clear from the start, made his opinions on the subject well known: the first black who invaded the first farm made a declaration of war. They should've taken care of business there and then. Not this cowardly sneaking about at night, clearing up after a boy's sloppy attempt. As a matter of principle he'd almost said no to Mike when he'd phoned. Not his style, this afterthought business. He's only here now because he's pretty sure there'll be more action, that somewhere they'll be caught out and then these guys will need him to step in and take control. He's convinced they'll need him to sort things out the proper way.

Davey continues to stare at the curtains. He can't seem to take his eyes off them. Overhead the light stays on, spreading a certain kind of warmth. Even though it's the height of summer and ordinarily he'd be lying on top of his bed, shirtless, fanned, he huddles into himself, pulling the duvet up to his chest. His memory makes him cold, breaks goosebumps on his skin.

Eventually he and the piccanins go back. It hasn't been a particularly good catch – only three small bream that they dutifully released. At home Ma and Pa are waiting for him.

'Where have you been?' Ma says. 'We're going to the club for a braai.'

Shit. Why hadn't she mentioned it before? He hurries into his bedroom and changes – his best Nike sports shirt, parachute shorts, a pair of socks and tennis shoes. He searches under his bed for his racquet and goes into the bathroom to brush his teeth, style his hair, spray on deodorant, wash the thick grime of the muddy earthworms and the smell of fish off his fingers. The whole time in his mind is an image of Katie Hutchins, lovely, sexy Katie Hutchins. He only leaves his grooming after Ma yells out for the third time, 'Come on, it's only tennis at the club!'

They drive in the blue metallic Nissan V6 three-litre hardbody twin-cab four-by-four, Pa's pride and joy. It's only used for what Ma calls 'social occasions'. Davey's always proud when they pull up at school in it. Today Pa sails down the main road at a thunderous speed while Davey prods open the lid of the cooler box propped on the seat next to him. Inside is a heap of meat – steaks, pork chops, ribs, boerewors – all sitting in their plastic bags waiting for the braai. The steaks are leaking blood and he dips his finger to taste it – rich with the pepper and garlic marinade. Immediately he thinks of his teeth and lips and hopes he doesn't look like a vampire when he sees Katie Hutchins. He licks them vigorously.

At the club he's pleased to see a lot of the farming families and most of his mates from the district, one of the best things about the school holidays. He goes straight over to join them. There is a great deal of handclapping, exclamation, playfighting – they haven't seen one another for most of the school term. Soon they all disappear round the back of the fir trees and into a kind of den they've carved out over the years. One of the guys pulls out a box of smokes and they all take one, light up with an air of grown-up nonchalance. They exchange news and try to disguise their boasts about what they've been up to during the school term. Jackson 'pulled two hard babes in one night' and Richie talks about how 'motherless and wasted' he got drinking neat Sambuca shooters at a house party. Nick made the schools' districts rugby side and Shaun the junior national hockey team. They argue about whose school had the stronger sporting sides and talk about hunting, fishing, girls, but really none of them wants to be anywhere else right now.

Then one of the older boys, arrogant Tim Bartlet, remarks on Katie Hutchins and Davey is disappointed to hear she's already earmarked. He probably doesn't stand a chance now, not if the older guys are after her. They discuss her sexy figure, her breasts, her pretty face and one of them says he wouldn't mind a quick slice of action. They all agree. The common way she's discussed upsets him slightly and for a while sullies his opinion of her.

Like fucking used goods now, he thinks, although she's still the hottest chick around. When they finish their smokes and move off from the den, they all head to mingle with the congregation of fathers and farmers gathered along the breezy veranda of the club-house.

The braais have begun to smoke away and all the men gather round to start cooking. He loves the distinctive smell of braaing meat, the pungent blood juices sizzling away. Chilled beers are fished from cooler boxes in a seemingly endless supply and the sharp snap of bottle tops opening is a pleasant sound. The men stand about talking, planning, discussing, laughing, cajoling in their causal manner. For a while Davey stands amongst them, hoping Pa will invite him into the men's crowd by offering him a beer. Instead, he's insulted when Pa digs in the bag and holds out a Coke. 'No thanks,' he says stiffly.

The men talk more. As usual Pa is the most vocal of them all and has a lot to say about everything. They discuss crop prices and restrictions and the pathetic value of the currency which someone says is 'like second grade shit paper' and another adds, 'But would you even wipe your arse with it?' and there is a tumultuous roar of tough, manly laughter. Inevitably the touchy land issue is raised, but they all dismiss it, the mad logic of it.

'It can't be done.'

'Logistically impossible – just how the hell can they come and kick you off your land overnight?'

'Yes, how the hell?' Pa mutters. 'It's illegal anyway. That's what the law says.'

'Besides, if they take the farms, they'll stuff themselves up. Who's going to feed them then?'

'Ja, those bastards don't know a good thing when they see it. If it wasn't for us whites coming here in the first place, they'd all still be running round in bloody straw skirts, warrior stripes painted on their faces.'

'Fucking right. Worst thing we ever did was hand them independence. Look what a mess they've made of it.'

Their confidence impresses him. More and more he wants to be like them; confident in his own patch of paradise.

He sees Katie amongst a crowd of women organizing the salad and bread rolls table. His memory hasn't let him down – but she has outstripped it. She has become startlingly attractive and suddenly he finds himself desperately craving her, wanting her, this wonderful, blissful thing. She's so hot in her short tennis skirt, tight top which slips over her slender stomach so alluringly. He wishes he were older as he sees Tim Bartlet move in, start to flirt with her. She smiles at him, appears to laugh at one of his jokes. He seems to have all the slick moves and will probably succeed in getting his bit of holiday fun. That'll be all it is to him, whereas for Davey it would have meant so much more, the culmination of a term's desires. It's just not fair.

The place is teeming with people and they braai and feast and drink and are merry for the afternoon. A while later the more sober of the gathering take to the tennis courts as sets of mixed doubles are arranged.

From his seat beside the court, he notices Ma looking a bit downcast. He can always tell – not that it's in any way obvious to the untrained eye. She remains cheerful and sociable, but behind her appearance of congeniality he can see she's disappointed about something. It's a look he sees from time to time. Instinctively he searches for Aunt Marsha in the gathering but already knows he won't find her – that's what Ma's look always means. It's strange, Aunt Marsha and Uncle Mike hardly ever miss a braai at the club. Aunt Marsha and Ma are like sisters; Ma's never truly happy in a crowd unless she's talking and gossiping with her. With all the other farmwives, Ma gets along famously – he's come to see that she's universally popular – but there's just something a bit different, reserved about her when Aunt Marsha fails to turn up. He hopes she's not going to become all moody later on.

Later on, by luck, he gets his chance to talk alone with Katie Hutchins, when he gets to go on with her in a set of mixed doubles. He is complimentary about her game throughout but as they're coming off he can't think what to say to her. His mind has gone blank and he's sure he comes across as confused, clumsy. Like a child. All he can think of is to offer her a drink, but she politely declines and soon disappears, his one chance having whipped by before he can make something of it.

This time in the car Ma sits in the back and giggles a great deal. Looks like she's had too much white wine with lunch. Drowning her sorrows, he's tempted to think. Pa has certainly had his fair share of beers and is in good spirits too, humming and singing along to the Don Williams tape. 'Amanda, light of my life, fate should have made you a gentleman's wife.'

As they fly along the road, he continues to think about his missed chance with Katie. He's pissed off with himself for being so timid, for not making more of his opportunities. The school holidays are only four weeks after all. He ought to have been bolder, more sure of himself. He shouldn't have let some nobody like Tim Bartlet get his prize.

'Pa,' he says, 'how big is the Bartlets' farm?'

'What makes you ask that?'

'Just wondering. I mean, compared to Edenfields?'

A half-grin widens on Pa's face. 'No no, son, there's no comparison size wise. I'd say about a tenth, if that.'

'A tenth? And the Hutchins' farm?'

'It's also pretty small.'

'Why does it matter?' Ma asks from the back.

'I was just wondering that's all.'

'Don't forget,' Pa says, 'many of the newer farms are just offshoots from Edenfields. Your grandpa sold a chunk of it years ago that was divided up into four or five smaller farms.'

'Why did he sell it off?'

'Practical reasons.'

'Like?'

Pa sighs. 'Well in the old days, the farm was as big as a small country. Literally. It was just too much land for one family to handle. It wasn't being utilized.'

'Don't you remember,' Ma says, 'the story about how Eden's View got its name?'

'Ja, Ja.'

He knows the story well; he doesn't need Ma to tell him. In fact, now that he thinks about it, he'll put it into his history essay. The story of old Oupa Jack who climbed to the top of the kopje and was struck by the magnificent views out over the land, how the farm seemed to stretch as far as the eye can see. He had named the place Eden's View because he'd said to himself that he could plant as far as that view and no further; the view was the boundary to the farm.

It pleases him to think that Edenfields is by far the biggest farm in the district and that if it wasn't for Grandpa's generosity in selling off part of their land, people like the Bartlets wouldn't be farming here right now. Katie will know that as the future owner of Edenfields, he's got far more to give her. And she should know, too, that her farm used to be part of Edenfields, that their families have been connected for years anyway. He sits and thinks how nice it would be to take her up to Eden's View, to stand and show her everything you can see from there. That'll certainly impress her. That'll make her see just how lame Tim Bartlet is in comparison; a mere tenth of him.

He wonders whether that's how old Oupa Jack impressed the ladies all those years ago. He can't imagine them trailing up there in their long flowing dresses and those old-fashioned shoes.

'What was the farm like at the beginning?'

'The beginning?' Pa says, a bit impatiently.

'You know, the very first time someone came here.'

'Well there was nothing but bush, of course – miles and miles and miles of long, dry bush. Those frontier guys took this land between them and carved out the farms literally with their bare hands. Well, they had the blacks to help. They were co-opted on to the farms as labourers.'

He knows about all that too. He wonders whether that should go in the essay; his great-grandfather's philosophy of farming with a sjambok, nailing the blacks if they dared to step out of line, showing them who's boss, the old saying that control and authority is the farmer's golden creed.

He would ask more questions, but Pa, it seems, doesn't want to talk any more and turns up Don Williams again. For the rest of the journey home he thinks about the first days of the farm, imagining old Oupa Jack arriving with his Scottish bride on the back of a wagon drawn by two old horses, or maybe mules. It must have been strange at the start, and difficult. He wonders how they managed without any running water, electricity, the house. He would like to ask Pa, but maybe later on. Instead, he pictures them living in a small shack made from mud, cattle shit. God, it must've stunk. And what did they do for a loo? They must've dug a pit latrine, he assumes, away from the house, down hill from any water supply because that's what he's been taught at school about shitting and sanitation. He also pictures them hacking down the bush in order to plant the first batch of crops, driving oxen over the hard dry barren land with only an old hand driven plough like he's seen in pictures at Aunt Marsha and Uncle Mike's place.

Thank God things have changed. Katie and he will have it good. They'll carry on the farm, have children, raise them, pass on their heritage.

'As hostess and household manager, Adelia did well by Benjamin Chase. She prided herself on her taste, and my grandfather deferred to her in this because her taste was one of the things he'd married her for.'

Marsha just can't read. Why's she trying? She discards the book again, props herself up on her pillows. She places her reading glasses on the bedside table under the lamp. The clock says 11:24. She wonders again about Davey in the next-door room. She really should check up on him. She thinks of the men, and her worries return. Yet, somehow that's not true. It's not really worry over the risks involved, the danger, just anxiousness to hear that they've made it. She wants it all over, but can't really imagine they'll run into any trouble, any danger. The warm air in the room tells her this, the quietness outside too.

The windows are open behind the drawn curtains. She'd become aware of it earlier: the looming silence of the night. She's surrounded by millions, millions of living things, no matter how large, how microscopic. Yet none of them stir. Isn't that strange? Not even the elements: wind, rain, air.

What it suggests to her is that everything has inhaled, everything has taken shelter, recoiled, fallen to rest and is waiting, waiting patiently, for it all to be over.

She fiddles with the bed covers, touches her arm. No surprise. It's cold. Still.

\*

She sits perfectly still for a while, covering her eyes with her hands, trying to pinpoint her misgivings. She looks within, searching for snatches, visions, answers: anything that will provide some solace in her heart. But there is little that is new, little that is genuinely revealing: just the knowledge that she can't repress, the simple truth that she can't mourn the Bakers. She can't mourn the loss of her friends – not even Leigh – or Davey's current state. Something in her remains untouched – she has been unable to press the sharp point of their fate against that great reservoir of emotion in her core. She has had no release. Even on this night, some two and a half months later, what grips her more acutely than anything else is the awareness of this lack, an overwhelming guilt.

There's some obstruction, some resentment between them left unresolved, something that needed clearing up.

She presses herself to think about painful memories, the early days, the old atmosphere of the farms. She and Leigh were brought together by a kind of happenstance – destiny if such a thing exists – as the two women of the great district farms. Edenfields and Summerville were, without obvious ostentation, set apart from the other farms by their pure scale and size, their history and heritage. But just as the wide expanse of Broadlands Dam joined the two farms together, she'd honestly believed that something intrinsic, something unspoken and feminine, had linked her and Leigh.

They were both initially outsiders to the district. Marsha remembers her own transformation with a smile, how she'd been raised a town girl, the daughter of a civil servant and a dutiful housewife. She'd shown an early aptitude for music, singing lullabies the local nannies taught her, whistling songs off the wireless with perfect pitch. She went for formal piano lessons from an early age and played beautifully. Eisteddfod cups soon littered the cabinet in the lounge, honours certificates, distinctions from posh overseas exam- ining boards. At sixteen she gave a recital: Bach preludes, Chopin waltzes, a Liszt transcription. A year later she performed an entire Beethoven sonata at the Annual Young Soloists' Competition. She won silver, coming second to a lanky teenage violinist whose wild mop of hair was enough to convince the judges of his brilliance. The chief adjudicator praised her technical dexterity, her subtle phrasing, the warm full-bodied richness of her tone. Then her proudest moment: a scholarship to the Royal Academy in London. Once there, things changed. There were so many talented young people, such a big city. Such a big world. And it seemed she was just an invisible speck on a grimy, sleeted pavement.

She dropped out after a year, returned depressed, disillusioned and met Mike at the theatre of all places, at a repertory performance of *Hamlet*. He'd come along in the hope of finding himself a girl, informed that the evening was a gala performance to raise money for the women's hockey league. It wasn't and instead he'd veered off to the pub where she'd gone afterwards, determined to latch on to the first figure she saw so she could commiserate about the way Claudius had been portrayed. The poor, sweet bloke. How she'd tried to antagonize him, pick a fight so she could call him a typical male chauvinist pig. But instead something about his steady response to her questions, his grave acknowledgement of his igno- rance on any subject not connected to the farm, calmed her. She stopped to look at him, and at herself. What was she doing? She wasn't in London any more. She didn't have to compete for an opinion amongst the snooty intelligentsia. At once her heart soft- ened, exhaled months of stuffiness and disillusionment. The man in front of her had brought her home, back to Africa.

And then the hullabaloo over their wedding. He (and his

mother) had started to arrange the church service; she said she wanted to be married in a cave lit by a circle of virgin white candles. Again they moved towards each other, and were married outside, on a small island in a nearby game park, exchanging slightly modernized vows on a carpet of white rose petals. She had written a very verbose poem that she had thought deeply moving. He meekly read a Bible verse or two. She remembers how his mother remained wide-eyed and tight-lipped throughout, as though she was witnessing a satanic rite. Dear old Mrs De Wet; a difficult, trying woman, yet ultimately good-intentioned. She passed away a few years later.

At the start she had found farming life confining, daunting. It was summer, and the heat was relentless. She remembers an unbelievable infestation of insects. Their buzzing, crawling, darting about surprising her at every turn: it was something you never got used to. She had thought they'd be together on the farm, but Mike worked from sunrise to sunset. Those first days were a baptism of fire and sometimes she'd permit herself a few well-controlled sobs to quench the loneliness. She battled on, waging war against endless monotony. But in due course she fell into line, coming to love the land, the untainted country air. She became a true farmwife, caring for orphaned lambs with warm milk bottles, finding herself deeply, unfathomably upset when one died suddenly in the night, snake-bit or sickened, so that now, thinking back, she can't believe she's the same person at all. Almost unimaginable to her are her wild hippie days, her feminist utterances, her outspoken, flagrant ways.

Mike and Joe, of course, had grown up together. They were the same age, were notoriously mischievous as boys, went to boarding school together, played in the same cricket teams, rugby teams, went off to agricultural college, inherited the farms, even went and did call-ups together during the bush war. They were always like brothers, and had the association of home and land that brothers so naturally enjoy, take for granted.

And then Leigh arrived. Joe met her under more civil circumstances than she had met Mike. It was a few years later, in the days when both men were still young and fit enough to play districts rugby. They had all gone up to a mining town for a rare weekend away from the farms and there, squinting in a drunken haze, Joe caught sight of Leigh amongst a crowd at a braai. It was quite a festive weekend – miners vs. farmers always was – and (in what became the standing joke ever since) she'd told Joe in the car on the way up that he'd get himself hitched. She sympathized with the poor guy, sweating it out all day, every day on that great big farm without anyone to come home to at night, without any companion to keep him from brooding. Joe cut a lonely, despairing figure back then. He'd inherited the farm after his father had died young from a heart attack and his mother smoked herself into an early grave. He needed looking after, and she wasn't going to do all his mending and darning for ever. Anyway, she'd nudged him and said that the rugby weekend was his chance, and sure enough through the silvery screen of smoky braai fumes he'd caught a glimpse of Leigh dancing to a makeshift disco. Marsha knew at once how smitten he was: he made his way over, tentatively joined in the dancing – not Joe's style at all – and afterwards shyly introduced himself, offering Leigh ghastly white wine in a grubby plastic cup. By the end of the weekend he'd plucked up the nerve to ask for her phone number and invite her to the drive-in the next time he was in town. The very next week he was off, all spruced up and eager.

Their wedding was comfortably conventional: a flowered church, waffling minister, muted organ tones. She remembers being envious, mildly regretting the botch she'd insisted on. Mike's mother was there, shedding a quiet tear, no doubt thinking the same. The May weather was idyllic after the brutal, oppressive heat had passed. Iced beer bottles were clutched in every man's hand, several pigs slowly roasted away on spits over smouldering coals. The speeches were brief and funny, slightly below the belt. The whole thing was just, well just perfect!

And so, suddenly, there was a confidante close by, just the next farm away: another woman, a friend. They'd both been town girls, knew friends of friends, played giggly games of tennis, relished getting involved in district fêtes, gymkhanas, market days. Yet there was more to it than the simple luxury of friendship, and this is what concerns Marsha now, alone, bereft, unsettled. There was something deeper between them, this connection, like the settled waters of a dam linking the two farms, a river of maternal love, a still lake of dissolved pain.

Yes, there was something deeper between them: Marsha knows full well she is breaking her promise, her solemn promise to Leigh that she'd care for Davey, be a mother to him.

How Leigh struggled to bring him into the world. It was a terrible pregnancy – the poor girl almost miscarried twice and had to spend the last two months lying on her back virtually immobile. Marsha had gone over to Edenfields every day to sit with her, talk with her. And this was when their true bond developed. It was during this time that they became as close as sisters, as twins even.

They found solace in one another, a certain faith – so much so that in the periods when Leigh was most in pain, Marsha would place her hands on the swollen egg of Leigh's belly and, sometimes climbing on the bed to lie beside her, work them over that tight stomach, rubbing some peace back into her. They would say nothing. They both seemed to recognize that silence – apart from the odd groan or sigh – somehow sanctified these moments, and Marsha came to understand that it was essential, as much a part of the treatment as her hands moving over her friend's body, and the body inside it.

Afterwards, Leigh would murmur to her, half in and out of sleep, relaxed into a trance-like tiredness, 'Your hands, they're so hot.'

In due course she and Mike became godparents to Davey. An August christening saw the four of them dutifully serene before the altar dish, laughing over the baby's untimely howling when doused. Davey was an attractive child from the start: compliant, rewarding, infinitely surprising. There was an unspoken understanding that he was a child to be doted on, shared almost, by all. She wonders now whether Leigh hadn't known even then that she and Mike wouldn't have children of their own. Marsha and Mike became constant figures in Davey's life. He'd come to stay weekends. Mike taught him the basics of rugby and she'd introduced him to Kipling at bedtimes. How the zebra got its stripes. How the elephant got its trunk. And there was a time when Davey stayed with them permanently, kept away from Edenfields.

It was breast cancer. The Bakers had been vacationing in Mauritius after a particularly good year when Leigh suddenly became uncomfortable, noticed a hardness in her chest. Back home, Marsha urged her to go for a checkup. They found two malignant tumours, quickly spreading, and performed an instant mastectomy. Leigh had months of intensive chemotherapy. Davey was six.

Leigh paled, lost weight rapidly, her thick crop of hair vanished almost overnight. It was a bitch of an illness – that's how Joe always referred to it. It got her hard. Her regular trips to the specialists became successively less optimistic, and after one particularly pernicious round of treatment left her convulsing, screaming in agony when she wasn't vomiting into a bucket, Marsha had insisted she take Davey away. 'He's too young to have to see this,' she said, 'he'll never get over it.'

And so the poor kid was installed at Summerville. Mike kept him by his side during the day, taking him round the farm, showing him the various crops and fascinating mechanical contraptions while she stayed most of the time at Edenfields, nursing her beloved Leigh with the only tools the doctor could recommend, a moist cloth to her brow, soothing words of comfort for her heart. But it wasn't working. The sordid signs of death appeared: a coldness in the room, a whitening of Leigh's skin as her life drained away. She could sense it, anticipate it. A morphine drip alleviated the pain, but seemed to carry Leigh off into a distant, surreal fog. For most of the time she was incoherent, not knowing who or where she was, not remembering that she even had a young son, a devoted husband, a wide, wondrous farm.

From time to time there would be a gap in the fog, and Marsha would see her friend look through at her for a while, sometimes even smiling. In one of these gaps, she pulled Marsha close and whispered that she wanted a promise from her, a promise to look after Davey. She couldn't say much, was barely audible, but Marsha understood perfectly. 'I promise,' she mouthed, her eyes welling up with tears. 'I promise.' Leigh reached for Marsha's hands, and for a moment the warmth of Marsha's touch seemed to transcend Leigh's pain – Marsha could visibly see the relief in her taut face, the instant clearing in her eyes – leaving her stunned and overcome. She moved Marsha's hand up her body, towards her deflated, drained, emaciated chest. For a moment Marsha was struck with horror, but then she seemed to pass through the horror into calmness, a sudden full understanding of Leigh's suffering; as if for an unreal moment she'd been handed the dead weight of her illness in a silver clinical bowl, the disease-riddled organs and tissues, so she could judge the extent of what was consuming her, discern it tangibly, comprehend it.

And so Marsha touched Leigh, who lay whispering, writhing under the spread of her glowing hands, the warmth unfurling far across her body, deep inside her flesh, dissolving the illness.

'So hot,' she breathed.

It was her hands that did it. That's what Leigh always swore after her inexplicable eleventh-hour recovery. 'It's your hands, I know it.' Marsha herself didn't think much of the whole hands palaver; not until much later at least. And, of course, neither did Joe or Mike. 'She's just overcome by being cured,' Marsha said. 'She just needs to believe in something.'

Privately, the idea that she might have what the blacks called healing hands unnerved her. Looking back over her childhood, she saw that once or twice she'd had a particular touch with the family pets; her beloved white tabby cat with a blocked stomach the vet said would never heal. They were about to take him to be put down when she'd held him on her lap the whole way to the veterinary surgery, crying and crying, clutching him tight to her chest, stroking his tight, furry stomach. When they arrived, the vet couldn't understand it: the cat appeared fine, the stomach unblocked. She recalled something too about the pet spaniel with distemper. And in her teens, when the baby piccanin of the family's loyal nanny, Gertrude, came down with a bad case of malaria, she'd gone to the kia, simply ran her fingers a few times across the infant's feverish brow. On the farm, well, it went without saying that she had nursed sick animals now and again.

But it wasn't something she could take seriously. She didn't want to be labelled a freak, as being odd, different, witch-like as no doubt some of the more staunch members of the Dutch Reformed De Wet family would claim. No, she just wanted to be herself, a normal person, a farmwife. And perhaps the gift was, in fact, a curse. If it were true, if she could somehow heal by touch, then why was her own womb, which she'd laid her hands over many a late night after Mike had fallen off to sleep beside her, still so cold, so barren? And now, of course, it was too late.

Yes, the whole thing was bizarre, wicked even, if it couldn't bring her what she wanted most. There were times when she resented it. There were times when dark thoughts entered her mind and she even resented Leigh; for being healed, for having it all.

So Leigh had miraculously gone into remission, and Davey over the years grew into someone innocently beautiful, then gorgeously handsome as maturity set in – those emerald eyes, that darkened skin, the wavy hair, the firm athletic build – and she, well, she took up gardening as a substitute, investing all her time and devotion, crassly calling it her baby, her family. Christ almighty! Of course, everything she touched grew magnificently. Those green fingers. Those hot hands.

She gets out of bed, goes into the bathroom, peels a Disprin and dissolves it in a tumbler of water. There is a dull tension holding her eyes. If I don't deal with it now, she thinks, it'll only get worse. She knocks back the frothy mixture. Bitter/sweet. No, maybe that's wrong, it should really be sweet/bitter. She shrugs it off.

She returns to the bedroom. She hasn't heard anything further from Jen Smit. She can imagine they're worrying like hell, particularly young Annie. Shame, it can't be easy for a young girl, newly married, from the city. It's certainly not the best time to go marrying a farmer. Still, you make your choices, the bed you lie in.

She thinks she should phone them up, but doesn't.

All of a sudden something in her shifts, and instead of finding the bedroom the comfortable seat of her memories, it becomes suffocating – restricted, confined, like a tomb. It's keeping her from the rest of the world, the magnitude of things, the big wide world Mike and the boys are battling to put right. She has an instant desire to get out, out into a wider, freer place so that she can sense the tone of the night, be in the same air they're in. She walks down the passage, doesn't stop at the door to the room where poor Davey must be struggling to exorcize the horrors from his mind. Instead, she goes through to the lounge, unlocks the French doors, opens them out on to the veranda, and breathes deeply, as if she's just emerged from a ward of invalids, infections, dying things.

When they drive up the hill to the farmhouse they notice at once that something is wrong. A big black Mercedes Benz is parked outside and two blacks in suits stand by, hovering ominously.

'Jesus,' says Pa, 'what's this?'

As they get out Pa asks the men what they want, but they just smirk, pointing towards the house. As they approach the back door, Phineas comes out looking anxious. 'Sorry baas,' he says again and again.

'What's going on?'

From down the passage they hear a loud woman's voice laughing and exclaiming. Pa stalks down the passage. He and Ma follow, curious and tentative. The voice doesn't come from the lounge or the office or any of the smaller rooms – it leads them towards the main bedroom. 'What the hell?' Pa mutters, bewildered. As they enter the room they see the huge bulk of a black woman sprawled out over the end of the bed, talking furiously on her mobile phone. In her hand she clutches an item of clothing. At once Ma gasps: it's her Indian silk shawl, the one Aunt Marsha gave her years ago. They notice the cupboard door standing open, exposing all Ma's clothes and accessories.

For a moment they stand aghast, the sight an unreal swelling in the room. As the fat woman sees them she raises her hand telling them to wait while she finishes her conversation. She speaks in the local dialect, assuming that they can't understand. But they can. She's talking of fashion, of possessions, of Ma's wardrobe as she kneads the shawl in her bulging, bright-red-nail-polished hands.

183

'Now just a minute,' Pa shouts, recovering himself and striding towards her. 'What the hell do you think you're doing?'

She brings the phone down and stares at them indignantly. 'Ah, what is this – can you not see I am busy?'

'What the hell are you doing in my house?'

'That can wait for now – I am occupied. You cannot disturb me.'

They stand, lost for words, shocked. As she starts her conversation again, Pa moves forward and tries to wrench the phone out of her hand. She exclaims loudly, slapping at him.

'Joe,' Ma says, 'just be careful.'

But Pa is already fuming. He pulls the woman by the arm and yanks her off the bed to her feet. The phone crashes to the floor. He and Ma stand almost frozen. The tussle is already over. She bends to pick up her phone. Pa steps back looking bemused, bewildered. They cannot understand what is going on.

'You cannot do this,' she says, sternly, controlled. 'It is not for a man to assault a woman. I would not assault you.'

'What are you doing in my house, my bedroom, going through my wife's clothes?'

'Do not adopt that attitude with me. Do you not know that you are meant to be off?'

'Off? Off what?'

'Off this farm. You are meant to be off already.'

'What! What are you talking about?'

'Do you not know that you are meant to be off this farm by now? You are meant to be off two weeks ago already and I am losing my patience with you.'

Pa can't understand what the woman is saying. But her tone is enough to enrage him further.

'Look. My name is Joseph Baker and I am the owner of this land, Edenfields Estate. I have title deeds. Either leave my property now, or I'll call the police.'

She lets out a short cackle. 'Do not bother telling me this. Do you think I am stupid? It is a mistake to think that I am stupid but it is typical of you people – you think we are all stupid. Your title deeds are meaningless to me. They will not save you now.'

'Didn't you hear me – either leave or I'll call the police!'

'Call them. Be my guest. I am the owner of this land. I'll simply instruct them to have you removed.'

'Fine, I'll bloody remove you myself. Now go.'

She chuckles at his anger, dismissing it with a cursory shrug.

Pa breathes in. He's about to snap – really snap – Davey can sense it. The woman scratches around in her handbag producing a brown envelope. She waves it in Pa's face and his temper flares up another notch immediately. 'All you have to know is that this document tells you to be off two weeks ago and still you are here. That is now against the law and I am not prepared to entertain you any further.'

'We never got any letter,' Ma says.

'Do not try and worm your way out of it. That will not solve the issue. The fact is that you should be off this property by now. I am not responsible for getting the document to you. You are now on my land as of two weeks ago and I have already been more than patient with you.'

Pa snaps. 'Just get yourself off my land.' He breathes in heavily. 'Now!' he screams.

But the woman just laughs. 'That is not going to work.' She takes out the document from the envelope and opens it. 'This is it – it says so right here. This is now my farm and you must be off.'

'How dare you,' Pa shouts, lost to his rage. 'This is my farm, you hear? My farm! You just get in your car and get the hell off.' He steps towards her.

'Joe careful,' Ma says. The fat woman stands her ground and waves the document at Pa; Pa slaps it out of her hand. She laughs again, undeterred.

'It is so typical of you people that you do not want to know the truth. It is now a simple issue that you must leave. I was hoping to start taking over this farm even from today and now I come to find you have disobeyed the law.'

'Just get one thing right woman,' Pa hisses, leaning into her face. 'You'll never have this land. Never. It's mine you hear and you can't take it.' He kicks the document lying on the floor and it tears under his shoe. As much as anything that's happened, this shocks Davey. Why is Pa bothering to talk to her, why doesn't he just kick her out, chase her off with the shotgun?

She chuckles again, grinning. 'You can do that if you want but it is only paper and I can easily get another one printed just like that.' She snaps her fingers in his face. Pa's head jerks back instinctively; Ma knows him well enough to move in to restrain him.

Suddenly the woman changes her tone, dropping her air of amused tolerance. She plants her feet and puts her hands on her hips, taking possession of the ground. 'And I am now wasting my time. You have one week to move off. One week. I am being nice. Otherwise I cannot say what course the law will take if you choose to disobey it and stay here illegally. But it will be severe. Even now I am most put out because I have to go back to town when I was expecting to stay here from today. It is most unfortunate for me. So there you have it – one week. And do not think you can try and negotiate. I do not negotiate with racists. That document which you – not I – have rubbed in the ground says everything you need to know. You are selfish to assume you can own all of this by yourselves. This is why measures have been taken to put land like this back into the hands of its rightful owners. You are strangers and you are already very lucky that I am not going to press charges against you for being here illegally on my property when you were supposed to be off two weeks ago. It is because I am fair and considerate that you are here now but beware of what may happen. I am one of many more who intend to come and live in this district soon so you cannot win. We are in control now. It is over for racists like you.'

She walks out of the room, down the passage, turns into the hallway and storms out of the front door. What the fuck entitles her to use the front door? Davey thinks, following her at a distance. One of the dogs growls at her. She lets out a short cry of fright and moves round the house quickly towards her big black car, pressing buttons on her phone as she does.

Pa suddenly rushes out of the back door and screams at her, 'Get off my farm you bloody black bitch!'

'Joe, shut up for God's sake,' Ma shouts, going after him.

The men in suits look at each other, and then make tentative steps towards Pa, but the dogs growl viciously.

'Just get in,' the woman shouts from the car. 'Let us go. Let us go.'

They drive off. In the meantime a long white truck has appeared down the hill. Davey can see a few suspicious looking men hanging round it. As the Mercedes passes it slows and stops, and he sees the fat woman lean out the window to shout brief instructions before her Mercedes lumbers off again, kicking up dust. The truck makes a U-turn to follow after.

They make progress, good progress, constantly alert. It's not a race, a game: it's survival. You don't get frustrated trying to survive.

Eventually there are suggestions they are coming towards the heart of the farm. Mike realizes it first: the gradient's slightly steeper, his body knows the sharp bends in the road well, the bush is thinning. And sure enough, they all begin to discern a gradual ascent. At the first sight of a farm building – in this instance the tall bulk of a tobacco barn ahead round the next corner – they stop, turn off the engine.

For a few seconds a pause. Then Mike says, 'This is it guys.'

Gus and Dirk get out, guns in hand. They will creep ahead, cut through the bushes and survey the path. They plan to run a relay, making bird calls to signal a safe passage, baboon grunts to signal danger. Terry hops on to the back of the truck, lies down and positions himself with the rifle. Mike will drive. It's all been worked out.

Gus and Dirk peel through the bush, moving quickly. The faster they move the more likely they'll sound like small animals scurrying in the undergrowth. If they stalk, it will arouse suspicion. Gus stations himself about twenty metres in, Dirk shoots all the way through and rejoins the curve of the road, just in front of where the tobacco barns stand. He crouches beneath a tree, looks. He can't see anyone, and that's enough – they have to be decisive, the more they spread apart and the longer the time they aren't together as a unit, the weaker they become.

He calls his bird call, loudly. Gus hears it, calls on. Terry hears it, calls back to signal they've heard. Mike turns the ignition. They creep on round the corner. Gus in the meantime dashes through to join up with Dirk. The truck comes round. The unit is together again.

The next stretch: past the tobacco barns. The truck is silenced. Dirk runs ahead, Gus follows, stations himself after the first barn. Dirk runs the full length of all four barns. He peers round the side, up to the house. It's clear. He calls back. Gus calls. Terry calls. They move on, join up. So far they haven't come across another living thing. So far so good.

In the midst of this, Dirk, with his schoolboyish nature, can't deny the thrill of the experience. He doesn't have history chained to his ankles like the other men. He's too young to have been caught up in the liberation war, he's too young to know the reverberations of that time, it's thrum of distant echoes that have become so loud. Also, in a disenchanted way, he's already acknowledged his own displacement. All this doesn't affect him personally; unlike these men, he has nothing personally to lose. He's just a bystander. He's just a rookie, trying his hand at helping out on a farm, floating along, killing a few easy years until something better turns up or Gus and Jen are kicked off. He'd dreamt of owning his own farm one day, but that isn't bloody likely now.

So to him, there is a touch of the absurd about all this. Like they're kids, stalking and scuttling round in a weird, surreal, fragmented game of hide and seek. In a morbid way, he's eager to see who's going to find whom first.

*

They move to within a stone's throw of the farmhouse. So far it's been quiet, no trouble – they are both relieved and disconcerted. Are they expected after all? Is a gang of thugs lurking in the shadows, waiting for them? Eventually, the truck pulls up right outside the kitchen door, and reverses. The closer it is the better.

Terry jumps off the back and at once flashes the barrel of the gun at the stillness of the dark night. Mike gets out. Dirk and Gus trot up by foot. They look round cautiously. As a precaution they spend a few minutes scouting the yard, the perimeter of the house. The kitchen light is on, a beacon drawing them in. Is that part of the plan, the trap? There is an almost static quietness. Mike grows increasingly disturbed. It was exactly the same the night of the attack. When they join up again outside the kitchen door, he says, 'Just watch it guys.' They all stiffen. 'I'll go first.' Mike knows this is now more his task than anyone else's. This is something he owes Joe, Leigh, Davey, his parents, their parents, their grandparents, and this place too, Edenfields: all that it is and has been. A certain pride, mixed with an unrelenting throb of nervousness, drums through him. The others step aside for him to enter the kitchen. The door is open. 'Just as Davey must've left it last night,' he says quietly.

'Davey, or someone else,' Terry suggests.

True. He notices the counter on the stove flashing a steady pulse, but there is no one else waiting for them. Not here at least.

Marsha sits for a while on the veranda in her wicker chair. Facing Edenfields, over the hills, she thinks of how many times Leigh has faced the other way, unsettled, pensive, wondering why Marsha had withdrawn from her in the last few years.

Well, she'd made a conscious decision of it. Mike and her, they had their own lives. She had her husband, the farm, the garden, the bougainvilleas, her music, her books. The reason was Davey: she couldn't allow herself to fall in love with someone else's child. She had come to see herself as nothing more than an extension of Leigh, something parasitic, like a leech. Even though she wanted more than anything else to invest herself entirely in their happiness, to share in what she'd helped bring into the world – this child, this boy wonder – she just knew it wasn't right, wasn't fair to anyone. He'd never be her child, her son. He'd never look on her as Ma, mum, mother. And all the while she had to contend with her own private turmoil, the dryness inside of her.

So she withdrew, forced herself to sever that imaginary umbilical cord. She did it quietly. They didn't see any less of one another; the Bakers and the De Wets, Edenfields and Summerville were still inseparable, she saw Davey all the time, watched him grow like a proud, doting godparent, and Leigh and she still remained the closest of confidantes, sisterly.

But the fervency with which they had understood one another before, communicated so intuitively, waned and withdrew into each of them. And now, only now, does she suddenly see the bigger picture, the reason for Leigh's disquiet, her unsettledness and longing. She wanted me, Marsha considers, and I neglected her. She can see it here, now, in Leigh's still eyes – the look of an orphan, unsure, unknowing as to why she'd been abandoned, why she'd been discarded at a time when she needed Marsha most, at the hour of her fate, that dreadful night.

Marsha hasn't been able to bear looking into these visions, this reel of horror her mind has been playing all this while, but knows now she has to let it come, timidly, hesitantly. It is a clear, sharp, striking image of the Bakers on that night, at that tragic juncture between life and death, existence and non-existence. She sees Leigh – dear Leigh – getting out the bath, towelling herself, doing womanly things – applying moisturizer and lotions in soft circular gestures to her well-aged, supple skin, dusting her armpits white with lavender talc, brushing her hair even though she'll soon be going to bed, thinking of things simple and domestic: a chore to do in the morning, baking biscuits for church tea. Then, robed in lilac, looking fresh, smelling perfumed (the memory of that smell is with Marsha now), she walks through from the bathroom to the bed-room. Joe sits in bed, strangely frozen, still as a statue, the crisp look of shock set on his face. Despite what is about to happen, he is doing all he can to look normal, unaffected. He is a decent ordinary man, just a minute from death, trying to shelter his wife's peace of mind, protect her from that thousand foot drop into panic and despair. His love for Leigh is ceaseless, an almost tangible devotion, and Marsha is overwhelmed to have seen this now, in her vision, this unbridled act of devotion, this unity.

But these are mere seconds of grace, before she sees Leigh sens-ing something in the room, the weight of some alien presence lurking in the darkness where the bedside lamps cast no light. A step further into the room confirms it: her family is in danger, her home has been invaded. What does Leigh see? Three featureless shapes soon appear in the scene; three men, their figures heavy, weighted with a certain something, a certain heavy inner ... but no, in fact they are light, they are insignificant, there is no substance to their presence. Just as a litter of dead leaves has no right to lie in a pristine garden, or a run of scorched grass to spoil the lush carpet of a lawn. These men contain a drought.

Leigh looks pale, a white sheet. She says nothing, does nothing. The room is still: five stone figures, a bizarre, stunted awkwardness shifting coldly between them. And then Marsha sees the axe – not glinting in the light, or threatening, just another shape in the room. These men, whoever they are, these three youths, they've come here with nothing but the permission to kill. Someone, somewhere has issued an instruction, spoken a few cursory words. Kill them, get them out, get them off my land, do what it takes. So they have arrived, entered the house, made themselves a fatal presence in this room. But despite their power and authority, they do not have an answer. They can offer no motive, no plot, no reason that explains the act they're about to perform. And in the immediate surge of panic that grips Leigh and Joe, and even in the surreal, momentary aftermath of accepting their fate, there is no attempt to request an explanation, and no attempt to plead.

And so it only takes an instant: quiet, swift, final. And for them – who were surely, she hopes, dead mere seconds later – there seems to be in that last moment a sense of controlled acceptance, almost as if they both know to be quiet, to go silently in that final, loving sacrifice.

Marsha flees inside, to the bathroom. The ghastly, nightmarish vision of all that the Bakers went through, all they suffered, culminates in a rush of agony that hits her like a blow to the skull. She sits on the loo, dabs her tears. Inside she's shaking to her core. Her stomach climbs into her throat, sifts down, lurches up again. But she knows she must get a grip of herself. She sniffles, breathes deeply the loitering fragrance of pot-pourri, peers ahead absently at a stark blue National Foods Pork calendar pinned on the back of the door. She lets the tears run a bit more, tells herself this is finally part of the healing process, hoping it's true.

The phone rings, bringing her back at once into the present world, the men and their dangerous mission, this night. She blows her nose one more time, gets up off the loo seat and walks through to the hallway.

'Hello,' she says, unable to cover the emotion settled in her throat. It's Jen Smit.

'Marsha, any news?'

'No, not yet.'

'God, the more I think of it, the more stupid I think the whole thing is. I'm a bloody nervous wreck.'

'I know Jen, I know.'

Jen bursts into tears. 'They shouldn't have rushed into this like schoolboys. I couldn't bear for something to happen to Gus, not like this. It's our thirtieth wedding anniversary next month, Marsha, thirty years. We just want to be left in peace. We've already survived one bush war. We can't face another.'

'Now, just calm down,' Marsha says, her own voice cracking again. 'It's all going to be fine after tonight. Just fine.'

They speak for another few minutes, reassuring one another, telling each other that no matter what happens on the farms no one can take away what they've had all these years: true happiness, a farm in Africa.

*

Marsha goes into the lounge, looking for solace. She is drawn to the stereo. How she's missed her music. She looks at her collection of CDs, picks one, puts it in the machine and eases up the volume. She closes her eyes, allows the sound of the chamber music to massage her mind. Is she soothed? She's uncertain at first, but after a while she is still uneasy – not because she's seen Leigh, or because the farm's in disarray or her garden's dead, but because in this mad sad world, and in times of adversity, such pure beauty exists as Yo Yo Ma playing the Bach solo cello suites.

Yes, such beauty. She waits for it to bring her solace.

Pa and Ma stand shocked, numbed. They exchange brief shattered glances, but nothing is said. Pa wanders off into the house and Ma quietly follows him. Davey remains at the door, watching the Mercedes and the truck crawl away out of sight. He notices his heart beating, thudding against his chest and he is breathing in short gasps. He has never seen Pa so furious, never.

He goes into the kitchen, sees Phineas cowering by the sink. 'Sorry baas,' he says. 'Sorry.' Davey ignores him and goes over to the fridge to pour himself a glass of milk. His hands are shaking and his stomach is tight and hard. He ends up pouring half the glass down the sink. He moves out of the kitchen, through the dining room, wanders about the house. He finds he can't think what to do, where to settle. He wants to keep out of Pa's way. He knows that they're in the office – Ma and Pa – and soon there's a horrible shouting match that puts him even more on edge.

Ma's trying her best to calm Pa down. 'Just relax Joe, just relax.' But it's not working. Instead Pa's shouting louder and louder, cursing, swearing. 'Just calm down for God's sake,' she shouts, 'just now you'll have a bloody heart attack!' But he continues to shout and scream – not at Ma, of course not at Ma – but at the sudden situation, the predicament, the fat woman. It has all come about so instantly, a great tragic disaster, and yet the world still surrounds them, breathing and carrying on. None of them can comprehend it.

He can't sit. He walks about the house pointlessly. The dogs trail after him, following him with their usual curiosity. Lucky bastards to be spared having to deal with all this bullshit! In the kitchen again he tells Phineas to make him a cup of tea. 'Quick,' he shouts when he sees the old man hobbling about slowly. 'Yes baas.' Shortly Phineas brings the cup of tea to the lounge where he has stationed himself on one of the sofas, staring vacantly at the music channel on the TV. He takes one sip, throws the rest into a nearby pot plant. Too damn hot for tea!

He drifts about the house again, unnerved by Pa's continued shouting from the office. He finds himself drawn to the half-open door. Soon though there is a lull, a break in Pa's tirade, and he hears Ma sobbing – loud, unsteady, uncontrollable sobs.

'We should have seen it coming,' she manages.

'Christ – what were we supposed to do?'

'I just can't believe it,' she says, her crying now less wrenching. 'Maybe we should have tried, tried to reason with her at least.'

There is a pause before Pa says, with more control in his voice, 'Yes perhaps. But do you really think that would have made a difference?'

In a second Davey's nervousness has turned to anger, anger at Ma's softness. She always bloody ends up crying, he thinks, she always makes it personal. She's not the only bloody one affected. He reckons it'll make Pa even more furious, more enraged. He wants to storm into the office and tell her to grow up, that now isn't the time for womanly weakness, that it's no use crying and crying. But he doesn't dare.

For a few moments there's a dead silence in the house. Ma's loud blubbering has stopped and Davey inches nearer the door to see for himself what's changed. Ma's still sobbing, but quietly now, and as he glances in he sees Pa cradling her to his chest, soothing her, patting her gently on the back.

'There, there Leigh, we'll get through this, we'll make it. Got to be strong. We'll survive, like we always have, don't worry.'

He is surprised by the tenderness in Pa's voice; it catches him off guard. He doesn't know what to make of it. He feels a little betrayed. What's wrong with him? he wonders. Pa's always been so tough, so strong, so unflinchingly controlled. What's wrong with him?

Ma continues to sob quietly and Pa consoles her. Davey's not sure what to do. He feels awkward standing at the door, so near to this scene. It's a dimension to his parents that he's never before witnessed, or maybe never before acknowledged. Pa has always seemed to him so unemotional, and Ma has always just been a woman doing what women do. He'd never thought about this sort of thing. But he supposes it's always been there, hidden away, discreet, displayed behind the bedroom door late at night, early in the morning at the break of day, during the term time perhaps when he's not around.

And now he's glad that he's seen it, despite the circumstances that have brought it out into the open. He's glad for them.

Davey retreats from the passage outside the office, and goes into the lounge. He's a lot calmer now and skips through channels on the TV. Pa comes in looking pale. He sits in his wide-winged armchair and takes over the remote control, settling on a live rugby match between the Springboks and the All Blacks. It's not like Pa to watch TV during the day. He thinks he should say something, something to make Pa realize that he's just as concerned, just as shocked and distraught.

'Jesus Pa.'

'It's okay son. It's just a lot of hot air. We'll be fine. Promise.'

Pa doesn't seem to be in the mood for talking. They just sit in the

lounge. Father and son. Still. Unblinking. They're not really watching the rugby; all they register is the animated sound of the
commentator, the intermittent blow of the ref's whistle, the festive
cheer of the crowd. In a while Ma comes in carrying the carrot
cake, Phineas trailing after her with the tea tray. She looks just as
white as Pa.

'Tea guys,' Ma says quietly, going through to the veranda. They
get up to follow her. Outside the blue sky is starting to dim, lose its
white hot brilliance. He looks at his watch, sees it's going on half
past five. They sit, drink tea, eat cake. Time passes and no one says
much, but eventually Pa announces he's going out to check on the
sties before sunset.

'For the meantime,' he tells them, 'let's not mention this whole
business to anyone. It'll just get everyone up to ninety, okay?'

He and Ma agree and once Pa's gone Davey leaves Ma sitting on
the veranda, looking contemplatively out over the lands. There is
no wind to bring the sounds from far away — not even a rustle
through the trees — but he knows what she's listening out for. She's
listening for the faint sounds of Aunt Marsha's music carrying to
her in short, indistinct phrases. Ma swears she can actually hear it
occasionally and that it always lifts her spirits, as if she's received a
letter from a long lost friend overseas. He's always quick to tell her
that she's just imagining it — that the sheer distance from
Summerville to Edenfields makes it physically impossible — and she
always replies, 'No I'm not,' sounding a little hurt. But today he
leaves her to think what she wants, whatever's going to make her
happy.

In his bedroom he lies on his bed, listening to a CD. The music
thuds away, a fast wave of metallic sound. He stares up at the

ceiling. He can't get the awful words of that fat woman out of his head. The arrogance of it, the fucking nerve. He thinks about the farm, Edenfields, the farm that his great-grandfather built from nothing with his own bare hands, the sweat of his brow. He thinks of Pa – how hard he works on the farm, from dawn till dusk. In time, he'll work just as hard himself. He thinks about time – one week, seven days, and the clock ticking down all the while, tick, tick. He just can't comprehend what it all means. It seems so unreal, impossible. They can't just pack up everything in one week! It'll never be enough time. Well, it just won't happen. It's just purely impossible. They'll never come and take over his farm. Pa won't allow them for a start. Neither will he. It's against the law, it's illegal. Pa has all the official papers. The farm belongs to them and always has and always will.

He dozes off into a light, restless kind of sleep, waking when he hears Pa get back from the sties. Outside the night is falling more quickly now and he gets off his bed to look out of the window. The darkness seems to sneak in between the spiky branches of the gum trees and then swamp them, obscuring the last listless mist. He draws the curtains, cancelling it out. Suddenly he's angry. He's woken up muzzy, in a foul mood. It's been a shit day, to say the least. The mess up with the gun, his botch with Katie Hutchins, the fat bitch demanding the farm, Pa ranting and raving, Ma crying and crying. He thinks about the gun a bit, decides that he'd better do something before that's the next thing to cause a scene.

In the kitchen, a while later, Ma has another go at him again about his poor school report. She seems even tenser than he is. Obviously she didn't hear the music coming from Aunt Marsha's garden. She goes on about how much money they're spending on him each term, about the need for a decent education, that he won't get anywhere in life without one. He takes most of it well, trying not to overreact to her provoking accusations. But when she mentions the farm and what she calls 'the unsettled future', he takes exception.

'Don't bring that up,' he snaps, 'it's got nothing to do with school work.'

'It's got everything to do with school work,' she retorts. 'There may just be no farm to take over and then what the hell are you going to do?'

'Don't ever say that, it's not going to bloody happen! Okay?'

He storms out of the kitchen, slams the door of his bedroom. Ma comes barging in.

'Don't you dare take that tone with me mister!' she shouts.

'What tone?'

'That precise tone!'

He ignores her, turning on his CD player. The loud, aggressive rock music scrambles the room.

'Hey – just watch yourself young man!'

Pa storms in. 'Turn that bloody noise down!' he yells. Davey obeys at once and sits on his bed looking ashamed. 'Don't you dare shout at your mother, you hear me?'

'Yes Pa.'

'We're all under enough bloody stress as it is.'

'Sorry Pa.'

He storms out, but Ma stays. 'Did you hear that – let's all buckle down together, and that means school work as well.'

'Fine.'

She goes out but he can see she's upset again. As usual. He turns up the music and sits on his bed, sulking. A few minutes later he hears Ma call dinner, but decides to make her wait. A minute later Pa bursts in, almost screaming, 'Your mother called you for dinner, now hurry the hell up!' He goes at once, swiftly into the dining room. Pa glowers angrily at him across the table. Ma still looks upset.

They bow their heads and Pa says Grace. 'For what we are about to receive may the Lord make us truly grateful.'

'Amen,' they all say.

They start eating, picking at their crumbed pork fillets and vegetables quietly, unspeaking. Eventually Pa puts his fork down, inhales. 'Now listen – we've all had a bad day. I know we're all anxious and stressed out, but let's just try to deal with it coolly and calmly, okay?'

Ma and he agree.

'Tomorrow,' he continues, 'we're going to church, all of us – yes, you included David. And we're going to take the time to relax and come to terms with things. We're all getting far too carried away by all this shit.' He pauses. He's never heard Pa swear at the dinner table before, never. It's quite shocking. 'Nothing's going to happen. We're not leaving this farm. Never. Do you hear me?'

He slams his fist on the table. Ma is visibly shaken, about to start crying again. Pa lifts his hands to apologize for the outburst and begins to pick at his food. They all carry on quietly, their heads bowed, reluctant to look at one another. But suddenly Pa shakes his head and throws his fork on to his plate, pushing it away. 'I want to see you in my office straight after dinner,' he says, getting up.

'Yes Pa.' The gun, he thinks, Pa's found out about the gun. He'll be in for it now. He braces himself, nervousness spreads through his stomach, making it impossible to finish his dinner. He pushes it around his plate until Ma says, 'Just leave it.'

*

He gets up and walks slowly to the office. Pa tells him to shut the door, his face taut with anger.

'Now you listen to me good and proper boy – I'm not going to have you speak to your mother like that ever again. Hear me? I don't want to hear another word of disrespect – you know she's been through hell. You know that – you just be grateful she's still here on this earth, looking after us. It could be a very different story.'

'Yes Pa. Sorry Pa.'

Pa walks up and down. 'Right, let's get this over and done with.'

He knows what to do. He walks to the desk, takes down his pants and bends over, clutching the side of the desk. He hears the clinking of the belt, the buckle, the hard, stinging leather in Pa's hand. The first strike is always the worst, the most prepared for but least expected. It's a fierce sting. The second is harder and the third he thinks has cut his skin. It's intense pain, fierce pain. But Pa doesn't stop. Four. Five. Six. Seven. Jesus Christ! He's seething. Eight. Nine. Suddenly, through his clenched mind, he understands what Pa's doing. He's not beating him, he's just beating. He's doing it for sake of it. Ten. Eleven. Each blow is an explosion of fire in his back, his legs, his head. It's as if Pa can't stop himself, as if he sees the fat woman trying to take over the farm and is beating her, stopping her. Twelve. Thirteen. His head is light. The floor seems to be dissolving. His grip on the desk is all that keeps him anchored in the room. Fourteen. His eyes are shut tight, his face clenched, finally, finally hearing Pa pull back, breathing hard.

He waits, petrified. The tears are streaming, streaming down his cheeks. His chest is heaving, his backside is on fire. Hovering above his tortured body, his mind swimming, he knows that something more than punishment has taken place. Through these blows, he has been purified. The beating has taken him beyond paying for his various crimes, beyond atonement and forgiveness. He has shed his guilt. He can't be touched. As he slowly straightens up, he is innocent again.

He turns from the desk and at once goes weak at the knees. He gropes for his pants, easing them up. He's crying steadily, like a lost child, but trying desperately hard not to. He wants more than anything to be tough in front of his father. It means so much to him to show Pa how strong he is.

But Pa is crying himself, piteously, collapsed in the sofa, the belt lying across his lap. Davey looks at him, seeking him out, demanding an explanation. Pa looks at him too. Disbelief looks at itself like looking in a mirror. He makes towards the door, limping.

'Son,' Pa calls out, softly, 'I'm sorry son.'

He turns briefly. 'Yes Pa.'

He walks out, and finds he's in complete shock. This is the greater pain – that Pa has broken, that Pa isn't strong enough. He goes into his bedroom, falls on to the bed and sobs and sobs into the bedspread. He doesn't care who hears him. He's not ashamed to be seen crying, not after this, not after Pa's been crying too. He has no one not to cry in front of now. He's aware of Ma's presence lurking about the passage, passing the door every now and then. After a while he gets up, slams the door shut, then falls back on to the bed.

But, in fact, it's not confinement he wants, it's freedom, and a sudden urge comes to him to get out of the house, to put it all behind him. He opens the door, walks through to the kitchen. The door to the office is standing half open, just as he left it and he assumes Pa's still in there. He wonders whether he's still crying, weeping like a small weak child, a boy, a woman.

He's become furious. The pain has dulled, through shock, but by

God he's going to suffer in the morning. In the kitchen he notices the radio receiver bleeping. He walks over to it and slaps off the power switch. Fuck whoever it is. He's not going in to call Pa now, not after this. Fuck Pa too.

Outside he plays with the dogs. They're surprised, elated to see him. He hits old tennis balls for them with a warped wooden racquet high into the dark sky. For a moment they're genuinely confused and rush about, knocking into one another. Only when the ball lands with a distinctive thud down the hill do they go charging after it, leaping and sniffing about.

Phineas and George appear, walking briskly up the hill. They both look flustered, perturbed. What the hell do they want? he thinks.

'Baas, baas,' Phineas says, 'where's the Big Baas please?'

'Why?'

'We must speak to him at once baas, please.'

'I don't know. He's probably gone to bed. Why?'

'Then you tell him baas, please, very important.'

'Tell him what?'

George speaks. 'They say there is trouble coming baas. All farms must be told. Very important. Trouble coming. Big trouble.'

'Trouble? What, a fire?' He looks to the horizon, but can't see the ominous ruddy glow, the scourge of farmers. 'What trouble?'

'There big big trouble coming. They say so at shebeen. They talk about it all day. Now please, you go and tell the Big Baas.'

'Yeah, okay I'll go just now.'

'Please, you go and tell the Big Baas straight away. Big trouble. Very big trouble in area. They say very dangerous.'

'Okay – I heard you for fuck's sake. I'll tell him.' He throws down the tennis racquet. The two old guys are probably pissed if they've been down at the local shebeen all afternoon. Fucking

annoying that they have to come and disturb him, asking for help.
He storms back into the house, going at once to the lounge where
he finds Ma watching a movie on the TV.

'Where's Pa?'

'He's gone to bed. Why?'

'Never mind. I'll tell him tomorrow.'

He turns to leave but Ma calls after him. 'Sunshine, everything's
okay, right?'

'Fine,' he calls, going down the passage.

Outside he tells Phineas and George that he's spoken to the Big
Baas. They both seem greatly relieved and promptly disappear
back down the hill. Drunken cunts, he thinks. They can sort out
whatever it is by themselves. He goes back to the dogs.

Back inside again he hears Ma in the bath. He'd better deal with this
gun, he decides. He doesn't know how long Ma's been in the bath for
and if she came out and caught him in the act, then what? He'd
better have a back-up plan. And if he comes across Pa … He enters
the bathroom, looks up at the trap door. It hits him – the geyser. He
turns on the water and waits until it starts to drum against the tiled
surface of the shower. 'The geyser's not working again,' he says loudly
so that he'll be heard. He walks out of the bathroom, down the passage, into the laundry room where he fetches a spanner, a screwdriver,
a pair of pliers and then goes back towards the bathroom. Outside, in
the courtyard, the dogs are barking. 'Shut up,' he calls to them. The
last thing he needs is for the dogs to alert Pa and spoil his plan. He
throws them a handful of biscuits from the tin to keep them occupied.

In the bathroom he climbs up on to the basin, pushes the trap
door aside. He taps around for the gun but there is nothing. Odd.
He pats all over but there is no trace of it at all. Where the hell is it?

•

He stands on the toilet cistern and pulls himself up into the ceiling where it is hot and stuffy. The geyser rumbles beside him and he looks around in the cobwebbed dark for the gun. Then he sees it – it's slid off the rafters and is now lying a foot or two inside the ceiling. He reaches over for it and is about to descend when he squints through the trap door, seeing a figure pass by the door. Ma on her way back from the kitchen where she's fetched her glass of water. He sits back, waits. He peers down again. He is expecting her to pop her head round the door to say goodnight, but instead notices that she passes by the door again, back towards her room. Then he hears a loud thud come from deep inside the house. Another series of thuds, this time more muffled. What are they up to? Perhaps Pa's slapping at mosquitoes with a towel. When he peers through the trap door again he sees Ma pass by yet another time – a dark shape in the passage. He sits back, waits for a good few minutes.

Soon, however, he cannot tolerate the heat in the ceiling any longer and decides that Ma must've settled down by now. He inches down with the gun, careful not to put too much weight on to the enamel toilet cistern, and jumps gently on to the bathroom mat. Only when he's on the floor does he register how absolutely still the house has become.

When he enters the passage he immediately sees a trail of blood streaking along the stone floor. Jesus. One of the dogs must have got caught in the barbed-wire fence and cut itself to shreds. There is a great amount of blood, pools and pools of it winding away. He follows the trail through to the lounge where the blood is streaked across the carpet. Ma's going to go ballistic! The trail leads on to the veranda and he peers out.

In the far corner he sees some activity, figures moving about, a shape on the ground, something that looks like a backside moving through the air, an action like fucking. He sees Ma's shape lying beneath a man. Something sticks out from the top of her body. An axe. A river of blood.

He stumbles back through the passage and the next thing he knows he's in Ma and Pa's bedroom, fallen against the cupboards below the red bed, before he finds himself back in the ceiling, hugging the gun, his mind on fire. His hands work furiously, disconnecting and reconnecting the geyser wires. Red, blue, black. Red, blue, black. Which goes where? Which is live, which earth? It perplexes him entirely, this great enigma, until sometime later someone comes up into the ceiling and finds him, tempts him down.

The rest is a blur. There is nothing he remembers or registers for a long while – a gap of complete blankness – and a while later, he sees only fragmented images as bodies hustle in and out of Aunt Marsha and Uncle Mike's house throughout the night. Featureless bodies, like targets at a shooting range, their faces pale discs, a drone that might be voices. There is coldness prodding him on the shoulder, a tight clenching of his hand every now and then.

But otherwise: nothing.

Now he is studying the curtains, trying not to cry, but his eyes are beginning to strain, tire, so he looks down at last. There are only so many herds of zebra he can imagine painted into this fabric, only so many pots of relish. It's odd, he suddenly thinks, zebras and pots! What a bizarre combination. Only now does it click: Aunt Marsha's sewed together two different fabrics. He looks again, more closely. Yes, he can see the seams. It pleases him, enthrals him, the sudden solving of the puzzle. Now that it's done, he can leave it.

He looks up at the light. It's too bright, hurts his eyes. He looks at the posters Aunt Marsha had put up on the cupboards. It was nice of her to think of him. He hadn't, in fact, really bothered to look at them before. There're a few nice chicks, a few cool bikes, cars. He finds neither satisfying, interesting, comforting. Neither touches him. He doesn't picture himself with any of the girls, or on the bikes either, beating the dust, rushing into the wind. He shifts his eyes away, settles them on the white wall instead.

Fiddling in the bedside drawer he comes across a packet of cigarettes, a box of matches. He'd brought them back with him one rebellious weekend. He remembers an uproar in church, and he's faintly embarrassed now.

But he lights a smoke anyway. He does it to instigate something. He knows Ma would kill him if she were alive and knew. She abhorred smoking, the easiest way to cancer. He can imagine the outcry, the concern.

Now he wants to vex her, to provoke a response from beyond the grave. It's ludicrous, but any gesture would mean something: the packet suddenly falling to the floor, the cigarette burning his hands, the box of matches exploding in automatic combustion. But nothing. Nothing. Of course.

He smokes, draws the tobacco deep into his throat, exhales slowly. He flicks the ash into the bedside drawer. He taps his fingers against his knee. He's awake, alert, and becoming restless. He can't bear it, this void. Into the emptiness of the room, appearing from the silvery spiral of smoke, the stark truth of what he's done forms before him again. He pictures the vengeance, the violence he'll be the cause of, and he can't bear to think how they'll sort this all out, how they'll cover it up. He wants to recoil from this burden he's placed upon himself, this responsibility. It's not fair, he's too young.

He walks out of the room, and hears music. He'd assumed Uncle Mike and Aunt Marsha were asleep. He enters the lounge, sees Aunt Marsha sitting, listening to some classical CD. He doesn't disturb her. He walks down the passage, enters the bathroom, looks at himself in the mirror. He sees red round his eyes, a pale blotchiness about his lips and chin. He is still shaky from the journey, but steady enough to study himself for a minute. His reflection looks back.

In the hallway, he sees the phone. He kneels on the rug, picks up the receiver. An impulse takes him, rises up. 'Hello,' he says. 'Hello, hello.' He listens for a reply. He wants Ma to be on the other side, speaking to him, reaching out to him. 'Hello. Hello.' He stays on his knees for a long time, listening to the silence: a vague, dead nothingness, perhaps a slight distant hissing. A wind through the wheat fields. Nothing motherly, nothing comforting. Just a sullen taunting lament.

He slaps the receiver down. Aunt Marsha's not in the lounge as he passes back through. He falls back on to the bed, looks at the curtains and thinks this is the tedium stars endure while waiting a hundred billion years to experience death by imploding.

Mike shines his torch into the gloom of the rest of the house. It beams away down the passage, shining a tunnel before them. In the dark, the house seems small, confined. They don't really know where to look. They move in deeper, probing rooms, like ancient chambers asleep for thousands of years. There is a wooden caution in their step, hollowness in their thoughts and assumptions. They just don't know what to expect, what will suddenly be thrust at them in the dark.

The tension weaves and winds around them, stirring up a sense of strangeness, of chilling realizations. Gus is beginning to grow steadily more uneasy, a sharp tightness stabs at his stomach, his fingers tingle. Prodding his mind from all angles, like snatches of blue light, is the memory of the night the guerrilla fighters came into his place during the bush war. They'd crept into the house without a sound, stalked, like they're stalking now, down the passage, entered rooms, pointed rifles at sleeping bodies; Brendon in his cot, Lara clutching her teddy bear, Jen and him lying side by side on white sheets under the beating of a fan. Gus, battling through the thick fog of sleep, had heard a sound, a trail of footsteps, a careless movement and had got up. But they'd gone: food, drink, money, the guns. And the next night, a blast of brick and timber, a blaze; they'd come back, thrown a petrol bomb at the tobacco barns.

The thought sends a quiver of shock down Gus' spine. What it must've been like, to be those men, as they are now – Mike, Dirk, Terry and him – going in to a sleeping house, armed, intent,

211

hateful, how easy it would've been for each of them to stand at an opened door, squeeze the trigger, pump a bullet into a bed. Gus sees here, in this dark, haunting trail, the stark possibility of his own family's death that night, twenty-five years ago. And now they're here, to do the same thing. An inversion has taken place, a perverse turning of the tables. And he doesn't like it. Not one bit.

But they proceed. Room after room, each simply adding to the puzzle, to the maze of uncertainty and dread. The house seems empty. Slowly they're being drawn to the last place she could be, the main bedroom. Its door stands open, the entrance to a dark crypt. They go in single file, slowly, like a procession. They enter the bedroom, stand still. They listen for signs of breathing, of life. Terry raises his gun to shoot if anything moves. But there is no breathing in the room, no sign of someone lying before them, asleep, alive. Mike shines the torch at the bed, finding the body. He flicks it off. A startled moment. The physical truth. They all seem to back off slightly, retreat in the dark. It's not because of the snatched sight of the body on the bed. It's not even because they now know it's true after all. It's because suddenly they realize that they've confronted the shape of their own turmoil, their own nightmares. This thing, this weight has brought them here to do unspeakable things, things ordinary men like them shouldn't have to do. They don't know whether they have the strength left to at last confront her, take back what she's taken.

Mike says, 'Right boys, let's do this. Turn the light on.'

Dirk gropes for the light switch with both hands, presses it down. The brightness temporarily blinds them. Mike's initial reaction is to recoil, even though he knows she can't do anything to him now. He breathes in deeply, prepares to confront the body on the bed, the cause of all this. It's big and bulky and still. As he gets closer he realizes something's not right. Her face is expressionless, even tranquil – it doesn't look like the face of someone who spent her last moments staring down the barrel of a shotgun. Was she asleep when he shot her? But, more tellingly, there's no blood, not a drop, simply a large guttered hole in her stomach. They all know what this means.

'Jesus, she was already dead.'

'Must've been.'

This changes things. 'How the hell did she die?' Dirk asks. They can't fathom it. She looks like she died in her sleep. Just their bloody luck, Mike thinks, all of this for nothing. But really it doesn't change the situation. They've still got a dead black woman with a white man's bullet in her stomach.

'We have to carry on,' Mike says.

'Yeah,' Gus agrees. They move round the bed. Now she merely disgusts them, her weight suggestive of her greed, her stubbornness.

'Jesus, she's like a blinking pig,' Terry remarks.

'Two blinking pigs,' Dirk jokes. They laugh.

Gus says, 'Enough joking around. Let's just get on with it.'

Mike can't actually think how they will manage it. 'She must weigh a frigging ton,' he says. He steps back from the bed, considering what to do. 'Right, on the count of three.'

They close in on the bed again. One man per limb: Mike and Terry on the arms, Gus and Dirk on the legs. One, two, three. They heave. She hardly budges. Immediately they break off. 'My God, this is going to be a mission,' Terry says. They all know it. But there is nothing for it. They close in again, lift, strain. They get her up, carry her off the bed, put her down. They lift again, lug her off the carpet as far as the passage.

'Right,' Gus says, 'we'll drag her. It'll be easier.'

Gus and Dirk pick up a leg each and proceed to pull. She goes sliding easily enough across the polished stone floor.

Mike goes back into the room and straightens things out: the sheets, the bedspread. Without any blood, there's a chance they'll be able to obliterate any evidence of her. There are piles of clothes draped about, cosmetics, brushes, lotions. Messy bitch, he thinks, but typical. He clatters everything together and dumps it in the wardrobe. He looks round the room one last time. Suddenly there is an ache in his heart, not just the physical pain that's getting more and more intense as this mission goes on, but a low, slow plunge in his mood. This is the place Joe and Leigh were murdered. This is where the bodies had laid slain, the scene of the crime. Morbidly he finds himself squinting down at the beige carpet. It appears clean, a consistent light shade. Now how the hell did they get all the blood out? he wonders dimly. The splinters of bone, chunks of brain? Christ almighty, Phineas must have spent hours and hours scrubbing his poor heart out. Revulsion takes over. He can no longer stomach the thoughts, the sight of death around him. He leaves the room, flicks off the light, catches up to the others. 'For Christ's sake, let's get this over and done with,' he says.

They are able to drag her right through the kitchen and into the laundry room. Occasionally they have to move odd bits of furniture, but by and large it's easier than it had seemed at first. The truck is only ten steps away from the laundry-room door. They reposition themselves as before and on the count of three, all heave and lift, wobbling away with her to the opened back of the truck, trying not to make a noise as they dump her dead bulk. They drape the boat cover over her, and fall away panting and tired. Terry scans the darkness with the gun again, making sure no one is about to creep up on them. It's occurred to him that she's been killed by her own gang – an easy way to get hold of her property, and an easy way to blame it all on the whites.

'Right, two more things to do,' Mike says.

They climb back into the truck and inch down the hill. At the gate, Dirk and Gus get out and proceed as before, looking and calling, looking and calling. They can't be too sure.

Then, it all happens. Suddenly there's a loud, startling knock on the back window of the truck. Mike and Terry spin round. There is a tremendous report. Terry has fired a shot at a figure in the dark.

Marsha listens to the music – bits of Beethoven, bits of Brahms – pouring from the speakers: crisp, melodic, digital, mechanical, distant, unreachable.

Then something occurs to her, something she needs to know. She turns down the stereo, walks to Davey's room, knocks gently, opens the door. He can't be asleep: not tonight, with a resolution so close at hand. He is lying on his side on the bed, shirtless, the duvet half on, half off, staring ahead vacantly.

He doesn't acknowledge her or even blink. 'Davey,' she says, gently. 'Davey.'

'Yes.' His voice is hoarse, dry sounding. She moves further into the room, sits on the end of the bed.

'Davey, there's something I want to know.' He looks at her, prompted by the seriousness in her voice. 'How did you come to do it? I mean, what made you decide?'

For a second he pretends to be confused, but he knows exactly what she's talking about. 'What?'

'What made you decide on what you did? To the woman?'

He looks at her, unblinking. 'I just did.' She's not convinced, he can tell. 'I just had to do it. I couldn't see what else to do. That's all.'

She stares at him. 'But there was something specific, wasn't there? Something that made you decide to do it now. What was it?'

'I don't know. I just told you – it was just something I had to do. I couldn't think of anything else.'

She moves forward. She's about to touch him on the shoulder, but thinks twice. He doesn't want to be startled by her cold hands. Not now. 'Davey I know there was more to it than that.'

And he knows she knows. He can't avoid telling her, not Aunt Marsha: she knows everything.

'A few nights ago at school, I saved one of the rabbits. The guys were playing with them, looking after them, to feed to the snake.'

Marsha waits for a moment.

'How did you save it, Davey?'

'I killed it – but I didn't let them feed it to the snake.'

'Did that make you feel better?'

'Yes.' She can see the tears in his eyes.

'And that's the same night you phoned me?'

He nods. She contemplates for a moment what he's told her.

'Come with me,' she says.

She leads him outside via the veranda. She doesn't want him to see the men's cars in the driveway and become worried. She takes him down through the dry garden, past the stables, coops, pens. He follows, not asking or caring where they are going. They stop outside a pen. It's fairly big, hooded in the night. He can see a covering of tin at the far end, the dim outline of water bowls, feeding bowls. Lying underneath the covering he can make out the faint shape of a small animal. It's too large to be a goat, too slender to be a sheep. It's not a colt or a filly either.

He turns to Marsha for the answer.

'Go inside,' she says.

She unlatches the gate for him. He enters, unsure of what's expected. He walks forward, the animal stirs, lifts its head. Only when he's much closer does he see what it is – a small buck. Strangely, it stays lying down, then he sees it can't get up – its back legs seem lame. He puts his hand out, expecting it to cringe away, but it stretches its neck forwards, wanting to sniff him. He sees it strain. For some reason it's trying to come to him. It lifts itself on its forelegs, but buckles. So it just lies on its bed of straw and blankets, sniffing his scent. He reaches out, touches it on its cold wet nose, strokes its ears. It carries on sniffing him.

Marsha has approached from behind. He turns to her. He's still unsure. He waits for an explanation.

'This buck, she was found the day after your parents were killed. One of the workers found her close to one of our fields. They brought her here. She'd been shot in the left back leg. You see, I was so distraught about what had happened the night before, I just couldn't deal with it. I told them to put her here. I forgot about her. Really, I should have told them to kill her, put her out of her misery, but I forgot all about her.'

He looks at the buck, impartially.

Then Marsha says, 'Davey, you shot this buck didn't you?'

The words sink in. He hadn't wanted her to say it. But suddenly it's all there – that day he'd gone hunting, taken a pot shot at it in the bushes, not caring whether he got it or not, in a hurry to get home to his breakfast. And here it is. He is all of a sudden soaked with sweat, brought hard up against that day, himself. He wants to kick it, blame it for living so long, curse it for accusing him. And there are other acts he regrets, the list of charges suddenly streams out at him. When he was younger he'd doused a chicken in paraffin, set it alight out of curiosity. It fluttered round the coop, its head stretching and gawking, its feathers alight. It only took a few minutes before its lungs gave in, but he remembers the smell, a living thing floundering in fire.

He leaves the buck, stands up, turns to her. 'Yes, I shot it.'

'You know, if things were different, if none of this had happened, I probably could have healed this buck the day it was brought to me.'

'Yes.' He knows her so well. 'The way you saved Ma.'

'Maybe,' she says. 'But then, you know, if I had done that, then I would've become a part of its life. I would have given something of myself to it and so it would have come to depend on me and I'd have been responsible for it.'

He doesn't understand what she's getting at. He stands still, looking down.

'Your mother and I, we were so close, and she relied on me in certain ways, in ways maybe we didn't properly understand, and I ... I let her down. In these last years I wasn't there for her.'

'Yes you were.'

'No, not like I should have been.' She looks at him and is about to say, I became jealous of her life, of having you. But he's only a boy. He shouldn't be burdened with her guilt too.

But he surprises her by speaking. 'You know Aunt Marsha, you're wrong. Ma always knew you cared for her. She always knew because she could hear your music, the music you used to play in the garden, coming across the hills. She used to sit on the veranda and listen and say that you were talking to her, saying hello, telling her how you were through your music. It always made her happy. She'd say, listen to your other mother saying hello.'

In the faint light she moves a hand to her mouth, her chest working hard. He allows her this moment and looks down at the buck looking at him. The one contemplating the other.

Aunt Marsha and he walk back to the house, slowly. Soon, hopefully tomorrow, he will go far into the bush, get clear of everything to be by himself. He will have to do that.

At the shot, the lone figure drops to the ground, covering his head with his hands, shouting, 'Please baas, please!' It's Phineas. Terry lowers his gun, Mike pulls it away.

'For fuck's sake!' Mike shouts.

'What the hell's he creeping up on us for?' demands Terry, a little defensively. 'Could've been the fucking militia.'

Mike gets out and grabs Phineas by the arm, yanking him up. 'You okay?'

'Yes, baas,' he says.

'You sure?'

'Yes baas, we been waiting for you.'

'Yes?'

'Yes baas, please come with me.'

'What's going on?' demands Terry.

'Just please baas, come with me, it all right. We fix things. I show you the way.'

Phineas jumps in the back. They pick up Dirk and Gus further down the track.

'What the hell was that shot?' Gus asks, perturbed.

'False alarm,' Mike replies.

Phineas directs them a short way down. They take a left turn up a side road and soon come across the compound, a stretch of land cleared from the bush. But something's wrong. The first thing that strikes them is the heavy smell in the air, the thick, lung-grabbing smell of soot and ash. They park the truck, get out, straining to look beyond a large bonfire, to see into the gulf of darkness spread about them. Then they realize what's happened: they see the blackness of burnt wooden shells, frames of huts collapsed like a scattering of used matchsticks. A mass of charred straw, thatch is now a heap of mulch on the muddy ground. Gus shines his torch, picking out pieces of pots, bits of bedding, stools, racks and jugs scattered about, all flamed and grilled, coated in black.

People stand quiet, respectful round the bonfire. The flames reflect on their faces, lighting their solemn expressions.

Mike realizes that these are the farm workers. They look gaunt, traumatized, their faces drawn, their clothes ragged. Mike knew this sort of thing was going on, he fucking knew, but hadn't realized it was quite as bad, quite as shocking. Jesus Christ, he thinks, what have these people been through? Phineas, now that Mike observes him in the glow of the light, has obviously fared a little better, but he's also thin, skin and bones.

'They come last night,' Phineas says. 'They burn down houses. They beat people. They beat George.'

'George?' Mike asks, alarmed. He knows George well. Joe always spoke so highly of him. 'Best goddamn foreman you can get,' he'd say. Mike would beg to differ, but anyway. 'Where is he now?'

Phineas looks at him forlornly. 'He very sick baas, very very sick.'

'Where?'

Mike is led through the crowd, past the bonfire. Gus, Terry and Dirk hang back, look round a bit more, curse and mutter to themselves, commiserate with the workers.

Mike and Phineas walk along a short path, and after a passage through dense bush, come round the back into a smaller clearing where two tiny prefabricated breeze-block buildings stand. There is a small gathering holding a vigil outside. Women sob and pray under their breath, swaying backwards and forwards gently on the step and on the protruding roots of a tree. Mike goes in, squints under the dull naked bulb hanging from the low ceiling. There is George, a stiff, beaten body lying on the low, narrow bed.

Mike kneels down. The smell is foul and acrid. There is a tin bucket of bloody vomit standing on the rough cement floor. But Mike isn't repelled. A blanket is pulled up to George's chest; only his head sticks out, the swollen face Mike doesn't recognize, the bloated, cut skull resting on a blood-caked pillow.

'George,' he says, looking into his face. His eyes are closed slits. There are cuts everywhere. An exposed, red, raw gash runs from his right eye to his chin, the flap of his cheek swollen, leaking pus. Mike speaks in the local dialect, softly, as calmly as he can. George doesn't respond. He murmurs and mutters, spit and blood dribbling from his mouth. Mike tries to say something to him that will put him at ease, to make him know that it's all going to be okay. But will it? Will it ever be okay again after this? And what could he say? What suffering has he undergone that makes him a worthy comforter, a comrade? He suddenly realizes he's a fake amongst martyrs, a mouse amongst men.

Phineas, standing behind him, tells him that they're worried about George's stomach. Mike gently and slowly peels back the blanket, sees the extended abdomen, the egg-like swelling, the tight bruising, the deep lacerations. George whines a bit, grimaces in pain. The shock sits in Mike's throat, a looming bewilderment settles over him. He looks at the blood in the vomit. Internal haemorrhaging. He knows there's nothing he can do. Like the women outside, he can sense the fatal pull, the end drawing near. He eases the blanket up again, stands.

As he's about to turn and leave, George seems to hit upon a real-ization and weakly raises a hand. He mutters something again. Mike can't make it out. He lowers his head to hear. George is look-ing up, glancing at him through his glazed, slated eyes. 'Baas Baker,' he says, 'Big Baas Baker.'

No, Mike's about to say, it's not baas Baker, it's baas De Wet. But he doesn't. He lets him think he's Big Baas Baker if that's what's going to bring him comfort. He reaches down, briefly grips the outstretched hand.

As he's leaving the room, Mike hears another kind of whimpering, more sounds of suffering. He stops in his tracks, listens closer. Then Phineas explains. There is a boy, George's youngest son, in the next-door room. He's been badly injured too.

'Very very bad thing happen to him,' he reports.

Mike doesn't know if he can face it, but goes into the room. There is a boy lying on a bed, sweating and feverish, shaking with shock and pain. A woman holds a rag to his brow. When she sees Mike she looks up angrily, as if it's his fault and he's to blame. She shouts something, something Mike can't quite catch, and then whips away the blanket, ripping the bloodied bandage from the boy's groin. Mike looks down, sees the unimaginable gaping hole at the crotch, thick blood oozing. He turns at once to leave, dizzy, trembling.

He goes round the back of the buildings, out of sight from the quietly wailing women and the vigil keepers. He leans against the wall, clutches his chest as the pain shoots through him, worse than ever. At the same time he brings his other hand to his face to receive the first tears.

*

Back amongst the crowd at the compound, Phineas tells Mike and the guys that it's now all okay because he's gone and sorted everything out. How the hell can everything be okay? Mike thinks.

Gus says, 'Oh yes and how's that?'

Phineas gives a signal, calls out, and then, a few moments later, from deep in the bush, a procession appears walking towards the bonfire. At first the guys can't see what's there. They squint. Then they move towards the fire when it begins to become clearer, when they start to realize just what the trail of men carry between them, on racks of wood. Naked bodies. Six of them. All dead. Soon they are lowered on to beds of rock and stone, in a neat line.

'Here are the men you come for,' Phineas begins to explain. 'They beat and steal from us. They are evil. They not men of our country. Everyday they—'

Mike puts his hand up to shield himself. He doesn't want to hear it, doesn't want to hear what he's heard so many times before and hasn't done a damn thing to try to stop. 'These men – they were guarding the farm right?'

'Yes baas, they work for the new woman, the mad woman.'

'How did you kill them?' Gus asks.

'I put powder, powder from storeroom, in their tea. All of them. Yesterday morning. They all have tea up at the house every morning. That is when the mad woman she give them instruction. She was going to send them all over district to do this, to beat and burn. They be coming to all your farms soon. They start here because they want us off, but they want us off all farms too. We put powder in their tea. It work very quick baas, very quick.'

One of the workers brings forward a white powdered packet and gives it to Gus. Toxichlor. A pesticide. That'd do it.

'And young baas Davey?' Mike asks.

'Ah, yes baas, he here too. He was here last night when they start fire.'

'What – he was here then?'

'Yes baas. They have him. And then we no see him after fire, we look and look, but we no see him until later. I see what he do at house. I knew he come to do that.'

'Yes. I see.'

'And then baas, we wait for you. We dig trench in road to stop others coming, but we knew you be coming. So we waited for you and now you here.'

They all walk along the rows of bodies. As ordinary men, men of the land and soil, they ought to be shocked by the sight of death. But they're not. The bodies look asleep, nothing more, resting on their stone beds. At the end of the line there's one mound empty.

'The woman,' Phineas explains, 'it's for the woman at the house.'

'She's in the back.'

Terry shouts instructions and a few workers go shuffling towards the truck. In the end it takes seven of them to carry her, put her on her mound; they're so thin, weak.

Presently three elders emerge from the wasteland. They wear white gowns, white hoods, and carry staffs in their hands. Slowly, they walk in amongst the bodies, up and down the rows, speaking softly, humming, singing occasionally, chanting. Mike and the other white men stand off to one side.

Mike watches them quietly. He knows that the bodies lying here are the same men who attacked the farm. They killed Joe. They killed Leigh. These are the savage fuckers who took a budza to them both. The pain crosses his chest, his breath quickens, he clenches his fists tight enough to know that if they were round two of these bastards' necks he'd suffocate the life from them, snap them, crunch them.

The elders go about their work. No one speaks. All the workers kneel as prayers to the ancestors and gods are said and offerings given. The ceremony takes about twenty minutes. A scrawny chicken is beheaded, its blood dripped over the bodies.

Mike expects there to be an outpouring of anger from the workers, a release of emotion for the suffering these men have inflicted. Standing here he longs for the throng of drums, a mock display of spear-pointing and warring songs. But it's not like that. Instead they remain calm and composed. They are stone-faced, watching as their aggressors are gradually, ritual by ritual, sent on their way to the next world, to purgatory, to face their judgements, account for their aberrations.

Mike watches it through, feeling a welcome easing in his chest when, finally, it's finished.

The priests trail off, disintegrating back into the wilderness. Mike and the guys move forward again. One last ritual, it seems, is being performed. Phineas and two others are pouring vast amounts of home-made beer over the woman, the bitch, the pig.

'Why are you doing that?' Dirk asks.

'It's for her in the spirit world baas,' Phineas explains. 'She is so greedy that she will get very thirsty very soon. She will have to have lots of beer to quench her great thirst.'

They all laugh. It's like a laugh they have been waiting centuries to release.

'That fucking figures,' says Terry.

They light the bodies with torches taken from the bonfire. They don't catch properly, a flat, disappointing finale to the whole thing.

'We might be able to help you out there,' Gus says. He goes to the truck, pulls out the jerry can.

Within seconds the bodies are roasting ablaze. Great singing and chanting erupts into the air — wailing, hooting, ululating — spreading far and wide.

Marsha takes Davey into the lounge.

'I want you to listen to this,' she says. 'I planned to play it to the bougainvilleas the day your parents died.' She puts the disc in the machine. It starts up. Without her telling him, he knows it's about death. The tone somehow suggests it. Then she tells him. It's a mass of delivery for those who have died.

They listen together. The soprano pleads, soars serenely. The four-part chorus chants round the chamber of the room.

*Libera me, Domine, de morte aeterna, in die illa tremenda quando coeli movendi sunt et terra, dum veneris judicare saeculum per ignem. Tremens factus sum ego et timeo, dum discussio venerit, atque ventura ira. Dies illa, dies irae, calamitatis et miseriae, dies magna et amara valde. Requiem aeternam dona eis, Domine, et lux perpetua luceat eis. Libera me, Domine, de morte aeterna, in die illa tremenda quando coeli movendi sunt et terra, dum veneris judicare saeculum per ignem …*

There is silence as the music fades, draws to its transcendental cadence. They reflect. In the distance, a few seconds later, the sound of the chanting and worshipping starts all across the land. Finally, Marsha thinks, the chanting is back. They move out, sit in the wicker chairs, absorb it.


The final part of the plan was to dispense of the black Mercedes Benz, make it appear as if she was never there, obliterate her. But that can wait, for now. They go home, each to his own struggling farm, his own uncertain life.

Dirk feels a strange mixture of exhilaration and disillusionment. Does he want his children to know, in ten, twelve years' time, what their father did tonight, the part he played? He and Annie sit in bed, drink coffee, talking about whether it's all worth it: a child in this time and place, in this world. But there is a time, he knows, in a day or two, when his mood will change, a point when his disquiet will ebb away, and the hardness of resolve will take over, a hardness that will lead him to Annie, to their marriage, to their bed, to family.

Gus puts away the shotgun, locks the cabinet, the heavy, deep steel click of the thick padlock an assurance to Jen that all went okay, that it's all over, they're all going to be fine. He's relieved nothing untoward occurred, more relieved than he lets on to Jen. She, nonetheless, makes some smart comment about how rash and bloody stupid they've all been. Something – not that he really bothers to listen – that contains the biggest irony of them all: 'You guys should realize that you just can't take the law into your own hands.' If only you knew, he mutters to himself.

Terry doesn't put his gun away. Alone in the farmhouse he sinks down in a deep armchair with a brandy and water, the gun nestled in his lap, his finger absently running along the trigger, the dim spread of the single lamp casting a circle, defining his small existence. Then, in the darkness beyond, come the faces that every night, or so it seems to him, appear. The clear hooded eyes. The piercing stares. The clean gauntness of his victims so that he sees in them a line to their ancestors, their never-to-be-born children. He sips the brandy, his finger playing against the trigger. It is no different now.

At Summerville, it's the early hours of the morning when Mike finally returns after seeing the men off. The house is quiet. Walking down the passage, Mike stops outside Davey's door. He raises his hand to the doorknob, tempted to go inside. He'd like to tell Davey that it's all okay, all fine now, because together they've saved the farm, Edenfields, taken it back, even if just for a day, for its rightful owners. This urge comes to him to go in and tell the kid that his old man would be proud of him, proud as hell. But he doesn't. The boy's probably asleep. And anyway he's tired.

In the bedroom he undresses, lies on the bed, holds Marsha. He strokes her thigh, cradles her. He tells her not to worry they've sorted everything out, they can rest now, rest. At some point he takes hold of her hand, weighing it in his own. He looks into her eyes. In the dim light he moves Marsha's hand to his chest, feels her fingers, her palm warm against his heart so that at once he feels soothed, his own mind put at ease, which is all he needs to finally fall asleep beside her.

In the spare room, Davey isn't asleep yet; not while Ma looms here in this quiet space. She is smiling, telling him stories, her hand on his leg as he lies in her lap. He's young, three or four, and this is the earliest memory he has of her, the purest, the most translucent. He is laughing, giggling.

And Pa has his hands round his shoulders, down on the muddy banks of Broadlands Dam, teaching him how to cast and reel for bream or bass. The expanse of water lies before them. It is still in the early morning, at break of day, always is. It is quiet too and Pa is at his happiest, before starting the day's work on the farm. When the sun comes up it's a golden strip cast from shore to shore. He is small, a young boy, and he asks Pa about this strip of gold. 'Who put that big light here?' Pa tells him that the sun is using the still water of the dam as a mirror to brush his hair so that he can go down to the sports club and chat up all the lady suns.

And a few years later, he's sitting here at dawn, a pleasant chill filling the air, a gradual brightness rising over the mirrored dam, the wide woven blanket of tobacco fields, revealing the landscape, the savannah, Africa. Pa and he are drinking strong coffee from a flask Phineas has made them and dipping Ma's condensed milk biscuits in it. The dogs lie on the banks, they roam the bushes, get muddied. He gets muddied too, the warm squish through his toes a delight, the reeds along the shore ticklish against his shins. He has his feet planted in the soil, and even as young as he was then, he knew, one day, he would be master of all that, of all the glory that surrounded him.

He fishes, pulling silvery fish into a net. He's young, carefree and when Pa rows them out into the middle of the lake (there being no crocodiles yet) he strips naked in the fleeting dawn light and slips his tanned body into the brown water.

They're happy. They're so happy. Pa is laughing, teasing him as he splashes about the boat. Soon, Ma will come down in the truck with the picnic basket, lay the blanket out over the short grass, or perhaps a wide flat rock. She'll no doubt be wearing the scarf on her bald head, the shawl Aunt Marsha gave her during her illness, the one she treasures so much. Ma's not ill any more and that's why Pa is so happy, so relaxed. For the first time in ages Ma's got the strength to come down and join them for a morning breakfast outside, down by the dam.

Where the orange sun meets the melting clouds a spray of pink is cast through the African sky. It is at these times that a kind of peace has been declared amongst the heavens. Ma always says this when she witnesses a spectacular sunrise or sunset. Today, like all other days, there is a serene silence through the haze of hills, the yellow bush, before the low sound of the truck is heard creeping along the bending road in the dust. Pa helps him back in the boat, puts a towel round him and rows them back towards the bank so that they can run ashore to meet Ma as she pulls up to greet them both.

He sits on the edge of the bed, swaying gently. He has seen them, seen his parents. They are here. Whole. Absolute. Real. He sifts through scenes from the past, this perfect haunting of memory. He closes his eyes, embracing the shudder inside him like a great, momentous swell. When he dares to open his eyes again they will be gone, they will be a haze, specks of multicoloured patterns, part of the print of the curtains.

As he lies down now, with the light finally out, he's still determined about tomorrow, the new day. He hopes to find himself
awake just before dawn so that he can slip from the house and go
down into the vlei to wait. He hopes that a buck will somehow
appear, walk into a clearing of the veldt, so that he will have the
chance to make amends: he will simply sit, observe it, spare it, give
it its life. He would feel good about doing that, it would mean a lot
to him. But he knows it'll probably never happen. Not in a million
years. Instead, he will be lucky if there's a flutter in the scrub that
may just be the stirring of a guinea fowl or two.

**4**

By the time he wakes the sun has reclined, and although sick and miserable from sunstroke, his head is a little clearer. He sits in the shade of a low squat tree for a while, thinking, regaining his senses. There's a different texture to the air now. It's calmer, cooler. The purpose of this journey, his goals, his intentions are clear in his mind, real and reachable.

He doesn't know where he is, but up and walking again, he becomes more aware of his physical surroundings. As the bush thins out, something about the land strikes him: the more he looks about, the more he begins to see patterns, familiar patterns, and soon realizes that what surrounds him is a farm. There is a road network, eroded with tractor-tyre footprints, and coming round a curve and out into the open, he is standing in a field: a desolate, ashen, unplanted field. His first and most urgent thought is of water: a farm's bound to have an irrigation system. He'll trace it down, find its source, drink, drink, drink.

Gradually landmarks, the general shape of things, become clearer. At first he thinks he's imagining it, or hallucinating, but eventually he understands with a soaring of his soul that this is Edenfields – he is home, even though it took him a long time to know it. And then a shock: the village that burnt down must have been the farm workers' compound. He must have known those people who were being tortured, evicted. That's why he knew that man. This whole horrific time he's been home, struggling deep in bush he's scouted and hunted his whole life. Rising ahead is the old fort-like kopje, the unmistakable Eden's View. Across from it is the hill where the house stands, the old Cape Dutch, a white palace on the slopes. Somewhere in between, over the rise, is Broadlands Dam.

As he walks he weeps briefly for the luck of it, and for the terrible raw wound that obscured the most familiar place in the world. But now the tables have turned. He's got his chance again to set it all right, to save the farm, save the workers, himself. They'd made a mistake picking on him and his farm workers. When he's done with the woman, he'll go on a rampage, soak the soil with their blood, strike them down one by one. He strides on, steadfast.

Soon he's walking up towards the hub of the farm, approaching the russet-bricked shells of the tobacco barns, and then the smaller clusters of tiny-windowed workshops, a few lime-green fertilizer bags heaped about. He passes the oil-drenched tractor sheds, the machines stagnant with disuse, and then the patched-up wire coops spilling with emptiness.

He moves up towards the homestead, defended by a barrier of spotted gum trees and the tall barbed-wired security fence. He doesn't enter via the main gates where the teak-engraved signpost reading EDENFIELDS still stands erect, but veers off round the back and comes up through the overgrown orchard, deserted by the fat black crows that used to gorge on the mangos and citrus, and sees, at last, the massive weed-ridden reservoir.

He hurries through the abandoned garden, desperate to get to the reservoir so that he can drink and wash in the dark cool water. He reaches it, almost collapses against its hard fur-lined walls. He sees the tap, grapples with it in a frantic ecstasy. He gulps, gulps. He can't make his hands lap the water to his mouth quick enough. He splashes his face, claws at his skin to remove some of the dirt. His fatigue, the exhaustion of the journey, also seems to wash away, leaving his skin tight, barely containing the bright spirit that now burns inside him.

He strides up through the line of fir trees, crosses the brown lawn, passes the black Mercedes parked in the driveway and walks through the courtyard to enter the house through the kitchen. He looks about, hiding at first behind the door. It's clear. He dashes through the kitchen and into the dining room, and then quickly down the passage to enter the bathroom, closing the door quietly behind him.

He climbs on to the basin, pushes the trap door aside, stands up on the toilet cistern and reaches inside for the gun. At once his hand finds it, its cold thin barrel, the wood of its shaft: a heavy tool, waiting. He brings it down carefully. It's heavier than he remembers, much heavier, weighed down by purity and power. It's covered in a thick mesh of dusty cobwebs. He breaks a stretch of tissue paper from the roll by the toilet and wipes it down. He wants it looking smooth and polished, pristine. He sits on the edge of the bath, cleaning, cleaning. He checks it: it's still loaded.

He opens the bathroom door, looks both ways down the passage. It's clear. He creeps towards the lounge, scanning the room with the barrel of the gun as he enters. It's empty, quiet and silent. He goes to the veranda door, squints through the glass. Not a soul. He heads back down the passage trying several of the doorknobs; the bedrooms are locked, the office too. He wonders where she is. She's sure to be here. She has to be here. She has to.

The door to the main bedroom lies open, drawing him in. He edges nearer, knowing that she has to be there, that he's being led, somehow, by something, to this place, this juncture. The silence gets louder, a shrill emptiness. The gun is growing heavier in his hands. He enters, and there she is, lying fat and asleep on the bed, a resting giant. Aiming the gun at her, he moves closer. She wears a cream-coloured dress. Her legs are straight, her arms rest on her great big chest, her hands cupped together. Her mop of hair is cushioned against the pillow. It looks oily, glistening under the light. Her face, her cheeks pout. She has a huge, flat nose, a true snout. All of it disgusts him. He stands for a while observing her, contemplating her. She doesn't snore. He somehow expects her to. Snorting through her fat nose. But no, she's quiet, still.

It's time. He closes in towards the bed.

'Wake up.'

She doesn't stir. He takes another step, closer to the bed.

'Wake up.'

Nothing. He prods her belly with the gun.

'Wake up!'

She remains asleep.

'Wake up. Wake up.'

This isn't right. He stands over her, calling out, nudging her repeatedly. He wants her awake. He wants to see her see him, to see him here.

But he knows she won't. He's seen the still heap of dead things all his life. And he's been a killer, too, for most of it, slaying bucks and boars, skinning them, slicing and delving into their bellies to bring out the liver, spleen, kidneys. He would rather have spared the lives of all those animals just to take hers, to experience again the ecstasy of a first kill, the thrill of taking life.

But now he's tired again. So so tired. And even though he vaguely wonders who's beaten him to his prize, or how it can be that she'd just died suddenly before his arriving to shoot her, he is overwhelmed by the whole flat, disappointing thing. Well, what does it matter? She's dead.

He lifts the gun, points it at her stomach, and just for the sake of it, fires.

The noise is deafening. It shakes him from the inside out. Her body jolts from the power of the bullet, which gives him a dull satisfaction. He lowers the gun. If she were alive, she'd have suffered a miserable death. And before the blast of the bullet ripping her stomach she'd have seen his suffering too, the faces of Ma and Pa in him. He'd have made sure of that.

Having completed his chore, he withdraws.

His ears are ringing. He's never fired a gun inside before. He shakes his head, walking down the passage and into the bathroom to splash some water over his face. He's sweating; happiness and relief drip from his brow. He bends down to dry his face on a towel – still his towel! A purple and yellow beach towel. He looks round. His deodorant still stands on the medicine chest, his shampoo is still perched on the shower ledge. He opens the chest: his sun cream, face cleanser, hair gel, heat rub. All his. Even pills for the back injury he'd picked up playing rugby last season. It has his name on the packet – Master David J. Baker.

He enters the lounge. The furniture stands untouched and unmoved. The lounge suite. The coffee tables. The paintings. Everything's just as it's always been. The bar is still lined with Pa's collection of colourful looking bottles, the tall glasses arranged just how he'd always had them. Like a museum, like a display for posterity. He is surprised. He'd expected her to trash the place up. But it's almost as if she'd just moved in, taken over their lives. It is almost as if she approved of their things, the nice possessions they had, the way Ma decorated the house.

At least she'd removed all the family photographs. He's pleased because he can't bear to think she'd been sitting there every evening looking at them, getting to know them.

He goes into his bedroom. It's musty, but cosy – homy, private. He opens the curtains and the windows. All his belongings are there, as if he'd never been away. His fishing rods still stand in the corner. His clothes are packed and folded in the cupboards. Gadgets clutter his bedside drawer. It could have been this morning that he'd woken up and snuck out to go hunting – he could be returning from his hunt right now, with a couple of hours still to go before breakfast. He lies down for a while and stares up at the walls with their posters of women and cars and sports heroes. His bed slips round his body, hugs him, the mattress making him want to fall straight off to sleep. It is so tempting for him to shut his eyes.

But he knows it's forbidden. He'll have to leave the house soon. His victory is only a matter of principle. He's done it only to set things right, complete the cycle, redeem himself. It's only a matter of time before someone comes visiting.

So he picks himself off his bed and goes back into the lounge. He sits in the wide-winged armchair, once Pa's own chair, and for a moment tells himself that he can feel the contours of Pa's body press into his skin, his distinctive shape moulded into the soft leather. Of course, he can't, but he sits for a while, waiting for another trace of nostalgia to grip him. Nothing. It seems he will have to be patient.

He spends a few more minutes dragging himself round the house, up and down the passage, in and out of rooms, and then finds himself standing back in the main bedroom. He tries not to look at the woman lying on the bed. Instead, he walks round the room, trying to sense them, his parents. He ravages at Ma's old clothes like a wild dog, sniffs deeply at her skirts, blouses, shorts, shirts, her silken panties, her lacy bras. In the bathroom he lines his teeth with her lipsticks, licks gently at the sickening cosmetic tang to see if it tastes of her lips. He pours Pa's aftershave over his body, rubbing it into his chest, his groin, over his face. He strokes his skin and hair with their combs and brushes. He powders his body with Ma's talc, smothers himself in Pa's shaving cream.

But nothing. Not a trace. He can't feel anything, anything at all. She is dead; he sees her dead with his own eyes. He's fired a bullet into her gut. But the floodgates haven't opened, the memories haven't come back. And in death she somehow seems more alive than ever, her actions, her deeds, and it's him who is still dead. His heart won't bleed.

He takes a bottle of rum when he leaves.

And so he walks out of the house carrying the bottle and the gun. He walks through the yard, down the hill. He walks in the near darkness along the old farm road, past field after field of once productive land. He walks all the way up to Eden's View. He climbs, goes up, goes up. Finally, at the summit, he searches for a place to sit, leaning against a rock. He's alone. Invisible. Inaudible. Surrounded by trees, bush, rocky outcrops, he's just a tiny speck of nothingness lost against the vast, unfeeling wilderness. A cry will bring no response. Another gunshot will alert no one. It'll only send scurrying the birds, bush mammals, feeding beasts. And he's been in their domain once too often as it is. To them, he's a trespasser, an encroacher, an assailant. He knows what he knows.

So he sits in the dark, lonely and regretful and unappeased, but with only the night lying before him, he breaks the seals on the rum bottle and waits patiently for Aunt Marsha to come in the morning to find him.